PRAISE FOR
HELEN HARDT

"I'm dead from the strongest book hangover ever. Helen exceeded every expectation I had for this book. It was heart pounding, heartbreaking, intense, full throttle genius."

~ Tina at Bookalicious Babes Blog

"Proving the masterful writer she is, Ms. Hardt continues to weave her beautifully constructed web of deceit, terror, disappointment, passion, love, and hope as if there was never a pause between releases. A true artist never reveals their secrets, and Ms. Hardt is definitely a true artist."

~ Bare Naked Words

"The love scenes are beautifully written and so scorching hot I'm fanning my face just thinking about them."

~ The Book Sirens

Daughters of the Prairie

of the

Prairie

A COLLECTION OF NOVELLAS

Daughters of the Prairie

A COLLECTION OF NOVELLAS

WATERHOUSE PRESS

The Outlaw's Angel

CHAPTER ONE

Dakota Territory, 1869

"I'm tellin' you, I didn't kill anyone!"

Bobby Morgan sat, his wrists bound behind him, looking at lean, red-faced Justin Stiles, Sheriff of Dugan, Dakota Territory. The muscles underneath his scalp pounded like a hammer into his brain, and his eyes stung from the rotgut whiskey that had trickled into them when a bottle had crashed onto his head.

"I got a saloon full of men say you did," the sheriff said.

"A saloon full of crazy drunks." Bobby shook his head. "What about Frank, the bartender? He'll vouch for me."

"Frank didn't see anything."

"The hell he didn't! He was behind the bar when this all happened."

"Says he took a break."

"Goddamn coward." Bobby was never setting foot in that saloon again. He exhaled sharply. "Then who was manning the bar?"

"Don't know. Don't care. But I got one man dead, and five witnesses who say you done the deed."

Bobby squirmed in the hard wooden chair. His jaw ached, his head throbbed, and his face still burned from the alcohol seeping into the lacerations. He let out a sarcastic chuckle.

After losing stage robber Jack Daily's trail, he'd stopped in Dugan for a drink. Worst decision he ever made. At least he'd finally gotten some sleep. Course he hadn't expected to wake up on the dirt floor of a jail cell.

"I'll say it again. He attacked *me*. And when I heard his pistol cock, I shot him in the foot. Through his boot. Just enough to take him down so I could get the hell out. That's it." He sighed. The coarse rope bit his wrists.

"These men just like to git rowdy," Stiles said. "I ain't never had a one of 'em in my jail for anything other than drunk and disorderly conduct."

"Really?" Bobby's tone was sardonic as he cocked his head to indicate the dozing drunks in the cell. "So none of them are in here for shooting anyone?"

"Nope. That'd be you, Mr. Morgan."

Bobby stretched his neck while fumbling with the rope ties behind his back. Were they loosening? Yup. The good folks of Dugan had elected a sheriff who couldn't tie a decent knot. He kept his facial expression noncommittal, and without moving his head, scanned his surroundings. He'd need the sheriff's gun, but it was holstered at his waist. Problematic. A blade would do, or something that could masquerade as one. Most likely the sheriff lived in the backroom.

There'd be a knife in there somewhere.

Idiot hadn't thought to bind his legs to the chair. What a greenhorn. The sheriff couldn't be more than twenty, twenty-two. Bobby had age and experience on his side, and he planned to use them.

But first he needed a diversion.

The other prisoners were out cold, so he couldn't depend on them. By the time a suitable diversion presented itself, he'd be back in lock up.

Damn.

He closed his eyes, and despite his thumping head, willed his mind to churn. He'd gotten out of some pretty sticky scrapes over the years. He'd get out of this one.

He breathed in deeply to clear his brain.

Lavender.

His mother's pretty face emerged in his mind, and he was a boy of ten again, before the Indians had stripped him of everything he held dear. He hadn't thought of her in years. How had he conjured her out of nothing? It was the lavender. His mother had smelled of lavender.

He opened his eyes, and before him stood an angel. Although her sable hair was bound in a tight knot, he imagined it flowing over shoulders the same creamy shade as her beautiful face. She was tall for a woman, and slender, but with full, luscious breasts. One pale hand curved around a wicker basket covered by a red-checkered cloth.

"M-Miss Blackburn"—the sheriff's face turned a deeper red—"I-I didn't expect you today."

"Pa heard in town this morning that you had to lock several men up last night." Her voice was smooth and just a little husky.

Bobby's curled his lips slightly upward.

The young woman's brown skirts rustled as she set a basket on the sheriff's desk. The earthy lavender scent wafted to Bobby again. It was her. The angel.

Then he noticed her eyes. He'd mistaken them for blue at first, but they were actually deep violet—the rich hue of his mother's amethyst brooch.

Course the Indians had stolen her prized possession

after they raped and slaughtered her.

He shook his head to dislodge the repugnant thoughts. He hadn't gone down that path in decades, and he wasn't about to start now. There were more important things at hand. His very life, for one. Keeping his body completely still, he pulled one hand free of the ropes.

Stiles hadn't responded to the lady's query about the prisoners. His mouth opened, shut, and opened again, and his cheeks reddened even further. If the man got much redder he'd surely explode.

Bobby chuckled under his breath. The sheriff was smitten. Smitten with this beautiful angel. Well, who wouldn't be?

"I take it this young man is one of your prisoners?" The lady nodded to Bobby.

"Yes, m-ma'am," Stiles stammered.

Young man? Bobby scoffed. He'd become a man at ten and seen twenty-two years past that. He'd shot and collected bounties on criminals this angel couldn't even imagine.

"I'm being held on a false report, ma'am," he said. "The sheriff here seems to think I killed a man last night. He is, however, mistaken. I am no murderer."

Truer words had never been spoken. He might be a killer, but he was no murderer. Not like the savages who'd murdered his ma in cold blood.

"Now I've told you, Morgan, I have witnesses." Stiles's voice cracked.

"Goodness, Sheriff," the woman said. "You might be a little more polite. If this young man says he didn't do it—"

"Naomi...er...Miss B-Blackburn—" Stiles sat down behind his desk and opened a drawer.

Bobby stopped listening to the conversation to inspect

the drawer's contents. The gleam of a mirror caught his eye. Next to it sat a leather strop.

Where there's smoke...

He waited. Seconds ticked by as his heart thundered so loudly he thought it might wake the other prisoners. There'd be a chance. He had to believe it. Stiles was so smitten with Miss Naomi Blackburn that he'd let his guard down eventually. Bobby just needed to be patient.

"I brought fresh bread for you," Naomi said as she removed the checkered cloth.

The yeasty aroma wafted toward Bobby, and he inhaled. Though the bread smelled good, and God knew he needed a decent meal, he was sorry it diluted her lavender fragrance.

"I'll enjoy that with my lunch, Miss Blackburn." Stiles cleared his throat. "Thank you."

"You are, of course, welcome to it, Sheriff," Naomi said, "but you are to share it with these men." She gestured to Bobby and then the others still snoozing in the cell. "That is on my pa's orders."

"Y-Yes, of course I will," Stiles said, still blushing. "Now please, let me see you to the door. This is no place for a lady." The sheriff rose and left the desk, taking Naomi's elbow, his back to Bobby.

Quick as a rattler yet quiet as a mouse, Bobby hopped from the chair and rummaged through the still open drawer. Underneath the mirror, partially hidden by the strop, was the sheriff's straight razor.

Eureka.

He grabbed it, crept toward the door where Stiles and Naomi stood, their backs to him, and whipped one arm around the woman's waist, the thick rope dangling from his wrist. With the other, he settled the razor against her neck.

"Oh!" Her husky voice rose an octave. "Sheriff...do something!"

"Now, Morgan, you don't want to hurt that lady." Stiles stepped forward, his hands trembling in front of him. One inched lower, toward his gun.

"You know better than that, Sheriff. Get your hands in the air, or I'll slit her throat." Bobby pressed the blade into that creamy neck, taking care not to scratch her skin. "You're right. I don't want to hurt her. But neither do I want to hang for a crime I didn't commit. Now you're going to get in that cell with the rest of those derelicts, and the lady and I are going to walk on out of here."

"I shoulda hog tied you, Morgan," Stiles said.

"But you didn't. Lesson learned for another time. Naomi, angel, we're going to walk toward the sheriff real slow like, and you're going to take his gun, you hear?"

"I...I..."

"Now don't you worry. It won't hurt you." He walked forward, the heat of her curves against him a lusty distraction, but he braced his nerves against the tightening in his britches. "There we are. Just reach out and put it in my hand."

Naomi shook as she complied. Soon Bobby held the gun in the hand at Naomi's waist. He continued to press the blade against her throat.

"Now his gunbelt, darlin'."

"But I—"

"You're not doin' anything improper. But I need the belt and the ammo."

Naomi deftly unfastened the belt.

"Just hold onto it for now, angel," Bobby said. "Empty

your pockets please, Sheriff. You know what I'm looking for."

"Morgan—"

"Now, or the lady takes a bath in her own blood."

Naomi's warm body trembled against him. She was scared, and he felt bad about that. He truly did. She was a beautiful angel and she didn't deserve to be in the middle of this mess. But he'd discovered long ago that life sometimes only coughs up one opportunity for each situation. He'd learned to identify it and take it. She was his opportunity to get the hell out of this town.

Stiles pulled out his ring of keys.

"Hand them to the lady, Sheriff, and show her which one opens the cell. Come on, you'd best hurry, before those drunks wake up."

The keys clanked together as he pressed them into Naomi's hand. "It's this one," Stiles said, indicating. "I'm so sorry about this, Naomi."

"Save it, Sheriff," Bobby said. "Now we're all going to walk nice and slow over to the cell, and Naomi, you're going to open it. All right?"

She nodded against his chest, and he caught a whiff of her scent. He shook his head to clear the fog. No time to get lost in a dream of lavender and soft woman.

They moved in tandem to the cell door, and Naomi's fingers trembled as she turned the key in the lock. Bobby held the razor steady at her neck, though sweat trickled from his forehead into his eyes and stung. He blinked, but the blade never wavered.

"Step inside, Sheriff."

Stiles obeyed, shutting the door behind him.

"Lock him up, angel."

Naomi's shaking hands turned the key with a clink.

"You got what you want, Morgan," Stiles said from the cell. "Now let her go."

Bobby chuckled, though he did let the blade rest a bit more lightly against her soft flesh. It'd be a shame to scar such a sleek, pretty neck. Such a neck was made for kissing and nibbling, not slicing to smithereens.

"'Fraid I can't do that, Sheriff. She'd go runnin' to her pa. And she still has the key." He lowered his voice, speaking into Naomi's ear. "How'd you get here, angel?"

"M-My pa's buckboard is outside. W-We live on a claim... too far to walk."

"Perfect. Your horse?" He backed away from the cell, dragging Naomi with him.

"A g-gelding. Barney. He's...gentle. Don't hurt him. Please."

What an innocent. A razor at her neck, and she was worried about a horse? He shook his head as they left the sheriff's office. Once outside in the warm summer air, he lowered the blade and pressed the pistol into Naomi's trembling back.

"You can let me go now, can't you? I won't go to my pa. You have my word, Mister—"

"Morgan. Robert Morgan. Call me Bobby. And though it pains me, I'm sorry, I can't let you go. You and I are going to take your horse on a ride out of this town."

"But...but you...you don't need me." Her husky voice rose again. "I promise I'll go straight home and I won't say a word. I'll give you time to escape. Please, Mr. Morgan."

Despite the gun in her back, she turned her head, and he nearly melted into her violet eyes. But he steeled his heart against her beauty and innocence. She was an insurance policy, nothing more.

He walked her to the gelding, removed the harness, and unhitched it from the buckboard. Quick as a flash of lightning, he set her on the horse and leaped up behind her. He took a few precious seconds to rub his stiff wrists, trying to ease the rope burn, before he used the razor to cut the reins shorter. A minute later, he'd hooked the sheriff's belt around his waist, stuffed the razor in his boot, and they were trotting quietly out of town.

"Just who is your pa, anyway, angel?" he asked against her soft neck after they'd escaped the town limits.

"H-He's the preacher, Mr. Morgan."

Damnation! He'd kidnapped the preacher's daughter. He kneed the horse into a gallop and sighed.

He may have avoided the hangman's noose, but he was surely set to burn in hell.

CHAPTER TWO

Naomi sat stiffly upon old Barney, her derriere sore from three hours of galloping with no saddle. Thankfully her skirt was full enough to allow her to straddle the horse without too much of her legs showing, but the unladylike position still bothered her. Fatigue enveloped her body, yet she held herself stationary, refusing to rest against the handsome outlaw's chest.

Handsome?

Had she just thought of Robert Morgan as handsome?

So he had clear amber eyes, unfashionably long chestnut hair, and full pink lips. Not to mention a face Michelangelo himself could have sculpted. She jerked forward, catching herself before she melted into his hard torso.

Fear coursed through her, and she shuddered. He'd said he wouldn't hurt her, but he was a criminal, an outlaw. Truth probably wasn't at the top of his list of priorities. Pa had taught her to love her fellow man, to practice forgiveness, but was it possible in this situation?

Still, he hadn't hurt her. Yet. And she was weary. So very weary, and her muscles ached from this difficult ride.

"Angel? You all right?"

She jerked forward again at the melodic sound of Robert Morgan's deep voice. Her pulse pounded in her neck and she fought to hold her tone steady. "Fine, Mr. Morgan. Why do you ask?"

"You leaned against me, darlin'." He chuckled. "You've been takin' such great care not to touch me, I figured something must be wrong."

"I...I'm simply exhausted. We've been riding for hours without a saddle, galloping a lot of the way. I ache in...places unmentionable. Could we stop for a while?"

"Yes, this old brute has had about all he's going to take for one day, I reckon," Bobby said. "Problem is, we don't have any supplies. No food. No bedding. No shelter. We've got to keep going until we find a place to settle in for the night."

Naomi gulped, and her hot, sticky body quivered. "The night?"

"Of course. You didn't think we'd ride all night, did you? Ol' Barney here would collapse in a heap."

"But all around us are the hills of the prairie," she said, taking in the straw-colored grasses, the ragweed and rushes. "Where will we—"

"Now hush, don't you worry," he said. "I know this land. I've kept off the trails to stay hidden, but I know exactly where we are. See how the rushes are getting thicker?"

Naomi followed the arrow of his thick forefinger.

"Up ahead about a mile, we'll find a freshwater creek, and we'll follow it to a small cave where we can take shelter for the night. The night'll be warm, and we'll be fine without provisions. I can probably catch us a fish, or maybe even a small rabbit."

Naomi winced as her stomach growled. She found herself suddenly famished. And while the thought of breaking bread with Mr. Morgan troubled her, her rumbling tummy didn't find the prospect near as disturbing.

"It's all right, you know." His voice clashed into her

thoughts.

"What is all right, Mr. Morgan?"

"You can lean on me. I know you're tired, and I don't mind."

"It would hardly be proper," Naomi said, straightening.

"Angel, we've been ridin' hard without a saddle, and we've got a mile to go."

Though his breath was warm against her neck, she shivered.

"I don't plan on keepin' you, you know."

"Wh-What?"

"We'll hit a railroad camp about midday tomorrow," he said. "The cook there—Bessie's her name—is a real nice lady. I'll leave you with her and make arrangements for someone to take you home."

"Oh." Naomi breathed in relief. "But a railroad camp. Mr. Morgan, I don't think—"

"Hush now. You'll be perfectly safe. I never meant you any harm, angel. I hope you believe that. I just had no choice."

"I..." She couldn't finish. A lump hardened in her throat.

"Just lean back. We'll be there soon."

Naomi sighed and let her body melt backward into his solid chest. She closed her eyes, Barney's trot a steady, soothing cadence.

★ ★ ★ ★

A soft whisper of breath caressed Naomi's cheek.

"Wake up, angel."

A strong hand gripped her upper arm. She opened her eyes to clear water trickling over silver stones. Her breath caught at the beauty.

"What is this place?"

"The creek I told you about," Bobby said. "It's fresh, and you must be thirsty. I know Barney here is. So let's get down so he can drink. Steady now."

He dismounted and pulled Naomi down. She slid off Barney's slick back and into the arms of her captor. Her breasts pressed into his hard chest and her skin tingled when she grasped his shoulders for support. Such hard, muscled shoulders. Her cheeks warmed as she raised her gaze to his manly face. His eyes had darkened to a rich brandy, and his mouth was slowly descending toward hers.

A kiss. He was going to steal a kiss.

The prospect of those full, firm lips on her own frightened her. And excited her. Which frightened her even more.

Her first kiss.

And it would be from a man who had abducted her. An outlaw accused of murder.

No. Absolutely not.

She stiffened in his arms. His eyes narrowed, their lighter color returning. The moment had passed.

She shivered, hoping he didn't notice how his touch had affected her. Relief swept through her as she loosened her grip on his shoulders and slid her hands down his arms. When she reached his hands, he clasped one of hers and led her to the creek.

Barney eagerly sucked at the cool water, but Naomi hesitated.

"It's cool and fresh," Bobby said, "Come on."

She knelt, cupped her hands, and let the crisp liquid soothe her parched throat. When she'd had enough, she rose and brushed her soiled skirts. She turned and breathed in the enticing woodsy fragrance of the little meadow. She had admired the endless prairie from her father's homestead claim but had never ventured outward to the land that called to her. How she'd longed, during her walks on Pa's claim, to run into the hills that beckoned her with their wildflowers and their chirping birds.

But though they held beauty, they also held dangers, her pa said. Wild animals, and worse. Indians.

She closed her eyes and inhaled. Pine. And fresh dirt. There were no wild animals here. No Indians.

Robert Morgan's voice cut into her daydream. "You all right, angel?"

She opened her eyes. "Yes, I'm fine. It's just...so beautiful."

"You mean you've never been here?"

"No. My pa wouldn't bring my sister and me, though we often begged him."

"That's a right shame," Bobby said. "This here's paradise." He cleared his throat. "Or as close as it comes, near as I can tell." He held out his hand. "Come here. I've got a surprise for you."

She shyly placed her small hand into his large tan one but then pulled it away. He nodded slightly, and he led her about a hundred yards to a bush.

"Oh! Raspberries!" Naomi knelt and gathered a handful of the plump dark pink berries. Their sweetness burst on her tongue.

Bobby chuckled behind her. "You really were hungry."

"I didn't get any lunch today," she said. "I'd planned to eat after I delivered the bread to..." No need to finish. He knew as well as she why she'd missed her noon meal.

"I'm sorry, angel. I should have asked when you'd last eaten."

Naomi swallowed another mouthful of sweet berries. "It's not your fault—" She stopped. As a preacher's daughter, she was used to making allowances. But it *was* his fault. This whole situation was his fault, and she'd do well to remember that. No matter how kind he was to her, he was still the enemy.

Bobby nibbled at a few berries.

"Aren't you hungry?" Naomi asked.

"Yeah. I haven't eaten in a while either. But I've a hankerin' for some meat. Problem is, I don't have my shotgun. That goddamn tenderfoot sheriff—"

His words angered Naomi, and she huffed. "Mr. Morgan, I'd appreciate it if you'd refrain from taking our Lord's name in vain."

His handsome face reddened, and Naomi fought a smile. She had embarrassed him.

"Sorry, angel." He smiled, and a shallow dimple appeared on his left cheek.

Naomi's pulse quickened.

"What I mean is, the sheriff's Colt isn't my first choice of weapon for hunting. He took my revolver and my shotgun and what money I had in my pockets. Even the dirty laundry in my saddlebags. And my horse. I've no idea where he is."

Naomi revolted against the pity edging into her heart for this man. Stripped of everything, but it was nothing less than he deserved. He was a criminal.

"Goodness, Mr. Morgan. The sheriff was doing his job. He is sworn to keep our growing town safe. His job is no easy task, what with that raucous saloon in town."

"Well, now"—he smiled again—"some folks say a man

who works hard all day is entitled to a little drink."

Naomi scoffed. "A man who works hard all day is entitled to come home to a hot meal and the love of his family. He should want nothing more." She filled her hands with more berries and walked back toward Barney. "Take the sheriff, for instance," she continued, speaking louder so he could hear her. "He's one of the hardest working men in town, with no family to go home to, but he never walks into that den of sin."

She jerked backward when Bobby grabbed her elbow. The berries tumbled to the mossy earth. Her hands, stained with red juice, trembled as warmth crept up her arm to where his hand held her.

"Are you sweet on the sheriff, Naomi?" Bobby's deep voice rasped.

Naomi opened her mouth but no sound emerged.

"I'll take that as a yes," Bobby said and released her elbow with what almost seemed like disgust.

Why on earth would he care if she was sweet on Justin Stiles? Truth was, she wasn't. *He* was sweet on *her*. But she'd never thought of him that way. Her heart didn't go pitter-pat when in his presence. Certainly not the way it was racing right now.

But that was only because she was in such a frightening situation. Surely she wasn't actually attracted to Mr. Morgan's rough male beauty.

"No." For some reason, Naomi wanted to explain. "I'm not at all sweet on Mr. Stiles, though why it's any of your business, Mr. Morgan, I'm not likely to know. He's tried to court me. He even talked to Pa. But I'm...well..."

"Well, what, angel?" His voice had softened, and his amber eyes smoked as they gazed into hers.

"I'm not inclined to settle, Mr. Morgan. Most ladies my age are already married, but I—" Why was she telling him this? What did he care that she was holding out for love?

"How old are you, Naomi?"

"I'm—" Her face warmed. "I'm nineteen. I know I'm an old maid. I-I've had plenty of chances."

"I have no doubt of that." Bobby reached toward her and trailed his finger from her eye to her cheek and down the curve of her jaw line, igniting sparks along the way. "You sure are pretty."

Her mouth gaped. She knew she was pretty. She'd heard it often enough over the years. But when Bobby Morgan said it she felt like Helen of Troy, beautiful enough to start a war.

Bobby brushed back some wisps of dark hair that had escaped from her bun during the long ride. Again, his touch seared her and her breathing grew shallow.

"Why do you wear your hair like this?"

"B-Because it's the proper way for a woman of my age to coif herself, Mr. Morgan."

Bobby shook his head. "It's so severe. I'm hardly an expert, but there are lots of styles that would flatter you more." He curled a lock around his finger. "And you'd look the best with it down, hanging around your shoulders in soft waves."

Naomi tried to speak, but her words caught. He was touching her hair, a sinful liberty, and instead of being shocked, all she could think about was how his silky brown locks would feel between her fingers. She cleared her throat. "That would hardly suit me."

Bobby reached behind her and fiddled with her hairpins. She swatted his hand away.

"Mr. Morgan!"

"Please, angel, call me Bobby." He smiled. "I promised you I wouldn't harm you, and I won't. I just want to take your hair down. You don't plan to sleep like that, do you?"

She tossed her head and harrumphed. "Perhaps I will."

"Have it your way, then." He lifted his lips in a lazy half-smile and patted the revolver in his holster. "I'm going to see if I can snag us a rabbit. Will you be fine here for a little while?"

"Of course." She blinked as her eyes shied away from him. "I'll do the best I can, though without my shotgun..."

He ambled off, whistling a lively tune she didn't recognize. One he'd no doubt heard in a saloon. She frowned.

But the frown ceased when her tummy rumbled. She headed back to the raspberry bush but knew the sugary fruit wouldn't satisfy her. She salivated at the image of a fat jackrabbit roasting over a campfire. The smoky aroma, the juicy meat...

She crammed berries into her mouth, the juice dribbling down her chin. Her ma had chided her about her appetite since she was little, but Naomi couldn't help it. She liked food. She liked to eat.

Please, God, let him get a rabbit.

CHAPTER THREE

"Exactly what else do you carry in your boots, Mr. Morgan?" Naomi asked as she bit into a rabbit leg.

Damn, that girl liked to eat. She'd matched him bite for bite so far. Watching her enjoy the meat made skinning it with that dull razor worth all the effort. He shook his head and grinned. If she weren't a preacher's daughter, and if he hadn't kidnapped her, and if he weren't a no good bounty hunter without a heart who was wanted for murder...

Bobby wiped the slate clean in his brain. Such thoughts had no place.

"Whatever I might need," he said.

Her giggle warmed him. He hadn't heard her laugh before, and a musical sound it was.

"I'm certainly glad you thought to carry matches down there. Otherwise, we wouldn't be enjoying this wonderful meal."

"I'll keep you fed, angel." His insides squirmed as she blushed a delectable pink. The same pink he'd seen every time he called her angel. He wasn't likely to stop. "And I wish you'd call me Bobby."

"It's not proper, and you know it, Mr. Morgan." Naomi took another bite.

"You can clean the bones like no man I know."

She blushed again and his groin tightened. Damn, she

was about the prettiest thing he'd ever seen.

"I have a healthy appetite," she said, her tone haughty. "I'll not apologize for it."

"Who asked for an apology?" He tossed his bones in the fire.

"It's difficult to eat without a plate," she said as she followed suit, flinging the remains of her meal into the flames. She stood. "If you'll excuse me, I'm going to get a drink from the creek."

"I'll come along." He rose. "The sun is settin' and I don't want you wanderin' about in the dark."

"For goodness' sake, Mr. Morgan, it won't be pitch dark for another hour or so. I'll be perfectly fine. The creek can't be more than five hundred yards away, and Barney's hobbled down there."

"I said I'm going with you, and that's that." He held out his arm.

And was beyond surprised when she took it.

Was she beginning to believe he meant her no harm? Maybe it was time to tell her again.

"Angel?"

"Yes?"

"I want you to know how sorry I am about all this. Really. If there'd been any other way—"

"There *was* another way, Mr. Morgan. See the system through to the end and let justice prevail."

"The system?" He stopped walking and turned Naomi to face him. He stared into the violet depths of her eyes as he grasped her arm hard.

She shrugged to free herself but he held fast.

"There ain't no system in these parts, darlin'. There's a

sheriff who don't know shit"—Naomi cringed against him—
"and a dirty jail cell in a podunk town where men shoot each
other for sport on a regular basis."

"Mr. Morgan, there is a judicial system in this country.
Our forefathers—"

"You're naive if you think our forefathers had the foresight
to understand what goes on out here. This is the west, angel,
not Philadelphia."

"Don't speak to me like I'm a child." She shook her arm
free, but only because he allowed her to. "I was graduated from
our county school, you know. I even took the state teacher's
examination and was awarded a second grade certificate. I
spoke on the history of our country at a school exhibition. I
know whereof I speak."

Bobby shook his head. "You know theory, Naomi.
Theory. Here's the reality. Dugan didn't even have law the last
time I passed through, and that was nigh six months ago. You
say I should trust the system. What kind of system locks up
an innocent man on the word of five drunks? And where's the
courthouse? You got no judge in Dugan. You'd have to send for
one. How long would that take? How long am I expected to
rot in that cell for a crime I didn't commit?" He kicked at the
dirt. "I got things to do. They took my guns and my horse. My
property. Left me without means to support myself."

Naomi's eyes widened, and black circles formed around
her amethyst irises. Bobby wanted to kick himself. He'd
gotten his dander up and he'd said too much. He knew what
was coming.

"Just how *do* you support yourself, Mr. Morgan?"

Bobby cleared his throat. He wasn't ashamed of the way
he made his living. He didn't steal—not any more—and he'd

given his share to help others over the years. He provided a valuable service to society.

"I hunt criminals," he said. "For money."

He waited for her reaction. He never apologized for his line of work, but for some unexplainable reason, he cared what Naomi might think.

"So you're a bounty hunter."

Her voice had deepened—only a touch, but he noticed. Truth be told, there were few things he wouldn't notice about Naomi. Question was, did the voice change signal acceptance or disgust?

"That's right."

Her hands whipped to her hips, and she stared straight into his eyes, fire blazing in her own. "Well, tell me this then, Mr. Morgan. Has it occurred to you that there might now be a bounty on *your* head?"

Looking into Naomi's glaring eyes, Bobby lost all rational thought. He seized her upper arms, pulled her to him, and crushed his mouth to hers.

Her full red lips were as sweet as he'd imagined. He nibbled across the upper and then the lower, tasting the remnants of the raspberries she'd eaten with her supper. Sweet, tangy, and oh, so perfect. He cherished each second of the kiss, knowing she'd break away at any time. Probably slap him across the face. It'd be no less than he deserved.

Instead, she wove her arms around his neck and whispered against his mouth, her voice a sensual caress.

"Bobby."

His name. How sweet the sound from her innocent lips. He was a goner now. His cock woke in his britches, and he pulled her against his arousal.

"Open, angel," he said against her rosebud mouth. "Open your lips and let me in."

"I don't know how—" She broke away and spoke into his chin. At the same time her fingers entwined in his hair. "Bobby. This isn't...proper."

"To hell with proper, darlin'. Kiss me back. Please. I'm aching for you." He found her mouth again and drank from her raspberry lips. "Open. Please."

A soft sigh escaped her throat as she parted her lips, just a touch, and he slipped his tongue between them. Every nerve in his body screamed for him to thrust into her mouth, to mimic what he wanted to do with another part of his body. But he held himself in check. Likely she'd never kissed a man before, and even if she had she was otherwise untouched. As much as he longed for her, he didn't want to scare her away.

But when the tip of her sweet tongue touched his, he shattered. He pulled her closer, reached behind her with one hand, and began plucking out those dratted hairpins. With his other hand, he held her back at the waist and pulled her against the throbbing in his groin. Soon he was tunneling his fingers through the thick sable waves. They were softer than he'd imagined, like fine oriental silk. A throaty groan rumbled from her chest, and like the waters through a damn breaking, he rushed forward, thrusting into her satiny mouth with urgent yet tender kisses. His tongue tangled with hers, and when she moaned again he deepened the kiss and tasted every crevice of her soft, sweet mouth.

The kiss went on and on, and when she finally broke away, her breath came in rapid puffs against his cheek.

"Angel," he whispered, "you're so beautiful. So perfect." He rained kisses across her cheek, her jawline, to the tender spot below her earlobe. Her lavender fragrance ensnared him, and he inhaled deeply. Still she panted against him, and he waited for her to stop him, almost *wanted* her to stop him, because if he didn't stop soon he wasn't sure he'd be able to.

"Bobby." Desire thickened her voice.

His cock responded. How he longed to set it free from its constraints, to watch her wrap her ruby lips around it and pleasure him. Then he'd bury his face between her creamy thighs and return the favor before plunging his hardness into her virgin depths.

But he couldn't do this.

She was too good for the likes of him. To soil her would be to bastardize perfection.

Once more, though. Just one more taste of those honeyed lips and then he'd stop. He nibbled at her neck, breathed in her lavender essence, and then trailed to her lips again.

"Naomi," he said, and bent to touch his mouth to hers.

She gasped, but before he could thrust his tongue into her, she broke away from him, turned, and ran toward the creek.

Who'd he been trying to kid?

If he'd tasted her again, he wouldn't have been able to stop.

CHAPTER FOUR

Naomi knelt in the soft mud and splashed her face with the crisp, clear water. She was burning inside, on fire, and she needed something, anything, to cool her off. Her heart pounded against her sternum, her skin rippled with heated chills, and the flutter between her legs had become unbearable in its intensity.

How had she let this happen? She knew better. She'd been raised better. What would Ma and Pa think of her brazen actions? She'd already succumbed to gluttony. And now lust?

More water. She splashed herself again and took a long drink. The liquid soothed her, but heat still flashed through her body. Every sense inside her screamed to run back into Bobby's arms. The sweet pressure of his hard body against hers. The spicy male aroma of his neck. The sleek texture of his beautiful brown hair. The rough stubble of his cheek against hers as he nibbled at her lips, her neck, her earlobe. The softness of his lips. She'd never imagined a man's lips could be so soft.

And his tongue. Smooth and delicious inside her mouth. Such an amazing sensation. More. She wanted more. So much more. His moist tongue trailing wetness across her neck, her shoulders, over the buds of her nipples which were tight and painful against her bodice.

Naomi forced the images from her mind. What she

desired would be sinful with a fine upstanding man.

And she wanted it with an outlaw.

She splashed her face once again, the fire still burning deep within her.

"Angel?" Bobby's voice had deepened.

Tingles raced across the back of Naomi's neck. Slick perspiration beaded on her forehead despite the coolness of the water. Her pulse raced.

"Angel," he said again, "are you all right?"

All right? She choked back a laugh that had seemingly come from nowhere. She doubted she'd ever be all right again. Heat scalded her face, and she couldn't turn to look at him. She was afraid of what she'd see in his eyes.

Of what he'd see in hers.

Within a few seconds he was next to her, his canvas-clad knees indenting the soft mud. He reached tentatively toward her and stroked her cheek. Such a tiny touch, barely palpable, yet it scorched a path of fire in its wake. What was wrong with her?

She brushed his hand away and reached for more water.

"It won't help," he said.

"Wh-What?"

"Trying to cool off." He chuckled and reached toward her again. She backed away.

"I know how you're feelin', darlin'. I'm feelin' the same. And I can guarantee you an ice bath wouldn't help me right now."

Naomi shivered at the thought of an ice bath, but then heated again as she gazed into his darkened amber eyes. She had to say something. But what? She'd never felt anything like this.

"I..."

"Don't worry, angel. I understand." He cupped his hands and took a long slow drink from the creek. Then he took her arm and helped her up. "We've made a mess of ourselves."

Naomi glanced at the muddy knees of his duckins and looked down at her brown work dress streaked with the same wet clay. Now what? They had nothing else to wear.

"Mr. Morgan—"

"Back to Mr. Morgan now, are we?"

"Well, I...I think it's only appropriate."

"Angel, my tongue was just in your mouth. I think we know each other well enough to be on a first name basis."

His bold words, though highly personal and improper, flashed across her hot body and landed between her legs. He caught her before she could drop down to the water again.

"We need to sleep now, darlin'. I want to get an early start tomorrow. By noon we'll hit the railroad camp, and you can be on your way home."

Home. Thank goodness. Home was where she could get back to her life. Back to life before Bobby Morgan. Had it only been a few hours ago? It seemed she'd spent a lifetime with this man. Wanted to spend another.

"I...Mr. Morgan, I'm so very sorry for..." For what? For letting him kiss her? The good Lord knew that was a lie. That kiss had been the most powerful experience of her life.

He smiled, and that adorable dimple twinkled at her. "I'm the one who's sorry. I promised I wouldn't harm you, and I'll keep that promise. I've learned how to control my actions. Trust in that, if nothing else."

Harm her? Is that what he thought he'd done? Her mouth dropped open but she shut it quickly. He was thinking about what came next between a man and a woman. After a kiss. Her married friends had told her how difficult, even painful, it could be for a man to stop. Had she caused him pain? The thought saddened her. She shouldn't have let the kiss happen. It definitely couldn't happen again.

"I don't think we need to find the cavern," he said. "It's a beautiful night. We can sleep under the stars. The ground's pretty flat over by those boulders." He pointed. "God knows I've slept on a lot worse, though I reckon this'll be pretty uncomfortable for a lady like you."

"I'm certain I'll be fine." Naomi stalked past him to the area he'd gestured to and lay down in her soiled dress.

Bobby lay down a good ten feet away from her, no doubt keeping his distance on purpose, for which she was grateful.

Her body ached from the time spent bareback, and she tossed around. She could handle the lumps on the ground, if only she had a soft place to rest her weary head.

In the darkness, the scent of spicy male assailed her. Ten feet away, and she was still hyper aware of him.

"Come here, angel." His voice traveled across the thickness of the humid air. "You can rest your head on my shoulder."

"I'm perfectly fine, thank you."

Bobby's chuckle rang out. "You're not used to this, and I'm not gonna get any shuteye with you thrashin' around like a bear in a beehive. Let me offer you a resting place. I'll keep my hands to myself."

"I said no thank you, Mr. Morgan." She turned away and burrowed her head into her upper arm. He kept his word and didn't touch her. Soon his breathing turned shallow and regular, and she knew he'd fallen asleep.

She struggled to get comfortable and said her prayers, begging for forgiveness for her wantonness in allowing that kiss. But the prayers gave way to images of Bobby caressing her, undressing her, loving her with that beautiful and sinful mouth of his. Flutters coursed through her belly as she recalled the sensual scraping of his chestnut stubble against her cheeks. He badly needed a shave. He did have that razor, perhaps she could...

Her body jerked. Where had such a sinful thought come from? And about her kidnapper, no less? Shaving a man was more intimate than a stolen kiss. It was a wifely duty.

A strange, yet not unpleasant, sensation spasmed in her belly at the thought of brushing lather onto his chiseled face and drawing the straight blade up against the hair growth.

He'd smile at her, those amber eyes twinkling, and she'd murmur something coquettish and then back away, embarrassed by her boldness.

Fire consumed her body. Again.

Truth be told, she was sorry he'd kept his promise not to touch her.

She clasped her hands together and prayed to be free from lustful thoughts.

CHAPTER FIVE

Naomi woke to the sun rising against a pink sky. She stretched and discovered new twinges in her already aching body. Where was Bobby? She smiled when she discovered he'd rolled up his shirt and placed it under her head.

But if his shirt was here...

She warmed. He'd haunted her dreams through the night. She'd awoken several times, drenched in sweat, images of their bodies entwined plaguing her, to find him still sleeping soundly. He was older than she, and more experienced. To him, she was no doubt just another woman of many. Clearly he'd had no problem sleeping.

She sat up and brought his shirt to her nose, inhaling his now familiar aroma. Would she ever be able to get enough of it?

"Stop," she said aloud, and tossed the shirt to the ground. She was behaving like a loose woman. She'd been raised better.

Naomi stood and brushed the now dried dirt from her dress.

And beheld a dazzling sight.

Bobby stood in the creek, his back to her, cleansing himself in the cool water. He was too far away for her to see much, and though she knew it a bad idea, her feet, seemingly disengaged from her brain, propelled her forward.

When she'd walked a few hundred feet, she plopped on

her fanny and appraised his male beauty with wide eyes. His hair was wet and clung to his thick neck. His golden back rippled with muscles, from the breadth of his strong shoulders to the leanness of his narrow hips. The smooth slopes of his buttocks shone with wetness. Two perfect globes. Her heart quickened and she lowered her eyes, only to raise them again, unable to look away. His legs were long and powerful, covered with fine brown hair, and when he squatted to rinse his face, the sinewy lines in his calves bulged.

As she considered averting her eyes, he stood tall and turned around, his eyes widening at the sight of her.

Brown hair, the same color as his head, scattered across his golden chest. Two copper nipples poked through, and she had the strangest urge to touch them. She gazed downward, to his flat belly, his navel, and the line of hair that ended where the male part of him hung loosely within a nest of chestnut curls.

It drew her eyes like a magnet.

"'Mornin', angel," he drawled, not seeming the least bit uncomfortable as he ambled out of the creek to his duckins which were draped across a rock. His legs still dripping, he scrambled into them, and she couldn't help thinking what a shame it was to cover such a paragon of manliness.

"Would you like to wash up? I'll give you some privacy." He chuckled. "Though you haven't afforded me the same courtesy."

Heat flooded Naomi's cheeks, and she glanced down at her soiled garments. She couldn't launder them. They'd never dry in time. But oh, to clean her clammy skin sounded like heaven on earth.

"I apologize, Mr. Morgan. I didn't know you were here,

and I wanted…needed a drink of water."

"Go ahead," he said, buttoning his trousers. "And wash up if you want. I'll pick us some berries for our breakfast."

Though she longed to cleanse her body, even with no soap, she couldn't undress with Bobby in such close proximity. "I'll just wash up my face and hands. I'll be fine."

"Suit yourself," he said, and he walked, barefoot, toward the boulders where his shirt lay.

Naomi stripped off her shoes and stockings and waded into the creek. The cool water lapped around her toes and ankles, tickling her. She let her skirts drop. So they'd be wet. They'd dry. She squatted and splashed water on her face and then palmed some sandy dirt from the creek bed and scrubbed her hands. When she'd drunk her fill of clean water, she returned to the creek bank, picked up her shoes and stockings, and headed to where Bobby sat on the dry dirt. She plunked down across from him and plaited her tangled tresses into a long braid.

"Here you go," he said, handing her some berries. Her fingers still stained from the previous evening, she popped a few into her mouth.

"I'll get you a clean dress when we get to the camp," Bobby said.

"That's not necessary."

"Of course it is," he said. "I can't send you home in that old brown thing." He cocked his head and raked his gaze over her, heating her skin. "You shouldn't wear such a drab color. Blue. You should wear blue, bright blue or violet, to bring out your pretty eyes."

Naomi looked away, embarrassed. "You won't be able to find a dress for me at a railroad camp."

"Oh, you'd be amazed what I can find," he said. "I just have to offer the right price."

Naomi dropped her mouth open. "But you said Sheriff Stiles took all your money."

"Correction, angel. I said he took the money in my pockets." He grinned. "Trust me, I keep the bare minimum in my pockets."

Naomi couldn't help but laugh. "Your boots."

He winked. "My boots. And honestly, if your sweet sheriff'd had a clue what he was doing, my boots would've been the first place he looked." He smirked. "But he didn't, lucky for you."

"And you."

"Yup. And me. I need a new horse and a new weapon. I could go for some clean duds myself. And I'll need money to pay your passage home."

"Just how much money do you have, Mr. Morgan?"

"Enough that you don't need to worry about me, darlin', if you'd been inclined to. Bounty huntin' can be pretty profitable. If you're good at it."

"And I suppose you're good at it," she said coyly.

"Angel, I'm the best."

★ ★ ★ ★

"Wh-Where exactly are we?" Naomi trembled and leaned back into the solid wall of Bobby's chest. Two rough men eyed them as they trotted through the dusty railroad camp. Naomi knew the railroad wouldn't reach Dakota Territory for a while. President Lincoln, may he rest in peace, had only signed the Railroad Act a few years ago. So what was this place?

"The workers have to blast through some of the rock here," Bobby said. "It's a dangerous job, but they're well paid. I've passed through here several times, and they're a good bunch of fellas, always willing to do some trading. I'm bankin' on that today."

Bobby stopped old Barney and hitched him to a post next to a ramshackle shanty. He helped Naomi down, squeezing her hand. She was strangely comforted by the gesture.

"I'll take you to Bessie. She feeds this mass of men. The foreman's name's Ike. He's a right nice fella. Married. A couple kids. He'll see you get home all right."

Naomi trembled and eased closer to Bobby. She wasn't sure about this. "Uh, Mr. Morgan? Bobby?"

He smiled down at her. "Hmm?"

"Please don't leave me here."

"Don't be scared, angel. Bessie and Ike'll take care of you. They know how to keep these hicks in line. They're all out workin' right now anyway. Come on. I'll take you in to meet them.

He led her into the building.

A plump woman standing over a cookstove greeted them. "Bobby Morgan, as I live and breathe."

"Hello, Bessie."

"And who's this pretty thing? Don't tell me you went and settled down."

"No." Bobby flushed.

Naomi's breath caught at the rosiness in his chiseled cheeks.

"You know me better than that. This here's Miss Naomi Blackburn. I need you to see to her, if you don't mind. And get

Ike to get her passage home. To Dugan. Her pa's the preacher there."

"And just how'd she end up with you? As if I didn't know."

"Take it easy. It was all a silly misunderstanding. Seems I was caught in the wrong place at the wrong time during a furlough in Dugan. This lady was my ticket out of town. I've taken good care of her, but I got to get back to work, and you know my work's no place for a lady. I need to sniff out Daily again before his trail gets cold."

"If you say so. Good Lord knows it ain't none of my business." Her double chin jiggled when she laughed. "But I'll ask anyway. Did this man hurt you, honey?"

Naomi gulped.

"Now, Bessie, you know I'd never hurt a lady," Bobby said. "Come on now."

"I'm sorry, Bobby, but there she stands in dirty clothes and her hair in a mussed braid. I need to hear it from her."

Bobby looked at her expectantly. She shook her head. "I'm fine, ma'am. Truly. I just...I just really want to go home."

Bessie's lips curved into a welcoming smile. "We'll take care of you, honey. We owe Bobby here that much. I think Ike's out in the office tent...nope, here he comes now."

"Morgan." A tall gray-haired man held out his hand. "Been a little while since we've seen you."

"Only 'bout a month, Ike. I need to do some transactin'."

Naomi shuddered as the older man's eyes raked over her body. They were ice blue and bloodshot. His gray moustache twitched, and he rubbed his hands over his soiled dungarees.

"What do you need?" he asked Bobby.

"A decent horse and saddle, and a piece, two if you can find 'em. Clothes. Some food to take with me. And a new dress for the lady."

Ike choked out a chortle and then spit on the ground. "Can't say I can find you a dress. She's a little smaller than Bessie."

"Really, Mr. Morgan, I don't need a dress," Naomi said, fingering her bedraggled garment. "This will do fine. I'll be home soon."

Bobby smiled at her and continued, "Blue, Ike. Blue or Violet. I'll make it worth your while. And I need you to get her home to Dugan. Her and her horse."

"That I can do. First thing tomorrow. I won't ask you what she's doin' here, Bobby, but I hope you've taken care of her. She reminds me of my oldest girl."

"I have. No harm has come to her. But she wants to go home."

"She can stay with Bessie tonight." Ike spit again, and though Naomi's stomach churned at the wad of tobacco that landed on the dirt floor of the shanty, her mind eased. This man had a daughter her age. She'd be safe with him. And Bobby trusted him. That fact soothed her even more.

"Thank you kindly," Bobby said. "Now about my other business."

"Go on out to the office, and I'll see what we can do for you. Bessie'll take care of your lady."

"Come on, honey." Bessie took Naomi's arm. "I'll show you where I bunk down. It ain't much, but you can clean yourself up a little, take care of necessary business. Then we'll see about getting you a snack. You hungry?"

Naomi let out a laugh. Always. "Yes, ma'am."

"Just Bessie, honey."

"All right...Bessie."

Bessie's room at the back of the cooking shanty was tiny, but Naomi gasped when she saw the washtub in the corner.

Bessie's brown eyes twinkled. "You'd fancy a bath, wouldn't you now?"

"Oh, no," Naomi said. "It's not necessary."

"I'll have Davey haul in some water. It won't be warm, but in this heat, I doubt you'll mind." She winked. "I even have some fancy soap my son sent me from New York. Can you believe it? New York?"

Naomi nodded. She knew all about New York. Had studied about it in school, but had never dreamed of actually visiting there. "Your son's in New York?"

"Yup. He's a gentleman's gentleman for some highfalutin lawyer. He sends me money every month." She beamed, pride evident in her eyes.

"How wonderful, but I can't use your gift from him."

"Pshaw. The stuff's made for a lady like you, not an old hen like me. It'd be my pleasure for you to use it."

"Miss Bessie?" A small voice beckoned as a knock sounded on the thin wood door separating Bessie's quarters from the kitchen.

"Yes, come in, Davey," Bessie said.

A small boy with skin brown as molasses entered, carrying an indigo bundle. "Mr. Ike said to bring this to you. It's for Mr. Bobby's lady."

"Thank you, honey," Bessie said, taking the bundle. "Now you run and fetch some water. Miss Naomi's going to have a bath."

"Yes'm." The boy trotted off, a smile on his elfin brown face.

"Davey wandered into the camp about a year ago," Bessie

said. "Skinny as a rail and covered in open sores. Ike took him into the camp and we nursed him back to health. Now he does odd jobs for us, and we feed him and let him sleep in the bunkhouse with the men."

Naomi nodded, hoping her shock wasn't evident on her face. She had never seen a Negro before.

Bessie held up the blue bundle, and Naomi gasped. The fine fabric of the dress fell in ripples to the floor. Small white flowers floated across the sea of blue-violet dimity.

Naomi's jaw dropped. She'd never seen such a lovely garment.

"I'll be," Bessie said. "This must be a gift for one of the workers' ladies. Bobby must have offered a fine sum for him to part with it." Her gaze wandered over Naomi's body. "Looks just about your size too."

"Oh my..."

"The boy's sweet on you, honey, that's for sure."

Naomi's cheeks warmed, and she reached to smooth the silky material. "It's beautiful."

"It'll suit you, no doubt," Bessie said, as she laid the dress across a wooden chair in the corner of the room. "Why don't you just rest your weary bones a little on my bed, until Davey gets the tub all filled."

Rest sounded like God's elixir to Naomi, who wondered if she'd ever be free from aches and pains again. She smiled at the older woman and lay down on the narrow quilt-covered bed.

Within seconds, a voice was buzzing in her ear. "Your bath's ready, honey."

She sat up, unaware, at first, of her surroundings.

"You done fell asleep, and I'm not surprised." Bessie

bustled about the washtub. "I've set out the soap for you. When you're finished, you just call me, and we'll get you outfitted in that pretty new dress, you hear?"

Naomi stifled a yawn and nodded. After Bessie left, she undressed quickly and lowered herself into the tin washtub. The water was cool, and though warm would be better on her aching bones, at least it was wet and would erase the grime from her weary body. She unwrapped Bessie's fancy soap and held it to her nose. Lavender and rose. Perfect. She smiled, thinking about smelling nice for Bobby when he saw her in the dress.

She rubbed the soap over her body and her hair, scrubbing voraciously. So wonderful to feel clean again! When the water had turned a dingy gray, Naomi stepped out and wrapped herself in the toweling Bessie had laid out. She squeezed as much moisture as she could from her hair and then dressed in her undergarments. Feeling bashful, she held the dress up against her body. Bessie had no looking glass, but Naomi knew the dress would flatter her.

"You decent, honey?" Bessie asked through the closed door.

"Yes, please come in," Naomi said.

Bessie helped Naomi don the new dress, brushed out her hair for her, and plaited it.

"You're as lovely as can be," Bessie said with a smile. "Now go on out there and show Bobby."

Anticipation coursed through Naomi's veins as she imagined Bobby's amber eyes glowing when he looked at her. "Oh, yes, Bessie. I'd like to. Where is he?"

"Well, I ain't seen him since he went to the office tent with Ike. I imagine he's still out there, transacting for all the stuff he needs." She smiled as she smoothed Naomi's collar. "Why don't you go out there and find him, honey?"

Naomi's feet raced as quickly as her heart as she sped to the canvas tent outside the shanty. Without thinking, she boldly strode in. Ike sat behind a makeshift desk.

"Well, you're a sight for sore eyes."

"Where's Bobby?" Naomi asked. "I want to thank him for the dress."

Ike rose and walked around the desk until he was standing in front of her. "He's gone, sweetheart."

"Gone?" An anvil settled in Naomi's stomach. Surely this was a mistake.

"'Fraid so, little lady. He couldn't stick around, but he did leave you a means home tomorrow."

Naomi's throat caught. He'd left her, and she'd never see him again. She wanted nothing more than to go home, but—

"Course—" Ike cleared his throat,

Naomi cringed, waiting for him to spit. He didn't.

"There's the matter of payment for your transport."

"D-Didn't Bobby take care of that?"

"In a manner of speaking." Ike grabbed her arm. "He left me you."

Naomi struggled, her heart racing. Bobby wouldn't. He couldn't. Surely Ike couldn't mean... He'd said she reminded him of his daughter!

"And you won't make a sound, you hear me?"

Ike's yellow teeth glowed when he smiled. A horrible, evil smile. He lowered his head until his mouth was only inches from hers. His sour breath assaulted her, and she gagged.

"Please." She coughed. "You can't."

"Oh, I can. It's due me. Bobby promised you'd cooperate,

and you will. You'll lie down and spread those thin legs, and you absolutely will not scream. Or I'll slit that pretty alabaster throat of yours. Do we understand each other?"

CHAPTER SIX

He'd left without saying goodbye. Bobby felt lower than a rattler's belly, but he hadn't had a choice. If he'd seen Naomi one more time, especially in that dress, he wouldn't have been able to leave her. Truth be told, he was having a darn hard time now. And that wasn't all. Something niggled at the back of his neck. A feeling. Call it intuition. His intuition was telling him to go back. That something wasn't right.

He'd learned long ago in his business never to ignore his intuition, but he was bound and determined to do so now. Naomi deserved better than a bounty hunter on the run. He'd never be able to properly care for her. She was a lady, and she needed a gentleman. That surely wasn't him.

Where were these ridiculous ideas coming from, anyway? He didn't want a woman tying him down. He wasn't capable of taking care of another person besides himself. And he sure as hell wasn't capable of loving someone else.

Was he?

He hadn't loved anyone since his mother had been taken from him all those years ago. He didn't even remember the emotion. Admittedly, he felt tenderness for Naomi. He was certainly willing to protect her at all costs. He ached for her kisses, and God knew he wanted to make love to her. His cock tightened at the thought.

Truth be told, if she were in danger, he'd willingly give his life for hers.

That wasn't love, was it?

He let out a whoop, as he turned the young stallion, Thor, around. He was headed back to the camp.

Back to the woman he loved.

★ ★ ★ ★

Ike forced Naomi against the desk, bending her over. "I'm gonna have you like this first, like a goddamned animal."

She struggled as he hiked up her skirts, tears streaming from her eyes. His strength defeated hers. Her heart raced, but she couldn't scream. She dared not. He'd said he'd kill her.

Damn Bobby Morgan for leaving her to this! She willingly thought the sinful curse. How had she ever had tender feelings for the man? He was a criminal. A kidnapper. An outlaw. He'd traded her virtue for her ticket home. Or maybe for a new gun. Or a new horse. Or money for his whores.

"Oh, yes." Ike's slimy voice dripped with lasciviousness as he thrust one hand into the slit in her drawers.

Acid rose in her throat.

"A little dry, but that don't bother me. You'll moisten up soon enough."

He ripped her drawers down to her knees, exposing her bare buttocks. His hand came down on her with a cool slap, and Naomi winced. Her married friends hadn't said anything about this. But then neither were they forced against their will.

She gritted her teeth, but a scream escaped.

"Damn it, bitch!" He slapped her buttocks again.

A tear fell down her cheek.

"I told you to keep quiet. He reached around and stuffed

a soiled handkerchief into her mouth. Naomi gagged as the rank taste of chewing tobacco and spittle seeped against her tongue.

She bit down, determined to bear whatever he had in store for her. She had to, if she ever hoped to see her ma, pa, and sister again.

She closed her eyes and pictured her pa's claim outside of Dugan. She imagined the protection of Pa's strong arms as they lifted her off the ground in a bear hug. The serenity of Ma's gentle smile as they kneaded bread together. The innocence her baby sister, Ruth, only fifteen, half child-half woman. Naomi had so much to teach her yet.

She'd see them again. All she had to do was endure hell.

As she steeled herself against the impending assault, Ike's hold loosened, and she fell forward onto the desk as a gunshot exploded.

"Ike Hawkins, you fuckin' son of a bitch."

Bobby's voice. Icy cold, as she'd never heard it. Then another shot, and a heavy thunk on the dirt.

Tears streamed down Naomi's face, and she choked through the handkerchief. Within seconds, Bobby's hand was in front of her, easing the dirty fabric from her parched mouth. With the most tender of touches, he placed her drawers back around her waist and pulled her skirt down so she was no longer shamefully exposed.

He turned her around and pulled her to him, crushing her against his body as though he couldn't get her close enough.

"Angel, angel," he whispered. "I'm so sorry. So goddamned sorry."

He held her for what seemed like an eternity while she sobbed into his shoulder, basking in his strength. She was safe.

Safe with Bobby.

Finally, when her sobs lessened a bit and she rubbed her nose on his shirt, he grasped her shoulders and pushed her away, but only far enough to gaze at her with angry, yet sad, amber eyes.

"Did he?" Bobby cleared his throat. "He didn't...did he?"

"N-No."

"Did he put anything inside you? His finger?"

Naomi trembled against his hard body. She couldn't say the horrible words. She shook her head slowly and broke into tears again.

"What on God's green earth?" Bessie burst into the office tent, Davey on her heels. "We heard gunshots. Oh, my!"

Naomi followed Bessie's gaze to Ike motionless on the dirt, crimson blood oozing through his cotton shirt and dungarees. Her throat constricted, and she buried her nose in Bobby's shirt again.

"What in the world happened here?" Bessie demanded.

"Ike tried to have his way with Naomi." His arms tightened around Naomi as he spoke. "Luckily I got here when I did."

Bessie knelt down and placed a hand on Ike's neck. "Christ, Bobby. He's dead."

Naomi gasped. Her stomach roiled with dread. Bobby had killed a man for sure this time.

For her.

His hard body stiffened against hers, though he continued to rub her back in soothing circles. "He sure as hell is. I know how to aim to kill. Truth be told, I wish he'd come back from the dead so I could kill him again with my bare hands. I'd make him pay for putting his filthy hands on her."

Naomi, her head still embedded in Bobby's shoulder, heard Bessie's soft sigh.

"I'm taking Naomi away from here," Bobby said. "I need you two to cover for us until nightfall. Don't call in the law. Trust me. Ike got what was comin' to him."

"Uh...well...I suppose." Bessie stood.

"It's not like me to be so wrong about a man. To think, I trusted that slug." Bobby caressed Naomi's neck, massaging some of the tension out of her.

His touch stilled her shivers and she sighed.

"To think we all did," Bessie said, and turned to Naomi. "Honey, are you all right?"

"Yes." It was a lie, but nothing else would come out.

"Come on. I'll take you back to my room to rest."

"N-No. Thank you, Bessie. All I want right now is to leave this place."

"I understand," Bessie said. "You take care of her, Bobby. She's gonna need a tender hand tonight."

"She'll have it." Bobby knelt down next to Ike's body and pulled a leather wallet out of his pocket. "The money I paid him for her transport," he said to Bessie as he counted out some bills.

"H-He said..." Naomi stammered, remembering Ike's foul words.

"What, angel?"

"He said you paid with me. That I had to..."

Bobby's face reddened, and the muscles in his jaw clenched visibly. "Bessie, Davey, don't expect to see me back here again. Come on, angel." He led her out of the tent and then turned back to Bessie. "If you can, send a wire to Dugan, to a Reverend Blackburn. Tell him Naomi is all right and she'll be home soon."

"Bobby—" Naomi said.

"Don't sign my name. I'm wanted there."

Naomi clamped her hand to Bobby's arm as they walked toward a beautiful roan stallion. He helped her onto the mount and swung up behind her.

"Angel, I'll take care of you," he said into her ear. "Whatever you need. I swear it."

Naomi choked back a sob. "You left without saying goodbye."

"I'm sorry for that. I was weak. I thought if I saw you I wouldn't be able to leave you. Turns out it didn't matter. I had to come back."

Naomi warmed, slightly, as she nestled back into his rock-hard chest. "I'm glad you came back. If you hadn't..."

"But I did. And in time, though I wish I'd been soon enough to stop him from tryin'..." He brushed his lips against her neck. "I won't leave you again. I promise. I'll personally take you home."

She shivered. "But what about you? They'll arrest you."

"I'll make them understand."

Battered and fatigued, she let herself believe the soothing words from this outlaw who'd kidnapped her. He'd come back for her. In this moment, that's all that mattered. She leaned back and closed her eyes as he nudged the horse into a gallop.

CHAPTER SEVEN

"I need two rooms, please," Bobby said to the clerk at the hotel in a small town Naomi had never heard of. Bobby laid some bills on the counter and took the two keys. "The lady'll need a bath sent up," he said over his shoulder as he led Naomi up the stairs. "And we'll both need supper."

"The kitchen's closed, sir," the clerk said.

Bobby dug into his pocket, turned, and tossed the clerk some coins. "Wake the cook. I'll expect a decent meal within the hour."

At any other time, Naomi would wince at the way Bobby literally threw money around. But right now her bones ached, and all she wanted was to erase the afternoon's events. Since that was impossible, she'd settle for a warm bed.

Bobby led her to her room and unlocked the door. "I'll be right down the hall if you need me," he said. "Your bath'll be up soon. I want you to relax."

Icy fingers of fear slithered across her skin. "Don't leave me alone. Please."

"Angel, I'll be right down the hall. I'll come eat supper with you if you like, but a hot bath is what you need right now."

Naomi launched herself into his arms. "What I need right now is you, Bobby Morgan. I..." She couldn't explain the fear she was feeling. She was safe. Safe behind a locked door with Bobby only a few feet down the hall. Why was she shivering at the thought of being left alone?

"You don't want me here while you bathe," he said.

"I don't need a bath. I don't need food. I need to be with you. I...I'm scared."

"Darlin', I won't let anything happen to you. I promise. Trust me."

"But you left me."

"I won't make that mistake again." He disengaged himself from her embrace and paced into the room, raking his fingers through his chestnut locks. He turned, and Naomi sighed at the sight of him. He was truly beautiful.

And troubled. The thin lines on his forehead gave him away.

"I'll never forgive myself for leaving you there. I wish I could change the last few days for you, angel."

"But then we wouldn't have met."

"That would have been better for you."

"No." Despite what had happened, the thought of being without Bobby felt all wrong, like a part of her would be missing. Naomi ran to his arms again, thunking her head into his chest so hard he let out an "oof."

"You promised you'd take care of me."

"All right." He sighed. "I won't leave you. But there's only one bed in here, darlin'. I guess I'll sleep on the floor."

"You don't have to. I trust you. We slept close last night, and you were a perfect gentleman."

"You have no idea how hard that was for me."

Naomi smiled against his chest. So he *had* wanted her. Maybe even as much as she'd wanted him. "You can turn your back while I bathe."

"Trust me, I'll have to"—he chuckled into her hair—"if

you expect me to behave myself."

True to his word, Bobby kept his eyes out the window while Naomi bathed. She scrubbed herself nearly raw. The whole of Dakota Territory didn't contain enough soap to erase the vileness of Ike Hawkins from her body. Yet still she scoured her skin, determined to cleanse every pore. When she was wrinkled as her granny, she stepped out of the washtub, toweled off, and slipped into the cotton nightdress a maid had provided.

All the time Bobby sat, his chin resting on his hands, his elbows on the window sill, gazing into the dark night.

"You can turn around now," Naomi said.

He did so and smiled. "That was one long bath, angel."

"I felt dirty." She looked down at her bare feet. "Like I'd been violated. I wanted to get clean."

"I understand." He nodded. "Our supper should be here soon. You hungry?"

Naomi grimaced. She *should* be hungry. She hadn't eaten since... Was it the raspberries that morning? But her hollow tummy didn't want food.

A knock on the door brought a maid carrying a tray. She set two plates on the small table in the room. Bobby thanked her and offered her a coin and then closed the door and turned to Naomi.

"You didn't answer me. I know you must be starving."

"No. Not really."

He winked. "You with the 'I'll not apologize for my appetite?'"

She forced a smile. "I'll try. I know I *should* eat." She took a seat at the table, and Bobby sat across from her. She removed the cloth napkin covering her plate to expose two pieces of fried chicken, fresh corn, and a roll. A glass of water sat next to the plate. She took a sip and inhaled. She normally loved fried chicken.

Bobby took a bite of chicken and smiled. "I've had better, but it's good. Try some. Please."

For him, she'd try. She picked up a drumstick and bit into it. And suddenly she was ravenous. She cleaned her plate and found Bobby, his plate still half full, showcasing his perfect white teeth in a gleeful smile.

"Now that's my angel," he said.

"I admit, I do feel better." Naomi drained her glass of water.

Bobby poured her another from the pitcher on the table. "Do you want some of mine?" Bobby indicated his plate.

She let out a giggle. "I may have an appetite, Bobby Morgan, but I'll never take food from a man. You've had a hard day too. Please, eat."

"If you're sure." His dimple flashed as he picked up a piece of chicken.

Naomi's body warmed, and she began to feel a little safer, a little more secure, in the presence of this man. He would let no harm come to her.

Something he'd said earlier tugged in her mind. "Bobby?"

"Hmm?"

"What did you mean when you said you understood?"

"Understood what, darlin'?"

Naomi cleared her throat and went on. "Understood when I said I felt like I was violated."

Bobby dropped his chicken leg, and his gaze. "I didn't mean anything."

"Please. Tell me. It'll help me, I think."

He raised his gaze and his eyes burned gold. "I don't speak of it."

Tiny invisible gnats crept over Naomi's skin. Though she knew she imagined them, she rubbed her arms to chase them away. "I-I didn't mean to upset you."

"You didn't." He shoved a fork full of corn into his mouth and swallowed, seemingly without chewing. "You sure you don't want anything else to eat?"

"I'm stuffed, really." She forced a smile. "But thank you for offering."

"I told you once I'd keep you fed, and I aim to."

"I know." Naomi stretched her arms over her head and stifled a yawn. "Goodness, I'm tired."

Bobby covered the rest of his supper with the napkin and stood. "You need to get some rest." He held out his hand. "Come on, I'll walk you to the outhouse. I don't want you going alone."

Naomi's cheeks heated at his allusion to such a private, though necessary, function. "I'd prefer not to leave the room. I'll use the chamber pot in the corner."

"Fine," he said. "I'll give you some privacy then. Will you be all right here alone for a few minutes?"

Naomi's skin turned cold, but she nodded, determined to be strong. "I'm sure I'll be fine. Please just make sure I'm locked in. And don't be too long?"

He smiled, and she breathed a little easier. It was a real smile. He wasn't upset with her.

"I won't be. Just long enough for you to take care of business, all right?" He leaned down and kissed the top of her head. "I told you I'd keep you safe, and I meant it."

He left the room, and the key clicked, locking her in. After taking care of all necessary business she snuggled into bed, leaving the kerosene lamp burning for Bobby.

A few moments later he entered, and she squeezed her eyes shut, feigning sleep. He moved quietly, no doubt to keep from disturbing her. When the bed sagged with his weight, she fought the impulse to turn into his arms.

CHAPTER EIGHT

Naomi woke, screaming. Someone was shaking her.

"Angel. Angel. It's only me." Bobby's deep voice, laced with concern, floated over her like a silken veil. Still she trembled, and perspiration dripped from her hairline.

"Was it a nightmare?" Bobby pulled her into his arms and kissed her clammy forehead.

His warm, hard body was like a rock in an ocean of torment. She clung to him, making no sound. Had it been a nightmare? She couldn't remember.

"It's all right now," he said.

His melodic voice soothed her, but still she shook. The inky blackness of the night frightened her. "Bobby?"

"What, angel?"

"C-Could you light the lamp?"

"Yes, but I'll have to let go of you for a minute."

She nodded against his hard chest and he released her. Within a minute, a flame flickered in the lamp on the night table and chased the eerie darkness away.

Naomi breathed easier and regarded Bobby's bare torso. She hadn't seen him unclothed since she'd come across him bathing in the creek. Had that been only a day ago? Naomi felt as though she'd aged a decade since then. That day he'd been far away. Now he was close, within arm's reach. The golden tone of his shoulders had darkened to honey-bronze in the glimmering lamplight. Curly dark hair dusted the sinewy muscle of his chest and abdomen, and his coppery nipples stared at her, begging to be touched. She reached for one with a shaky hand, but stopped herself. She dropped her gaze to his navel, to the line of hair leading to what she'd seen that day, to what his trousers now hid.

"Angel, you need to stop doing that."

Naomi lifted her gaze to his smoldering amber eyes. "Stop what?"

"Stop looking at me like you're starving and I'm a seven course feast."

Naomi's face heated. She was thankful Bobby's shadow cloaked her in darkness, hiding her warm blush. "I...I wasn't..." She gulped and surveyed his handsome stubbled face. Why lie? This man had witnessed her darkest moment. She had little to hide from him now.

"You are beautiful, Bobby Morgan. As finely made as any man."

A lazy smile curved his full, kissable lips. "You can't talk like that either, Naomi."

She smiled, but she knew when he called her Naomi, rather than angel, he was about to get serious.

"I mean it. You have no idea what you do to me, darlin'. And to know you...that you're..."

"That I'm what?"

"Damn, angel. You've been through hell today. I've got no right." He swung his feet to the side of the bed and sat up.

She touched his upper arm—how glorious the muscle felt beneath her fingers—to stop him. "No right to what, Bobby?"

He turned and met her gaze with his own. "To want you like this." He cupped her cheek and skimmed her lips with his thumb. "And I do want you. More than I've ever wanted a woman. More than..." His voice cracked.

"Don't be troubled, please." Naomi covered his hand with one of hers. His fingers were long and thick, and the hair on his knuckles tickled her palm. She gave his thumb a soft kiss. "I want you too."

He sighed, removing his hand. "Damn it, Naomi. You don't know what you're saying."

Naomi took his hand back and entwined their fingers together. His swearing no longer bothered her. It was just... Bobby. And she liked everything about Bobby. She liked... No. Warmth filled her body. She *loved* Bobby Morgan. Though they hadn't met under ideal circumstances, this man was her destiny. She knew it with her whole heart.

She smiled, hoping he could see the love in her eyes. "You think I don't understand what happens between a man and woman. I do. I have married friends. I know there's more than the kiss we shared."

"That kiss, angel, it was—"

"It wasn't a mistake. I thought it was at first. But it wasn't."

He chuckled and squeezed her hand. "I was going to say it was the best kiss of my life. No lie."

"Me too. Of course it was my only kiss." She smiled.

"Darlin'—" He cleared his throat. "You've been through a mighty hard thing today. You need time to heal. I can't. Not right after that. No matter how much I want to."

Naomi brought his hand to her lips and kissed each rough calloused finger. "You are so kind. So sweet. But Bobby, what happened with Ike today convinced me of something. I don't ever want to be in a situation again where a brute like him could take something I can only give once." Naomi took a deep cleansing breath and summoned courage for what she was about to say to this man she adored. "As God is my witness, I will be the one to choose when, where, and to whom I give myself for the first time." She breathed again, her pulse racing, as she unbuttoned her cotton gown and let it fall from her shoulders, exposing her bare breasts. "I choose here, and I choose now. And I choose *you*, Bobby Morgan."

"Damn!" Bobby stood up and raked his hand through his already tousled hair. "Naomi, I make my living hunting men. I kidnapped you. Now I've committed murder. I'm a fugitive runnin' from the law. I got nothin' to give you. Nothin'."

"You've got yourself. That's all I want. You."

He sighed and plunked back down on the bed, not facing her. "I got nothin'. No right at all to love you."

Naomi's heart jumped, but she held herself steady. She smoothed her palm over his sleek shoulder. "You've got the right to love whomever you please, Bobby. I'd be honored if it were me."

He turned then, and she saw the truth in his eyes before he said the words. Her insides melted.

"It is, darlin'. I haven't loved another in twenty-two years. Time was, I thought I might have forgotten how. But I love *you*, Naomi, with everything I am."

She leaned forward, kissed his lips and whispered, "I love you too. Only you."

He crushed her into his embrace. "I couldn't think straight when I saw Ike with his hands on you. You're mine. All mine. No other man will touch you as long as I live. I promise." He swallowed hard, his Adam's apple bobbing against her cheek. "If he'd harmed you—"

"He didn't," Naomi said. "You came for me. I trust you."

He took her mouth in a searing kiss so passionate and possessive that the cadence of his heartbeat sounded in her ears, in synchrony with her own. Their tongues mated and tangled, their moans answered each other. Bobby cupped one breast and flicked his thumb over her hardened nipple, igniting sparks along her flesh that traveled downward to the wet place between her legs. All the while he kissed her as if he couldn't get enough of kissing her. When he finally broke away, she panted, her breath puffing against his neck as he rained kisses over her shoulders, down to her swollen breasts.

"You're so beautiful, Naomi. I swear I've never seen a more perfect creature." He cupped both breasts and stared at them.

Naomi's skin rippled with tiny little shocks. "Now you're the one looking at me like I'm a feast," she said with a shaky giggle.

He didn't meet her gaze. Instead, he lingered over her bosoms, squeezing them, kneading them. "You *are* a feast, angel. For my eyes, my nose, my mouth, my hands." He raised his gaze then, a teasing smile gracing his mouth. He inhaled and plucked a nipple. "I bet these taste as sweet as your lips. Sweeter even."

Naomi gasped when he kissed one. First he licked it, and his tongue probing her sensitive nipple was a delicious sight. The tingles it sent through her heated her blood. But nothing compared to the exquisite sensation when he sucked it between his lips. She moaned, entangling her fingers in his hair, pulling him closer against her chest.

His suckling and tugging ignited a trail to her heated core. His rough beard scraped the delicate skin of her breasts as he nibbled, adding to the fiery sensation. Naomi wanted more, all he had to give.

When he reached between her legs and touched her there, she nearly jumped off the bed. Blazes ripped through her in a kaleidoscope of images so vibrant and bold, she was sure she'd flown out of her body and was soaring to the stars themselves. Her voice called out Bobby's name as she hurtled forward, backward, and then plummeted back to the bed where he was kissing the tops of her breasts and rubbing the smooth folds between her legs.

"Bobby." She panted, and her voice sounded not her own. "Bobby, that was so...so..."

He looked up and smiled. "That was only the beginning, darlin'. I'm gonna take you there and back again so many times you'll be plumb tuckered by the time we're through."

"Oh, my..."

Bobby slid her gown over her hips, down her legs, and tossed it to the floor. Naked, she lay before him, eager for him to see all she had to give.

He eyed her appreciatively, his amber orbs burning gold. "Like I said, a feast. A beautiful feast, Naomi Blackburn. From your violet eyes to your cherry lips to your sweet nipples to those gorgeous black curls between your legs, right down to your pretty little toes." His voice rasped. "If you want to stop, tell me now."

Stop? Had he lost his mind? "If you stop now, Bobby Morgan, I'll personally turn you over to the law."

"Thank God," he said, and slid down her body and spread her legs. "You'll like this, I think."

Like what? She closed her eyes and braced herself, figuring he was ready to take her. There would be pain when he came inside her. She accepted that. She also knew she'd bring him intense pleasure, and that pleased her. She wanted to please him more than anything in the world.

When nothing happened, she opened her eyes and found him staring between her legs.

"You sure are pretty down here, darlin'," he said.

He touched her, and a moan escaped her lips.

"And wet, too. So wet." His voice had changed again. It was even lower and raspier. Wild, almost. Primal. "I need to taste you."

He couldn't mean...

But he did. And he was. The soft strokes of his tongue against her private parts made her whole body sizzle, and when he sucked on her, licking a certain place, she was catapulted back into the frenzy of passion and emotion, only this time she soared even higher. She cried out his name as her body tingled and burned, and when she floated downward, she opened her eyes and met his gaze. He was smiling at her, and something moved inside her. It stretched her, but it was not unpleasant, and she realized it was his finger.

"I'm going to add another finger, angel. Don't be afraid. I want to stretch you first, to get you ready for me."

"I...all right. I trust you."

"I know you do, and you'll never know what a precious gift that is to me. That you want me to be the one who—" His voice wavered a little. "And after what you've been through. I love you so much. I'm going to make this good for you."

She smiled, wanting to abate his fear for her, trying to hide her own apprehension for his sake. He eased another finger inside her, and though it smarted at first, he moved it in patterns so gentle and touched a sensitive spot that made her shiver.

"You like that, angel?"

Embarrassment flooded through her. Oh, yes, she liked it. She liked everything he did to her. But could she say it? She squeezed her eyes shut. "Yes," she murmured.

"Don't be shy with me, darlin'. I love you. I want to make you feel good. It pleases me. So tell me if you like what I do to you." With his free hand, he squeezed hers. "Open your eyes, Naomi, and tell me how I make you feel."

"It...when you move your fingers like that..." Her voice trembled and she inhaled sharply and then exhaled, calming herself. "I like that, Bobby. I like your fingers inside me. It feels nice."

He smiled, his dimple twinkled, and his amber eyes looked genuinely happy. She hadn't often seen happiness on his handsome face. That she put it there thrilled her.

"I think you're ready for me now, angel." He dislodged his fingers and stood, his hands fumbling with his trousers. "It will still hurt, but I'll help you through it, all right?"

Naomi nodded, unable to tear her gaze from the bulge in his duckins. He pushed them downward, and his arousal sprang outward. Unable to stop herself, she gasped, and then clamped a hand over her mouth.

"Angel?"

"I'm sorry." She blinked. "It just...looks different."

He grinned. "This is how it looks when it's ready for you."

"But I don't see how—"

His chuckle eased her nerves. A bit. "People have been doing this since the dawn of time. It'll work. Trust me."

"I do."

Bobby shed his trousers and climbed in bed, his body covering hers. The hair on his chest tickled her nipples.

"Naomi."

"Yes?"

"When I come inside your body, that makes you mine. Do you understand?"

"Y-Yes, Bobby. I'm yours. I always was."

He cleared his throat, his swollen cock brushing against her wetness. Shivers raced through her.

"What I mean is, I love you. I want to take care of you, and I'll—"

She covered his lips with her fingers. "You're a good man, Bobby Morgan." She smiled, hoping he could see in her expression everything she felt for him but couldn't put into words. "Now take me quickly. I want you inside me."

He crushed his mouth to hers and thrust into her. His kisses muffled her cries from the pain. He stayed inside her, letting her get used to the fullness. All this time, he soothed her with numbing, drugging kisses, and her body changed, stretched, sheathed him, until she knew, in the depths of her soul, she'd been created for this moment.

For this man.

He seemed to know the exact instant she was ready, and he moved inside her, pulling himself out then pushing back in. The movement stung at first, and then burned, and then turned to a fierce wanting. She found herself meeting his thrusts with her hips, moaning into his mouth as he pumped into her, trembling as his chestnut curls brushed against that tiny nub that brought her pleasure.

When she shattered, he ripped his mouth from hers, groaned her name, and pushed into her with his whole body.

"I love you, angel. My God, I love you so much."

CHAPTER NINE

Bobby eased his body off Naomi's, careful not to hurt her. His blinding climax had surprised him. Though he'd had his share of conquests, he'd never experienced anything quite so intense. Naomi's tight body had sheathed him like no other woman, and when he released inside her, he knew he'd given her something he'd never given another.

So this was what true love, physical and emotional, felt like.

He smiled and gave her shoulder a light kiss. "Stay here, angel," he said. "I'll be right back."

He moistened a cloth in the tepid water in the basin and brought it to Naomi. "Spread your legs, darlin'. Let me take care of you."

The unwavering trust in her beautiful violet eyes humbled him.

"Did I bleed much?"

He wiped a few rust-colored smudges from the insides of her creamy thighs. "Not much." He pressed the cloth to her. "Does this hurt?"

"No. It's fine."

He wiped her gently. "You'll be sore for a little while. But the next time it won't hurt."

"It wasn't bad, Bobby," she said. "I...enjoyed it."

His blood boiled, and his cock stirred at her words. But

he couldn't have her again. Not for at least a day. Never had twenty-four hours seemed a lifetime.

Well, only once.

He obliterated that thought from his mind.

"It wasn't bad, huh?" He chuckled, rubbing the sweat from her belly and dragging the rag through her pretty triangle of black curls.

"Oh!" She clasped a hand to her mouth. "I didn't mean it like that. It was wonderful. Amazing. I went to heaven. Truly, I did."

"That's better." He grinned at her, admiring the healthy flush of her cheeks. She was so beautiful. His cock continued to grow. Had a damn mind of its own. He returned the cloth to the basin and crawled into bed next to her. She turned toward him and snuggled into his arms.

He sighed, content. Hell, he wasn't content. He was happy. Positively ecstatic.

All because of this pretty preacher's daughter with the soul of an angel. Such a wonderful woman. And she loved him. Robert Morgan. Bounty Hunter. Fugitive. Kidnapper. She'd gifted him with her body. More importantly, with her love. He wished he had a gift to give that was worthy of her.

There was one thing. Something he'd never given anyone. Something she'd asked for earlier.

"Naomi?"

"Hmm?" She kissed his chest and flicked her tongue over his nipple. There went his cock again. He gritted his teeth, willing it down. She blinked, and her long black eyelashes tickled his skin.

"You asked how I understood when you said you felt violated." He cleared his throat, his voice shaking. "It was twenty-two years ago. I was ten years old."

"Bobby, you don't have to."

"Shh. Yes, I do. I want to." He closed his eyes and let the visions appear. Images, sounds, smells he'd kept buried for over two decades. The acrid stench of beef flesh and manure burning in the barn. The guttural soul-wrenching screams of his mother. The cowardly pleas of the man who'd sired him. Then the war cry that closed his father's yellow eyes for the last time, never to see again the face of the son who was his spitting image. The soundless scalping, oozing blood, and then the sticky crimson liquid trickling down the bronze arm of the savage who carried his pa's light brown hair, as the other took his turn with his mother. Again, the war cry.

Always the war cry.

His voice shook. "I'd fetched some water for my ma. It was my pa's birthday and she was busy making a cake. She didn't have saleratus, though, so she used extra eggs for leavening." Strange he remembered that silly detail. He hadn't given it a thought in forever, but now it rushed into his mind like a freight train, with the vivid colors and actions of a stage play in New York City. The damn saleratus. He'd enjoyed helping his mother in the kitchen, even enduring his father's taunts of "sissy" and "mama's boy."

But it had been his father, the coward, who begged for his life at the hands of those brown invaders. Had offered his wife and son up on a platter, if only they'd let him live.

Who was the real sissy? Bobby had gotten out of his share of scrapes in the past two decades, and never once had he begged for his life. He took a long, deep breath.

"I came back up the trail to the house and heard my ma's screams. I...I dropped the water and ran to the window. Two

Indians were in the house, dressed in buckskins. I wanted to scream, but I was scared. I—" He breathed. "I should have helped my mother."

"You were a small boy, Bobby." Naomi fingered the hair on his chest. "Of course you were scared."

"That was the *last* time I was scared." He cleared his throat. "My pa came through the front door, and I watched as one Indian throttled him in the stomach and then held him with a hunting knife. He spoke foreign words, while the other—"

"The other what, Bobby?"

"He raped my mother."

"R-Raped?" Naomi's sweet voice trembled.

"It's what Ike tried to do to you, angel."

"Oh, my!" Naomi gasped and buried her head deeper into his chest.

Damn. He hadn't meant to upset her. "I'm sorry."

"No, no. I'm fine. It's just...your poor mother. Go on."

"I had no love for my pa. But my ma, she understood me. She loved me and I her. When that savage ripped her clothing and forced himself on her, in the midst of her screams, I wished for nothing more than to be big and strong like my father, so I could fight for her and protect her."

"Don't blame yourself. You were just a boy."

"A boy, yes. And small for my age. But my pa was huge. As tall as I am now and broader even. I knew he didn't love me, but I thought he loved my mother. So I thought to myself, 'don't worry, he'll save her. He'll fight for her.'"

"Did he?"

Bobby sighed, his pulse pounding. "No. He begged for his own life like a lily-livered pantywaist. Said they could have her if they'd spare his life. Said he'd throw in his little girl too."

"Little girl? You had a sister?"

"No." Bobby stiffened, remembering the tears that had formed at his father's words. The last tears he ever shed over the bastard. The last tears he'd ever shed, period. "He meant me."

"I don't understand."

"My father hated me, Naomi. He thought I was a sissy. A mama's boy."

"You?"

He chuckled. "I take it you don't agree?"

"Not at all. You're the most...well, I don't know how else to say it. You're the most manly man I've ever laid eyes on."

Bobby kissed the top of her head. "I saw his eyes through the window when he died. He had light brown eyes, lighter than mine, almost yellow, and they met mine with his last breath. I never felt remorse.

"The Indian who killed him handed him over to the other so he could have a turn with my mother. The other one scalped him."

"A-And your ma?"

"She stopped screaming during the second rape. I figure she died then. After he was finished, the Indians ransacked the house and took everything of value. My father's guns, his tobacco, the money my ma kept in a tin can on the high shelf of our pantry. She didn't have much jewelry, but they took the wedding ring off her finger, and they took her pride and joy."

"That would be you, Bobby. Did they take...you?"

"No." He fidgeted with her hair splayed on his chest. Naomi had such beautiful sable hair, like silk. "Her pride and joy was an amethyst brooch from her grandmother. The first time I saw you, your eyes reminded me of that brooch." He gulped. "I hadn't thought of it in years."

"I'm sorry. I didn't mean to remind you of something so painful."

"No, no, angel. God, no." He kissed her head again. "They went to the barn then, took our horses and milch cow. They left our old steer and set fire to the barn."

The steer's bawling had made his ears ache, but after listening to the screams of his mother as those savages violated her, the wretched cries of an animal hadn't touched his emotions.

He couldn't tell Naomi that he waited the rest of the day and then the night, outside. Scared to go in his house. Twenty-four long hours passed. Finally mustered the courage to sneak into his home and look upon his ma's lifeless body. He'd been a damn coward. But that was the last time.

He cleared his throat. "When I went into the house, there was nothing left. Nothing but the smell of my father's birthday cake that had burned in the stove before the fire went out. I scrounged what crumbs of food I could find, put as many clothes on my back as I could, and left.

"I left, angel, without even burying my ma's body."

"Oh, Bobby. How did you live?"

"The occasional odd job. Stealing mostly. I couldn't stay in one place too long or I risked being sent to an orphanage. I sure as hell wasn't going there."

"Would that have been so bad?"

"Yes."

She didn't ask why, and he was glad. He'd taken her innocence in so many ways already. He didn't want to tell her the truth about orphanages.

"Thank you for telling me," she said softly. "You really *did* understand about violation."

"I've never told another living soul that story, Naomi."

"I'm honored. Truly." She kissed his nipple. "You've been alone so long, but no longer."

A powerful surge traveled to his groin. "I can't ask you to stay with me. My life...it's no good for you."

"You don't want me?"

"God, yes, I want you. I don't want to live another second of my wretched life without you. But I've got nothing to offer you. Nothing."

"You have you."

"That's not enough."

"It's enough for me. I'm not leaving you."

"I can't let you—"

"Hush. It's not your decision to make. It's mine." She moved away from him then, sat up, and pierced him with her violet gaze. "Do you know where my name comes from?"

"Naomi?"

"Yes."

"No, I don't. But it's sure pretty. It fits you."

She flushed a beautiful strawberry color. "Thank you. It's from the Bible. My sister's name is Ruth. There's a story about two women named Ruth and Naomi."

"Can't say I know much about the good book, darlin'."

"I'm sure your mother would have taught you had she the chance," Naomi said. "In this story, Naomi loses almost everything—her homeland, her husband, her two sons. She's left with two daughters-in-law, and thinking of them, she releases them from their obligations to her and decides to return to her homeland of Israel. One of them, Ruth, remains devoted to Naomi, and speaks to her—my pa's favorite Bible verse.

"'Entreat me not to leave thee, or to return from following after thee: for whither thou goest, I will go; and where thou lodgest, I will lodge: thy people shall be my people, and thy God my God: Where thou diest, will I die, and there will I be buried: the Lord do so to me, and more also, if aught but death part thee and me.'"

The words, spoken in Naomi's husky, melodic voice, chorused into Bobby like sweet music. He said nothing, just stared into the beautiful eyes of the woman he loved. She took his hand and kissed his fingertips, then spoke.

"Whither thou goest, Bobby Morgan, I will go. Where thou lodgest, I will lodge. Aught but death shall part thee and me."

"You would sacrifice everything? To be with me?" Bobby's heart thundered. "I'm not worth it, Naomi."

She touched her fingers to his lips. "What was your ma's name?"

He wasn't certain he'd ever spoken his ma's name aloud. God knew he hadn't formed the thought of it in years. He spoke it now, in a grave tone that expressed what she had meant to him. "Her name was Ella. Ella Lane Morgan."

Naomi's eyes glowed. "There was a fine, strong woman named Ella who knew your worth. And now there's me. I'll spend the rest of my life proving to you how worthy you are, if you'll have me."

Could he? Could he be a husband? Could he be the man Naomi deserved? Living without her now would be to live as half a person.

"I love you," he said.

"Then don't even think of leaving me behind," she said. "Promise me."

Her words warmed him, and for once, he thought, maybe he could have something good. Something pure. He'd had a hard life. Surely he was entitled to happiness.

He cupped her flushed cheeks, lowered his mouth, and pressed his lips to hers.

"I promise."

CHAPTER TEN

Naomi woke to find Bobby standing at the basin shaving. Part of her saddened at the disappearance of his scratchy beard. She warmed, remembering the sensation of it scraping against her cheek, her thigh, her most private parts. Her belly fluttered, and she smiled.

She sat up and stretched. "Good morning."

"'Mornin', angel."

A sudden urge descended on her and she spoke boldly. "Bobby, may I do that for you?"

"Do what? Shave me?"

She nodded.

He chuckled. "Now angel, I doubt you've ever shaved a man before, and I can't say I relish the nicks and cuts you might give me."

"I'd never—"

"Don't get all upset on me. I'm almost done anyway. I'll let you do it next time."

"Promise?"

He sighed. "It ought to be clear to you by now that I can't deny you anything."

He wiped his face with a cloth and came toward her, sat down next to her, and gathered her in his arms. The cover fell away, revealing her bare breasts. He reached for one and tweaked her nipple. A jolt of pleasure coursed through her. He took his hand away, and she whimpered at the loss.

"We need to talk, darlin'."

"I know. We need to leave, don't we?"

Bobby nodded. "I'm wanted for murder in Dugan even though I'm innocent. I'm also wanted for kidnappin' you. I did murder a man at the camp, and the law's no doubt been called by now."

"But you're innocent of the charges in Dugan. And you were defending me at the camp. As for kidnapping, I'll say I went willingly, which is true, as of now, and—"

Bobby shook his head and interrupted her. "I'm not a paragon of society, angel. I'm a bounty hunter. I make a living huntin' men. It took most of my money to replenish my supplies at the camp."

"The dress!" Naomi flung her arms around him. "I never thanked you for the dress. You didn't need to spend so much on me."

"That was nothin', darlin'. Pennies, really, and worth every one. The point is, I'm runnin' low and I need to find a job."

"Another...bounty?"

"It's all I know."

Naomi nodded. "I understand."

"But that's no life for a woman, so I'll find somethin' else. But for now we need money, and it's the best way I know to earn it. I got some in a bank in Minnesota, but we got to get there." He shook his head, sighing. "Staying here for the night was a chance I had to take. You needed a warm bed after what you'd been through."

"This wasn't a mistake was it? Will they find us? Because we stayed here? Because of...because of me?"

"You needed to be taken care of, and I was honored to do it. So stop talking like that. I know how to keep the law off my tail. Remember, I grew up stealing. Anyway, we need to get to Minnesota, where my money is."

"All right, Bobby. I told you, I go where you go."

He nodded, his full lips pursed in a thin line. "I'm going to get dressed and go downstairs and talk to the clerk. See if there's any information on Jack Daily to be had. You get dressed. I'll see that some breakfast is brought up for you."

"Bobby?"

"Hell, angel, I'm sorry. You're scared to stay alone, aren't you?"

"Oh, no." She wasn't, strangely enough. Perhaps because it was daylight. Perhaps because she trusted fully in Bobby to keep her safe. "I was just going to say, if you'll give me a minute I'll come with you. I don't want to hold you up."

"That'd surely be a help if you can be ready."

"Just need to put on my dress and braid my hair. I won't be five minutes."

Naomi dressed quickly and left the room on Bobby's arm. He sent her into the dining room for breakfast while he talked to the desk clerk of the small hotel. The rolls with butter tasted like sawdust, and she shook her head at the serving girl offering her coffee, opting for water instead to sooth her dry mouth. What was keeping Bobby?

Finally he entered the dining room, looking handsome as ever in his shirt, trousers, and boots, his gunbelt slung low on his hips. When a young and pretty chambermaid turned her head to stare at him, Naomi winced as a jolt of jealousy struck her. Who did that woman think she was? Bobby, though, didn't give the young lady a look.

"Ready, angel?"

"Don't you want anything to eat?"

"I had a few slices of bread while I was doing business," he said.

"Any good news?"

"Well, if I'm wanted by the law, it hasn't come over the wire yet." He snickered. "Course the fella might've recognized me from my description and didn't let on, and he's callin' in the law as we speak."

Her heart lurched. "Oh, Bobby."

"I'm just teasin'. I can read a man good as a book. The fella's clueless. Let's go."

"All right." She stood and followed him out of the hotel where his horse was waiting, saddled and ready to go.

He helped her up and settled in behind her.

"Before we go— Never mind." She'd been thinking of Ma and Pa and Ruth, and how worried they must be. But if she wired them, she'd risk Bobby's life, and that she could not do. She'd find another way to communicate.

"We're headin' east, angel, to Minnesota. If I can't pick up some money on the way, it'll be slim livin' until we get there."

"I'm a preacher's daughter. I'm used to going without. I don't mind." And she didn't. "As long as I'm with you."

He kissed the side of her neck and kneed the horse into a canter.

★ ★ ★ ★

Bobby kept off the beaten trails, hoping to avoid any lawmen or bounty hunters who might be headed his way. He knew how to cover his tracks—a necessity in his line of business—and took extra care. He was now carrying precious cargo.

How could he ever become worthy of the gift Naomi had given him? Somehow he needed to find a way to make an honest living. Not that bounty hunting wasn't honest. No sirree. He prided himself on a job well done. The fewer criminals in the world the better. But it was no life for a woman. No life for *his* woman.

They'd been riding a while with only a short stop at noon to gnaw on some hardtack and drink from his canteen, when his ears perked at the rustling wheels of the afternoon stage. He slowed the horse and stayed off the trail, hiding in the tall grasses and cottonwoods, not wanting to attract attention.

"Angel?"

"Yes?"

"You feel like a rest?"

"I'm fine."

"Well, I think a rest would be good. There's a stage behind us, and I'd just as soon let it get ahead of us, if you understand my meanin'."

"You don't want to be seen. I understand."

He stopped the stallion and helped Naomi down. "Let's just lie low for a bit. Have a drink from the canteen if you want." He handed it to her and then dismounted himself.

Her thirsty gulps echoed in his ears as he concentrated on the approaching stage. It seemed off, as if it were coming up quicker than normal. Damn. Had they found him? He was ready to put Naomi on the stallion and tell her to ride like the wind when a gunshot rang from the direction of the stage. "Stay here," he hissed to Naomi, and he bounded through the grasses to get a better look.

The stage rolled into his view, the horses whinnying. A

mounted gunman trailed them. He fired again. A lone stranger.

Only one robber worked these parts and worked alone.

Jack Daily.

Within sight. He could get him.

He raced back to his horse and his woman. "Naomi, stay here. No matter what happens. Do not be seen."

"Bobby...what is it?" Her beautiful eyes were round as new nickels.

This bounty would give him the means to start a life with Naomi. A new life. The life she deserved.

"There's a gunman chasing the stage. He's alone. I know him. There's a bounty on his head of five hundred dollars. This is our chance, Naomi. *Our* chance. I can get him. I know it. Stay here and wait. I'll be back for you. I promise you that." He kissed her lips hard and fast, swung up on the horse, and galloped toward the action.

Bobby tried never to kill his prey. Live men were much easier to transport. He could tie them up and make them walk in front of him. One time, though, he'd inadvertently killed the man he was hunting. He'd tied him behind his horse and dragged him to the nearest town with wiring capabilities a hundred miles away. By the time he got there the body was so bedraggled to be nearly unidentifiable, and he'd had to fight for the right to collect his bounty. After that he took care to keep his quarries alive.

Daily, though, he'd have to kill. He couldn't risk keeping the dangerous man alive, not when he had Naomi to think of. He couldn't leave her vulnerable.

He didn't like to kill. Naomi would like it even less.

But it would be the last time.

The last bounty.

In a few seconds, he overtook Daily, who hadn't yet managed to stop the stage. They were perilously close to where Bobby had left Naomi, and that unnerved him, but it couldn't be helped. This was his one opportunity, and he'd learned long ago to take what fate offered.

Daily's revolver was trained on the driver of the coach, and though he turned to see Bobby and a flash of recognition crossed his stern features, Bobby was quicker. At this angle, he didn't have a good shot at the outlaw's heart. His Colt already drawn, Bobby aimed for Daily's upper arm, to dislodge him from his mount. He'd finish him off later.

He fired, and Daily fell to the ground, cursing. His horse galloped away, whinnying into the afternoon.

The stagecoach slowed, and Bobby shouted to the driver to pull back. That he was no threat.

Clearly the passengers weren't convinced. An arm stretched through the window, pointing a gun in Bobby's direction. Bobby swerved Thor to the right, missing the shot. No harm done.

Until a sound ripped through him.

The sound of heaven.

And of hell.

Naomi's voice.

Naomi's scream.

He turned toward it and his vision clouded. Naomi swayed, the blue fabric of her dress rippling in the soft prairie wind. Blood poured from her shoulder.

"No!" Bobby shouted, and raced toward her.

★ ★ ★ ★

Blinding, piercing pain shot into Naomi, and she heard Bobby's voice, deep and guttural.

"Noooooooooo...."

He rode toward her, his movements slow and deliberate, or was that in her mind? His beautiful face blurred, and then there were two of him, both catching her as she fell to the ground.

Her love.

The pain throbbed. She reached to touch it, to soothe it, and a sticky substance coated her fingers. Blood. Had Bobby been shot? Didn't matter. If he was leaving this earth, so was she. She wouldn't stay here without him.

She gazed into his amber eyes. Were those tears? Was he in pain? She reached to cup his clean shaven cheek. Drops of water tunneled through the red on his face. He was hurt. Her man was hurt.

"Whither thou goest..." she said, her own voice unrecognizable.

And then the curtain fell.

CHAPTER ELEVEN

"Naomi! No! No!" He shook her, trying to will life back into her body. "Damn it, woman. You can't leave me now!"

The stage rolled away rapidly, its wheels kicking up dust.

"Help me," Bobby shouted, cradling Naomi in his arms. But the stage kept going, and he knew the driver couldn't hear him anyway.

He touched her neck. Her pulse, though weak, lingered. Thank God. Quickly he reached under her skirts for her petticoats, ripped them, and tore them into strips. He bandaged Naomi's shoulder and then checked her pulse again.

The next town was over four hours away on horseback. Naomi wouldn't make it four hours, especially at the pace he'd need to keep.

There was a closer place to get the help she needed. Bobby grimaced, but he had no choice. He would go three miles north, to a Lakota encampment.

There he would beg the people he hated to help the woman he loved.

★ ★ ★ ★

Harnessing his anger and hatred, Bobby rode into the Lakota camp. Years had passed since the Dakota uprising, and though he wasn't certain it was the Sioux who had attacked his family all those years ago, he had his suspicions. He'd heard not all Indians practiced scalping, but that didn't matter. They were still red savages. He gritted his teeth and rode firmly. These people were all that stood between Naomi and death.

Conical tents surrounded the tamped down grasses of the camp, and several maidens carried water, lowering their eyes to Bobby's gaze. Barely clothed children stopped scurrying about and hid behind the women's fringed skirts. Braves, dressed in buckskins, met his gaze with mistrust and uncertainty in their dark eyes. Could they speak to him? Would they?

One large man, his ebony hair twisted into two thick braids, approached Bobby and held out a bronze hand to touch Thor's nose. His stern brown face exhibited an aquiline nose and high cheekbones.

"Why do you come here, white man?"

Bobby swallowed. He would not succumb to fear, doubt, or hatred. "I come for help. My woman has been shot."

The Indian nodded. "I am Standing Elk. My wife, Summer Breeze, is a healer. Come. I will take you to her."

Bobby followed on the stallion, ignoring the stares of the Indians. When they stopped in front of a large tipi, Standing Elk took Naomi from his arms. Bobby dismounted.

"You stay here," Standing Elk said. "This is the healing tent. I will take her to Summer Breeze."

Bobby shook his head. "I can't leave her."

"You must. My wife will not harm her." The Indian extended his arm forward, still holding Naomi. "Stay."

Though Standing Elk looked like a young man, possibly younger than Bobby himself, something in his demeanor commanded authority. Bobby nodded, and Standing Elk disappeared into the tipi with Naomi in his arms.

Everything in Bobby's soul screamed at him not to trust the Indian, but he had no choice. Naomi wouldn't have made it to the nearest settled town. These people were her only hope.

A young Indian boy, no more than three or four, appeared and scrambled around Bobby's legs and into the tipi.

Within minutes, Standing Elk emerged with the boy.

"Your woman is in the care of Summer Breeze and her mother, Laughing Sun, who is also a gifted healer."

"I need to see her."

"No. You must stay out here. They will fetch you when you can see her. They must remove the bullet from the white man's weapon. It is...a difficult task."

Bobby shivered. He knew what a difficult task it was. He'd had a few bullets removed from his own body in this lifetime. Agony coursed through him at the thought of Naomi having to endure such torture.

The little boy jabbered in Indian language to Standing Elk. After he responded, the boy ran away.

"My son, Silver Raven," Standing Elk said. "He wants his mother and doesn't understand that she is occupied." The Indian sighed. "Come." He gestured. "Let us see to your horse, and then we will speak."

Bobby nodded. What other choice did he have?

When Thor was taken care of, Bobby sat with Standing Elk. "It was right for you to come here," he said. "We have medicine that the white man does not. Your woman...what is her name?"

"Naomi."

"Naomi...will have all she needs to survive."

"And if she doesn't? Survive?"

"Then it is the will of the Great Spirit, and we have no choice in the matter." Black rubbed his temple, regarding Bobby with his black eyes. "What are you called, white man?"

"Morgan. Robert Morgan."

"Are you hungry, Robert Morgan?"

Bobby's stomach churned with a dull ache. "No."

"You must eat. You must remain strong for your woman. I will take you to my father, the chief of our tribe. His name is Black Wolf."

"I...I don't have much to offer him for Naomi's treatment. He can have my horse. My guns."

"He will not ask you for such."

"But...he is entitled to payment for his healers' services."

"We do not follow the way of the white man. We do not demand payment for what is our duty to give. The Great Spirit gifted Summer Breeze and Laughing Sun with their abilities to heal. It is their duty to use those gifts. To give where they are needed."

Bobby struggled to maintain composure. Worry for Naomi overwhelmed him, coupled with his inability to understand the philosophy this Indian man spouted. He spoke of duty, yet his people had raped and killed Bobby's ma, scalped his pa, stolen from them, set fire to their barn. None of this made any sense at all.

None of it mattered anyway. All that mattered was Naomi.

As they readied to meet the chief, an Indian maiden rushed from the tipi. She spoke to Standing Elk in her native language.

"Your woman, Naomi, lives for now," Standing Elk said to Bobby. "Summer Breeze has removed the bullet from her shoulder and sealed the wound. She is weak. But she lives."

Relief swept through him, but fear for what lay ahead consumed his innards. His bowels clenched, and he fought the nausea that rose in his throat. "I need to see her."

"She is with Laughing Sun. Summer Breeze says to expect fever. She will need to be watched closely."

"Damn it, I need to see her!"

"You will. She cannot be moved, so you may stay with her in the healing tent."

"Thank you." Bobby fidgeted, unsure of what else to say. "Why do you help me?"

"Because you need my help. Your woman needs the help of my healers."

"But you...your people...they've massacred white men. They've—"

"They've done what's been done to them. But not me, and not this tribe. We have chosen to abide the white man's laws, even if we do not agree with them. We have sought guidance from the Great Spirit. We move on when we must. We wish only to exist in peace."

"I don't understand."

"Do you judge all white men by the actions of some?"

"No. Of course not." Certainly not, in his line of work. Bobby knew some men were pure evil.

"Then why should it be so with red men?"

Bobby had no answer. Such a notion that had never occurred to him, and his mind was too full to ponder it now. He cleared his throat. "How is that you speak my language?"

Standing Elk turned, and his chin quivered slightly. "My mother, who learned it from her mother, my grandmother. She was the daughter of a white man."

★ ★ ★ ★

As darkness set in, Bobby sat on a fur in the corner of the healing tent. Summer Breeze, her long hair plaited into an onyx braid that hung nearly to her feet, tended Naomi. Summer Breeze did not speak English, but Bobby read her facial expression.

Naomi was in danger.

She slept fretfully and was not responsive. Her slender body shuddered, and perspiration poured from her. But still she was beautiful. And pure. And good.

Much too good for the likes of him.

Bobby clenched his hands into fists and squeezed his eyes shut. Fear absorbed him for the first time in decades.

Naomi was a preacher's daughter and she believed in God. Standing Elk spoke of the Great Spirit. Bobby's mother used to read from the Bible. Long, long ago.

The day Indians had taken her from him, God had abandoned Bobby, so he in turn abandoned God and never looked back.

Now, he prayed to a God he wasn't sure existed. But he had to try. God, the Great Spirit, whatever one called it, was his last hope.

Save her, he begged silently. *Save her, and I'll see her safely home to her pa. I know I was never meant to have her. Forgive me for trying to take what was never mine. I'll give her up, I swear it, if only you'll let her live.*

★ ★ ★ ★

Time passed like a locust caught in tree sap. Bobby lost track of the days, the nights. He ate smoked venison and corn because

Standing Elk insisted, but he had no appetite. He refused Black Wolf's pipe and drank only enough water to sustain himself. He had to live to see Naomi home once she recovered.

If she recovered.

After that, he didn't give a damn what happened to him.

The next morning, when Summer Breeze lifted a blood soaked cloth from Naomi's body, Bobby shuddered, and then relaxed, but only a bit. The cloth hadn't come from Naomi's wound. It had come from her private parts. She had started her courses.

Sadness, coupled with relief, enveloped him. The primal male part of him wished he'd impregnated her. Perhaps he'd have been able to keep her then, to watch her pretty belly swell with his child. But it was better this way. She could go on now, find someone worthy of her who could take care of her and keep her safe.

A knife settled in Bobby's gut at the thought of another man touching Naomi. Lying with her. Impregnating her.

He forced away the hurtful images. What was important was that she live. She'd be safer without him.

On the fourth day of fever, convulsions seized Naomi's weakened body. Bobby stiffened, fear pulsing through his veins. Summer Breeze ushered him out of the tent, jabbering in Lakota. She yelled something, and her little boy, Silver Raven, clad only in tan buckskins, came running. His cherubic tan face was solemn as he listened to his mother's rapid words and then sped off in a cloud of dust.

Bobby sat outside the tent, his head in his hands, oblivious to the goings-on in the camp. He didn't pray again. If God hadn't heard him the first time, he wasn't listening anyway.

At least his heart had stopped hammering. It had broken

days before, when he realized Naomi was no longer his.

Had never been his.

Standing Elk came forward, his son in tow. He didn't speak to Bobby as he passed him and entered the tipi.

Bobby had no idea how many hours had elapsed when Standing Elk finally emerged from the tent.

"Robert Morgan," he said, his firm hand a strangely soothing presence on Bobby's shoulder.

Bobby looked up, and to his surprise, a smile adorned the Indian's usually stern face.

"The fever has broken. Your woman, Naomi, will live."

CHAPTER TWELVE

"No, you will not take me back and leave me there!" Naomi threw a handful of parched corn at Bobby.

He'd held her, fed her, slept next to her for the several days it took for her body to gain enough strength to travel. He'd spoken to her words of his heart, words she needed to help her heal. He'd kissed her lips chastely when she asked him to, knowing she was too weak for anything more. He'd done so with his whole body and soul, needing to see her strong again, needing her goodness, her purity. To remember it during those long nights alone that were coming once he took her home.

Now, after several hours on horseback, they'd stopped for the noon meal, and standing over her, he'd told her the truth. He was taking her to her father.

And leaving her there.

She'd reacted pretty much like he expected. He steeled his body, his heart, against her pleas and concentrated on what she needed. What was best for her.

Never again would she be in danger because of him.

"You promised me, Bobby! You promised you wouldn't leave me!" She stood and ran into him, no doubt paining her shoulder, and pounded her fists against his chest. "I won't go. I won't. I'm not leaving you."

Her wet violet gaze met his, and he nearly lost his resolve. But no, he'd be strong. He had to. *For her sake.*

He grabbed her arms, mindful of her wound, but she squirmed against him, pressed her breasts into his chest, and laid her head against his heart. And she wept.

"Please, Bobby. I don't want to be without you. You said you loved me. You said you'd never leave me."

Bobby's heart thumped, and he gathered her close. God, how he loved this woman. She was so strong, so beautiful, so inherently good inside.

Which is why he had to let her go.

"Naomi, you know I'll be arrested as soon as we get to Dugan."

"Then we won't go to Dugan."

"Don't you want to see your ma and pa? Your sister?"

"Not if it means losing you. I choose you, Bobby. *You.* With all my heart."

"Angel, please. I can't let you."

Naomi seized his face in her hands and smashed his mouth down against hers. Her tongue licked the seam between his lips, and though he tried resisting, his body responded. He parted his lips and took her, tangling his tongue with hers, relishing the taste, the texture, the pure sweetness that was Naomi. A high-pitched moan escaped her throat and vibrated into his mouth.

He deepened the kiss, groaning, and pulled her against his arousal that pulsed in his britches.

If only...

He ripped his mouth from hers and regarded her beautiful face. A strawberry flush coated her cheeks and neck. Her violet eyes had darkened to a smoldering amethyst, and her lips—those lovely, soft lips—were scarlet and swollen from their passionate kiss.

"Bobby." Her husky voice spoke to his soul. "Bobby, if you're determined to leave me, at least make love to me one more time."

Her words sliced through him like a hunting blade. God, how he wanted it. To feel her body sheath him once more, to drown in her sweetness, in her passion. He might be able to exist a lifetime with only the memory to warm him.

But it couldn't happen. "I can't, angel. We can't risk—" He cleared his throat. "I can't give you a child."

She looked up and her beautiful eyes shone with triumph. "You may have already given me a child. What exactly are you going to do about that?"

"No." He caressed her back. "Don't you remember, darlin'? You had your courses during the fever."

"Oh." Her hand clamped to her lips.

Her moist eyes glistened with such agony, such torment, that Bobby's heart broke all over again.

"You can't even leave me with that little part of you?" She closed her eyes and two tears trickled down her soft cheeks.

Unable to stop himself, he leaned down and licked away first one, then the other tear. "I won't soil you further."

Naomi stopped badgering him then. She didn't speak for the rest of the trip back to Dugan.

They finally reached the town limits early the next morning. Naomi had insisted they ride straight through, and though Bobby was worried for her health, he relented, needing to finish this task as quickly as possible. They'd stopped only to give Naomi and Thor needed rest. Bobby did not sleep. A sword was lodged in his heart, and though he knew he'd never be free of it, being out of her presence might offer some small relief. So on they'd ridden toward the town of Dugan where

Bobby would leave his love and escape before the law could take him in.

But when they arrived at the small house on the edge of Naomi's father's claim, Sheriff Justin Stiles waited outside.

"Sheriff!" Naomi scrambled from Thor, not waiting for Bobby to help her dismount.

Bobby gritted his teeth as she ran into the other man's arms.

He took a deep breath and turned Thor, ready to gallop the hell out of this town, when the sheriff yelled at him.

"Morgan! Come back!"

Come back to get arrested and have his ass hauled off to that dirty cell again? The man was plumb *loco*. Bobby scrunched his knees together, ready to urge the stallion into a gallop, when the sheriff's voice rang out again.

"It's all right, Morgan. I know you're innocent. Come back! I have news!"

Bobby cringed, but thought he might bite. What the hell? He could still ride out of there quicker than this greenhorn could ever catch him. He turned and seethed at the sheriff still hugging Naomi. He dismounted and tied Thor next to a horse he assumed belonged to Stiles.

"What is it? I ain't got all day."

"I was just coming to see the reverend," Stiles said. "A wire came in late last night. Woke up ma at the store." Stiles stopped to catch his breath. "Sorry, I been up all night."

"That makes two of us," Bobby said. "Get on with it."

Naomi still hung onto the sheriff. Bobby glared at her. Her eyes glowed back a fiery purple.

"Came in from the railroad camp east of here. From the cook, Bessie. She'd wired last week to tell the preacher Naomi was safe and was comin' home."

"Yep. And here she is. Now I'll just be goin'."

"I'm so glad the wire came through, Sheriff," Naomi said. "I was afraid they'd be worried."

"Wire or no, they've been worried sick," Stiles said," as you can imagine. They'll be right glad to see you." He drew in another breath. "Anyway, like I said, another wire came in last night, and it got me to thinkin'—"

"Somethin' ought to," Bobby said under his breath.

"The wire mentioned you this time, Morgan. Said you were a good man, that you'd taken care of Naomi and were bringin' her home. So I thought maybe you'd been tellin' the truth. I hightailed it over to the saloon and dragged Frank outta bed with some whore—"

Naomi gasped and pulled away from the sheriff.

"Beg pardon, Miss Blackburn." The sheriff blushed a deep red.

Bobby thanked his stars for whores. Anything that got Naomi out of Stiles's arms.

"It's all right," Naomi said. "Please continue."

"So I dragged Frank outta bed and told him about the wire, and he admitted he'd seen what went on that night. That you hadn't killed anyone. Just shot some drunk in the foot when he pulled his gun on you. Claimed he didn't know who shot the dead man, though. I don't believe him. So I invited him to pack up his booze and his whores and leave this town. It's about time Dugan became respectable."

"Oh, Justin. Pa'll be so pleased!"

Justin. She called him Justin. Damn her.

"That's great, Sheriff. I'm innocent, so I'm just gonna be leavin' now if you don't mind."

"No, Morgan. There's more."

Bobby let out a heavy sigh. "What the hell is it?"

"The wire. From Bessie. Said the U.S. Marshal had been at the camp and there was a bounty you could collect on a man named Irving Hennessey."

"I don't know any Irving Hennessey. I been chasin' bounties for over ten years, so if I ain't heard of him, no one has."

"He was a southern war criminal. Been wanted down there for years. He disappeared in sixty-four without a trace. He was thought for dead, I guess, but evidently he was still around."

"I told you, I don't know him."

"Irving Hennessey. Also known as Ike Hawkins."

Ike? Bobby's mouth dropped. "Ike Hawkins is...er *was*...a foreman for the railroad. He's been at the camp at Little Oak, east of here, for a while. I met him a while ago, passin' through."

"Yup," the sheriff said, "he'd been hidin' in plain sight for years. But the bounty's still good, Morgan. Fifteen hundred dollars."

"Fifteen hundred dollars?" Bobby shook his head. "What the hell did he do down south?"

"I got a list back at the office that you are free to peruse. After readin' it, I'm damn glad you took him out."

Bobby grimaced. He didn't much care what was on those papers. Ike had deserved much worse than he got for hurting Naomi.

"Bobby?" Naomi's voice was tentative, inquiring.

He heard the question she didn't ask. Did this change anything for them? Would he stay with her?

It changed nothing. Her safety was still paramount.

"Let's go, Stiles, back to your office. And you can tell me how to go about collectin' this bounty.

★ ★ ★ ★

Three hours later, his nerves skittering, Bobby put down the list of Ike's alleged crimes. Damn. Stiles was right. Ike Hawkins had been one evil son of a bitch. Naomi would have never gotten away from him alive. His skin froze and his heart thudded. Bobby prided himself on his ability to read people. Ike had crept right under his brick wall. He'd entrusted him with something far more precious than gold.

Thank God he'd gone back for Naomi.

Thank God she was now safe with people who would care for her as she deserved.

The world was better off without Ike Hawkins. Bobby had done society a favor. Just like he always did.

Still, this was his last bounty.

He was tired. So tired. He'd find a farm somewhere in a remote area. Maybe claim a homestead under that act of Lincoln's. He'd head farther west, away from Naomi. He couldn't stay here and watch her be courted and wed to someone else. Probably the damn sheriff.

He'd raise some corn, some beef, and he'd grow old. And die.

Alone.

"That's about it, Morgan," Stiles said. "I'll wire the authorities down south and your money should be here within a couple weeks."

"I won't be here then."

"Well, where will you be? I got to send the money

somewhere."

Bobby sighed. "Hell if I know. Tell you what. I need to head to Minnesota, take care of a few things. I'll wire you when I'm settled in a hotel somewhere. Better yet"—he rubbed his stubbled jaw—"give the money to Naomi."

"Excuse me?"

"For her troubles. She's been through hell." He wished he could give her more—*everything*—but this would have to do.

The sheriff nodded. "That'll work. Sounds good." Stiles shuffled some papers on his desk, then looked up. "Oh. Morning, Reverend."

"Sheriff," a deep voice said from behind Bobby.

Naomi's father had no doubt come to demand his arrest. Not that Bobby blamed him. He'd probably do the same. But damned if he was going to let Stiles throw him back in that dirty cell.

"I need to speak to Mr. Morgan, if I may."

"Of course, Reverend," Stiles said, rising. "I got some things to take care of in the back. Take my chair."

Bobby flinched as a large, solid man walked around the sheriff's desk and sat. He was an older male version of his daughter. Hair the color of midnight, streaks of silver at the temples. A handsome face, with creases around the eyes and mouth. And violet eyes.

"I'm Charles Blackburn, Mr. Morgan. Naomi's father."

Bobby returned the man's gaze. "I know who you are."

"It seems I owe you my gratitude."

Gratitude? Was he serious? "For kidnapping your daughter? I don't think so, Reverend."

"She told me everything."

Everything? Bobby squirmed. She would have left out

the lovemaking, he hoped. "You mean you don't want me arrested?"

Blackburn cleared his throat. "I'd be lying if I said the thought hadn't crossed my mind. In fact, I've been plenty mad at you, though I was more worried about Naomi. But she wept in my arms this morning as she told me how you protected her from a rape. I'm forever indebted to you for that. And how you found help for her when she was injured. And you brought her home safely."

"It's the least I could do. If you'll excuse me—"

Bobby rose to leave, but the preacher held out a hand to stop him.

"I'm a forgiving man, Mr. Morgan, but even I have my limits. Please sit. We need to talk."

"I can't think what about."

"About my daughter. She's hurting. She says she loves you and that you love her. Is she mistaken?"

I should lie, Bobby thought. *For Naomi's sake.* But this was a man of the cloth. A holy man. A godly man, if such a thing existed. He'd never lied to Naomi. He'd never denied loving her. And he couldn't lie now. He didn't have it in him.

"Yes, sir. I love her. More than anything. More than I ever thought it was possible to love another person."

"Then why are you leaving?"

"I'm no good for her, Reverend. I'm a bounty hunter. She got hurt because I was doing my job."

"She claims you were going to stop hunting men and settle down with her."

"I had thought to, yes. But that was before she got shot." He winced as he said the words. He couldn't go through such torture again. Not and live to tell the tale.

"So because she was shot, you've decided to leave her."

"Yes, sir. Her safety is the most important thing."

"Morgan, I don't relish the idea of my daughter marrying a bounty hunter, but I do want her happiness. Do you have any idea how many men have tried to court Naomi?"

Bobby shook his head. Many, he was sure. He didn't want to hear about her courtships.

"There have been at least ten, starting when she was merely fourteen. She wanted no part of any of them. It seems, though, that you have succeeded where they could not. You have won Naomi's heart."

Bobby's heart raced and he clenched his hands into fists. "You don't understand."

"Understand what? You love my daughter and she loves you. What else is there to understand?"

"I made a promise."

"Yes. To my daughter."

"No. After that. I made a promise to your God. That if Naomi lived, I'd let her go. It's what's best for her."

Charles Blackburn eyed him sternly and coughed. "Even as a preacher, I don't claim to know what God thinks, so surely you shouldn't either. Just because God allowed Naomi to be healed doesn't mean she's better off without you."

Bobby shook his head. "I know she's better off without me. I knew it as soon as she got shot. In fact, I knew it all along. It doesn't matter to me what God thinks or what you think."

"What about what Naomi thinks?"

Bobby's heart lurched.

"Like I said," the reverend continued, "I'm a forgiving man, but if you break my daughter's heart, you'll have to depend on God for forgiveness. You won't get any from me. If you've captured Naomi's heart, you are what she needs. Don't let your own fears keep you from the happiness you both deserve." He rose, walked around from the desk, and held out his hand to Bobby. "Go to her. Take the opportunity you've both been given for happiness. Sometimes you only get one chance."

Bobby stood, his body trembling. Blackburn had spoken the words he'd told himself time and again. "Where is she? At home?"

The older man smiled. "She's right outside."

CHAPTER THIRTEEN

When Bobby appeared at the door of the sheriff's office, Naomi ran into his arms, ignoring the painful jolt in her shoulder. If Pa hadn't convinced him, she'd do it herself.

"Bobby, Bobby," she cried into his neck.

"God, I love you," he rasped, raining kisses over her cheeks, her jaw line, her neck.

She shuddered as his lips tormented her flesh. Her heart raced. It was now safe in his keeping. Where it was meant to be.

He took her lips and ravished her in a deep soul-searing kiss. His tongue danced around hers, surging, loving, until she had to rip her mouth away to take a breath.

"Marry me," he said into her ear, nipping her lobe. "Please."

Naomi melted at the words. "Oh, Bobby."

"I never meant to break my promise to you, angel."

"I know, I know."

His body trembled against hers, and she held him, tried to soothe him.

"It's all right. We'll be all right."

"I'll never break another promise to you. As long as I live, Naomi. I'll take care of you. I swear it. In my wretched thirty-two years, you're all I've ever wanted."

She smiled against his shoulder and inhaled, savoring the

spicy, salty male scent of him. He held her tight, as though he thought she might flee. Never. She'd spend the rest of her life convincing him of his worth. Of her love.

She pulled back slightly and gazed into his burning amber eyes. "So, when do you want to marry me?"

He grinned, his dimple flashing. "Is now too soon?"

"Not at all," she said. "Pa's waiting."

Bobby cupped her cheek, smoothing his calloused thumb over the tip of her nose and then over her lips that still stung from his passionate kisses. "I love you with all my heart, Naomi. Everything I have—everything I am—is yours."

"All I want is you, Bobby Morgan," she said, flicking her tongue on the pad of his thumb. "Whither thou goest, I will go."

He scooped her into his arms and carried her through the door.

Lessons

of the

Heart

CHAPTER ONE

Dakota Territory, 1876

"Mary Alice?"

The timid young girl looked up. Around her, Ruth's other students jarred their desks, gathered their books, writing tablets, and slates, and ran out into the sunshine. Another school day over.

"Yes, Miss Blackburn?"

"I need to speak to you, please."

The pretty—she'd be stunning if she ever smiled—eleven-year-old sullenly approached Ruth's desk.

"You missed five words on your spelling examination today."

"I-I'm sorry."

"You're a very bright girl, Mary Alice," Ruth said sternly. "I've let mediocre work slide in the past, and you've promised to do better."

She nodded.

"However, this approach is clearly not working. I'm afraid I must punish you."

She nodded again and her lips trembled. "I understand."

Ruth's spectacles slid down her nose a smidge, and she pushed them up. They'd only slide down again in a few moments. Perspiration covered her face. Spring heat in Dakota

Territory became unbearable inside the stifling schoolhouse.

"Have you been studying your speller?" she asked the child.

"Yes, Miss Blackburn."

"Well, then, I don't see how you can be doing so poorly. Perhaps copying the words onto the blackboard will help and will also serve as your punishment." Ruth cleared her throat, stood, and straightened into her firm teacher stance. "I want you to write each word you missed twenty-five times." She strode to the board, picked up a piece of chalk, and wrote *separate, desperate, appreciate, exhilarate,* and *educate* at the top of the board and then turned to face Mary Alice. "Just copy the words in columns underneath where I've written them."

The child chewed her lip. Such a timid little creature. Ruth's heart sank a little. She hated to punish her, but letting her continue to get away with mediocre work when she was capable of so much more would be a disservice to her student.

Ruth smiled. "Here's something that helped me when I was your age. Remember that there is 'a rat' in separate and exhilarate, but not in desperate." She held out the chalk.

Mary Alice didn't move.

"Come on, now. It won't take long."

Still no movement. "M-Miss Blackburn?"

"Yes?"

"Can I—"

"May I, Mary Alice."

The child's cheeks reddened. "May I do this tonight? On my tablet? I really need to get home, you see."

"I understand, but you must serve your punishment first."

"But ma'am, I have chores."

"You'll be done in two shakes of a lamb's tail," Ruth said.

"Your chores will still be there when you get home, and you'll know how to spell these words." She placed the chalk in Mary Alice's hand. "Go on."

The little girl sighed and trudged to the blackboard. Ruth sat back down behind her desk and shuffled the pile of compositions her upper class had written. She glanced at the first one. Neat penmanship, perfect grammar. But no vibrancy to the words. Ruth removed her spectacles and sighed. She considered the written word sacred and adored sharing her love of writing with her students. Clearly she wasn't reaching this one.

She blew on the lenses, polished them, and replaced the spectacles on her nose. She looked to the child at the board. Such a pretty little thing. Mary Alice Mackenzie's eyes were bronze and long-lashed. Her face was a perfect oval with high cheekbones, and her lustrous honey-blond hair hung in two long braids that fell nearly to her waist. A little skinny, though lots of pre-adolescent girls were thin. Mary Alice didn't talk about life at home much. Her father was widowed but seemed to be doing well enough on his small farm. Still, Ruth sometimes brought an extra cookie or a homemade turnover and slipped it to Mary Alice during lunchtime. The child's big brown eyes always glowed with thanks for the treat. She most likely didn't get such sweets often with no mother at home to bake them.

Mary Alice started on the third word. She wrote slowly, diligently, neatly. The girl was intelligent. And so pretty. The whole package, as far as Ruth was concerned.

She'd been intelligent. Always at the head of her class. But how she'd longed to be pretty. Her older sister, Naomi, was pretty. Beautiful even. Where Naomi's hair was a glossy sable,

Ruth's was mousy brown. Naomi's eyes gleamed a piercing violet. Ruth's were dark blue. Boring dark blue. Naomi's figure was perfectly proportioned, and though she was tall for a woman, her height wasn't a detriment, as most men still stood taller. Ruth, on the other hand, stood nearly six feet, dwarfing her tall sister and many of the men in town. She'd always felt she resembled an adolescent boy more than a woman. Though her breasts had finally made an appearance at sixteen, thank goodness.

Naomi was an *A*. A for excellent. Ruth was a *C*. C was average.

Men had started courting Naomi when she was merely fourteen, and she married the love of her life at nineteen. No man had courted Ruth. She was an old maid at twenty-two, still living with her parents on the homestead her preacher father now owned.

Ruth blew out a breath, turned back to the banal essay, and began marking. Boring verbs, inferior descriptions, no sensory detail at all. Grade: *C*. Average.

She shuffled to the next paper. Midway through her marks, heavy footsteps interrupted her. She looked up to see a big bear of a man walk into the schoolhouse.

"Mary Alice." His deep voice was stern.

The child at the blackboard turned. "Pa?"

"Where have you been, girl? You have chores."

"I-I..." the child stammered.

Ruth removed her spectacles and stood, her dander rising at the man. He hadn't even acknowledged her presence. She was the teacher in this school, for goodness' sake.

"Mr. Mackenzie, I presume?"

He turned, and his dark gaze raked up and down her

body. She warmed. This man was big as a mountain and more handsome than any in town. Thick blond hair the same hue as his daughter's brushed his broad shoulders in silky waves. Golden stubble covered his firm jawline and surrounded full dark red lips. His eyes were big and bronze like Mary Alice's, and his nose slightly crooked, as though it had been broken, maybe more than once. The small imperfection only added to his appeal.

Like his daughter, he'd be beautiful if he smiled.

But clearly that wasn't likely to happen.

He hadn't yet spoken, and Ruth cleared her throat. "I'd appreciate it if you'd remove your hat, sir."

The man ignored her. *The nerve.*

Ruth stood and walked toward him. Lord above, he was tall. Her eyes only reached the chin of this one.

Tall and mountainous he may be, but Ruth refused to put up with such discourtesy in her classroom. Not from a student, and not from a parent, no matter how good looking he was. A spark of anger fueling her, she reached forward and removed the cowboy hat from his tousled head.

"I said, please remove your hat in my classroom."

The man eyed her again. Was it her imagination, or did his gaze rest on her chest a little longer than normal? She resisted the urge to cross her arms. A good teacher needed to take a firm stance with students, and sometimes with parents as well. Give one inch, and they'd take a mile.

One side of his mouth edged upward, just a touch. Was that the beginning of a smile? It disappeared in an instant, so Ruth wasn't certain.

"Beg pardon, ma'am." He took the hat from her.

As his hand brushed hers, a flicker of warmth traveled up

her arm. Strange. And not unpleasant.

She cleared her throat. "I don't believe we've been properly introduced, sir. My name is Miss Ruth Blackburn, and I'm the schoolteacher here." She held out her hand.

"Garth Mackenzie." He didn't take her hand. "Why is my daughter still in school at this hour?"

"I'm afraid I had to punish her, Mr. Mackenzie. She missed five words on her spelling lesson. I've let it slide in the past, but I'm not doing her any favors by—"

"Favors?" Though he did not raise his voice, the tone was not kind. His handsome face tightened. "Her lot in life is to marry and bear children. She doesn't need to spell. She has chores to attend to at home, Miss—"

"Blackburn." Ruth's skin heated. Who did this man think he was? "And if that is what you envision as your daughter's future, sir, why send her to school at all? Why not keep her at home all day doing chores?"

"I've considered it, Miss Blackburn."

"And what stopped you?"

"That's not likely any of your business. Your business is to teach my child. It's what I pay all those damned property taxes for."

Rage surged through Ruth, and she whipped her hands to her hips. "You will not use such language in my classroom, Mr. Mackenzie. And as for teaching your child, that is why she has been kept after school. To learn the spelling lesson that she didn't learn the first time."

"Let me rephrase myself," Mackenzie said. "Your job is to teach my child during normal school hours. After those hours, she's needed at home."

"I understand that Mary Alice has chores to attend

to. All my pupils do, as do I. But learning comes first in this schoolhouse, Mr. Mackenzie. It's what the county pays me for, and I take my job seriously."

"If you'd taken your job seriously, ma'am, you'd be married with a family of your own by now."

His cruel words pierced her heart. Marriage and a family had always been her dream. But not her lot in life, it seemed. Her fate was to teach. A job that brought her both joy and frustration in equal amounts. She opened her mouth to respond but noticed Mary Alice had stiffened against the blackboard. The chalk fell from the girl's fingers, and she grasped the bottom ledge. Paleness crept into her cheeks.

"Goodness, Mary Alice." Ruth grasped the child's shoulders and steadied her. "Are you all right?"

"Yes, ma'am."

Ruth touched the girl's forehead. Clammy, but cool. "It's so hot in here, dear." She ushered her to a nearby desk. "You sit down for a moment."

"Of course it's hot in here," Mackenzie said, gesturing. "These windows are positioned all wrong. You can't even get a cross breeze. Who built this schoolhouse?"

"I'm sure I don't know, Mr. Mackenzie." Ruth rubbed Mary Alice's back in slow circles. "Whoever did so most likely did the best he could."

"You need better ventilation. Any fool can see that." He marched along the edge of the room, shaking his head. "What a waste of my good money. Damned taxes."

"Mr. Mackenzie! I'll not tell you again to refrain from profanity in this school."

"Miss Blackburn, I'm not your pupil. I'll speak how I like."

"Not in my classroom. And I should think you'd be a little

more concerned about your daughter. She nearly fainted. She requires medical attention."

"Don't put much stock in so-called medical science. She's fine."

"Then she's overworked. Just how many chores does she have at home?"

"That's not likely your business, ma'am."

"I consider the well being of my students to be my business, sir." She stood. "You stay here, Mary Alice. I'll run and get Doc Potter."

Mackenzie opened his mouth, but then seemed to think better of speaking and closed it. He nodded. "Get the doc. I'll stay here with Mary Alice."

Finally, some sense out of the man. If Garth Mackenzie couldn't afford to pay the doctor, Ruth would bake him a few pies. Doc Potter always raved about her cooking at the church picnics.

"There's a pump right outside, Mr. Mackenzie. Mary Alice could do with a dipper of cool water. I won't be long."

Ruth rushed out the door and down the steps of the schoolhouse. The general store was a block away, and Doc Potter kept his office in a room above.

Goodness, this heat. She swiped her forehead as she hurried down the dusty road. Several brown curls had come loose from the tight knot at the back of her head. They stuck to her neck and made her itch.

When she entered the store, cool air drifted over her heated face. Was this the cross breeze Mr. Mackenzie had mentioned? What a blessing that would be in the schoolhouse. Ruth pulled her handkerchief from the pocket of her dress and blotted her forehead.

Doc Potter stood by the counter speaking to Lula Stiles, the wife of the storekeeper.

"Good afternoon, Miss Blackburn." He smiled, his green eyes crinkling. Doc Potter was a nice looking man, but too short for Ruth. She towered above him by nearly two inches.

"Good afternoon. I require your assistance, Doc. One of my students had a near fainting spell. She's waiting in the schoolhouse with her father."

"Let's go," he said, grabbing his hat and black medical bag from the counter. "Give my best to Manny, Lula."

★ ★ ★ ★

Garth didn't like how the doctor looked at Miss Blackburn. Kind of like he wanted to eat her for dinner, and then again for breakfast. Was he courting the teacher? Garth stifled a small chuckle. Ruth Blackburn was strong and lovely and resembled an Amazonian warrior princess. Too tall for the diminutive doc.

Mary Alice was doing better, thank God. What would he do without his little girl? He'd had enough loss in his life for five lifetimes. This child was all he had left.

But he wouldn't let emotion get the best of him. He kept her at arm's length on purpose. He couldn't stand any more loss.

"She isn't drinking enough, is all," Doc Potter said, after examining Mary Alice. "Miss Blackburn, in this heat, your students need breaks to drink."

"I know that, Doc. I keep a basin of cool water and a dipper in the back of the classroom, as you can see. The students are allowed to drink as needed. One of the big boys keeps it filled."

"Well then, Mary Alice," the doctor said. "Are you getting up to drink as necessary?"

"I thought I was."

"If you're not using the outhouse several times a day, you're not drinking enough. In this heat, water intake is essential. Otherwise, you may faint, as you nearly did."

"Yes, sir," Mary Alice said.

"She's fine for now, Mr. Mackenzie," Doc Potter said. "You may take her home. But I want her to rest for the remainder of the day. No strenuous activity. And lots of cool water."

Garth nodded and cleared his throat. Damned doctors. Thought they knew everything. "If this schoolhouse had proper ventilation, it wouldn't be so hot."

Doc Potter nodded. "I can't argue with you there. But this is the schoolhouse we have, and the town is fortunate to have it. And we're indeed fortunate to have such a fine teacher as Miss Blackburn."

The doctor eyed the teacher again, and Garth's jaw tensed. He wasn't sure why.

"Perhaps you would be interested in making some adjustments to the schoolhouse, Mr. Mackenzie." The schoolteacher smiled. Such a pretty smile—full pink lips surrounding sparkling teeth. One of her front teeth overlapped the other just slightly. Garth had an overwhelming urge to run his tongue over the lovely imperfection.

He brushed the image away. A pretty smile, all right. A pretty smile with an ulterior motive attached.

The teacher continued, "That way, you can be assured your daughter and the other students won't suffer so much from the heat."

Yep, ulterior motive. Just as he'd suspected. "I'm sure

I don't have the time, ma'am." He turned to his daughter. "If you're feeling better, Mary Alice, we'd best get home."

"Yes, Pa."

"What do I owe you, Doctor?"

"For goodness' sake, don't worry about that," Miss Blackburn cut in. "I'll bake the doc a pie. This is my responsibility, as it happened in my schoolhouse."

Garth's muscles tightened, and he placed his hat on his head while still inside. "I pay my own debts, ma'am." He fished several coins out of his pocket and handed them to the doctor. "Will this cover it? If not, I'll make good tomorrow at the store."

Doc Potter took a few of the coins and placed the remainder back in Garth's hand. "This will do fine."

Garth nodded, took his daughter by the arm, and led her out of the schoolhouse, down the steps, and to his buckboard that was tied nearby.

He helped Mary Alice climb up and then attended the horses. His gaze drifted back to the schoolhouse. Miss Blackburn stood outside on the steps with Doc Potter, chatting and smiling. The doc appeared enraptured. How might if feel to gaze into those dark sapphire eyes? And he wouldn't have to look up, either.

The thought quickly vanished. The nerve of her, offering to pay his debt. What kind of woman was she, anyway? One who clearly didn't know her place.

But as he glimpsed Doc Potter rest his hand on her forearm, Garth's jaw tensed again. He shook his head and let out a breath he hadn't realized he'd been holding.

Time to go home. Chores weren't going to do themselves.

CHAPTER TWO

Ruth drew in a deep breath, gathered her courage, and knocked on the door. Driving out to the small Mackenzie farm had taken all the bravery she could muster. In the end, she'd had to come. Mary Alice hadn't been in school since the fainting spell three days ago, and Ruth was worried.

"Who is it?" Mary Alice's small voice asked through the door.

"It's Miss Blackburn, Mary Alice."

"Oh." The door opened slowly. "Good afternoon, ma'am."

"Good afternoon. May I come in?"

The child hedged. "I... Well, certainly, ma'am, I suppose."

Ruth entered the small cabin and gasped. Disarray would be a kind word.

"Have you been ill, dear? My goodness, this place is a travesty."

"I'm sorry, ma'am. I've had lots of chores around the farm, and there's no one but me to see to the housework. Pa sent me in early today to tidy up a little. I was just getting started. But dinner has to be made." The child sighed. "I don't know how my ma used to do it. She died, you know."

"Yes, I know." Ruth pushed a strand of hair out of Mary Alice's eyes. "I'm very sorry about that."

"It was a while ago."

"How old were you?"

"Seven."

Ruth took the child's hand and led her to a sofa buried in laundry. She edged some of it aside—*goodness, Mr. Mackenzie's unmentionables*—sat down, and pulled Mary Alice down beside her. "Mary Alice, your mother was a grown woman. You're eleven years old. Of course you don't know how she did it. A child can't do what an adult does, and she shouldn't have to."

"But Pa says—"

"I don't care what your pa says." Ruth was overstepping her boundaries and she knew it, but she couldn't ignore the look of quiet desperation on the child's face. "I'll speak to him. Or perhaps my father could."

"The preacher?"

"Yes. Your pa might listen to him."

"I don't know..."

"Well, it's worth a try." Ruth stood and steadied Mary Alice on the ground. "For now, chip chop. Let's get this place in order, and I'll help you cook supper. How does that sound?"

"I don't know if Pa would like it."

"Well, Pa's not here, is he?" Ruth sighed and looked around. Goodness, where to start? "You finish folding that laundry and put it away." Mary Alice had to do that herself. Ruth couldn't bear the thought of handling Garth Mackenzie's drawers. The idea made her skin heat. "I'll dust and sweep the floor. Then we'll tackle the kitchen and start supper. Where do you keep your rags, Mary Alice?"

"Off the kitchen, ma'am. In the lean-to."

Ruth scurried through the front room into the small kitchen. *Land sakes.* Soiled dishes and linens covered the small table. A cast iron skillet crusted with what looked like the remains of salt pork and beans lazed in a basin of cold water. Half a loaf of dense bread lay next to the basin.

Dusting and sweeping could wait. Ruth was needed here.

She spied a wrinkled calico apron hanging from a nail, grabbed it, and tied it around her waist. She started a fire in the cold stove. First things first. The child and her father needed fresh bread for supper. Fresh bread that would not masquerade as a brick.

Ruth walked into the lean-to to check supplies. She didn't have time to make a yeast bread. The small pantry housed plenty of saleratus, though, and cornmeal. She'd make a nice fluffy cornbread flavored with some of the maple sugar sitting next to the wheat flour. Sighing, she grabbed the flour as well. She'd put a loaf to rise and make sure Mary Alice knew when to bake it. They'd have fresh bread in the morning for breakfast.

Ruth cleared a space on the table and set to work. Soon her loaf, covered with a cotton rag, sat next to the stove to rise. Next she tackled some of the disorder. She cleaned the skillet of the bean mess, dipped another rag in the tepid water and washed the dishes remaining on the table, and then the table itself.

She piled the soiled linens in the lean-to and replaced them with wrinkled though fresh-smelling ones. A quick sweep of the kitchen floor with the broom, and she was ready to cook supper.

Back to the pantry, she surveyed the meager offerings. Dried beans, of course, but they'd need to soak overnight.

"I'm done with the laundry, ma'am."

"Perfect, Mary Alice." Ruth turned and regarded the child's fatigued, yet somehow content, face. Dark circles under her bronze eyes marred their perfection. Mary Alice needed rest. But alas, the front room needed to be swept and dusted. "Now you can dust and sweep the front room." She handed her the broom she'd used in the kitchen. "Then I don't want you working any more today."

"There's supper, ma'am..."

"I'm taking care of that. Tell me, what do you and your pa like to eat for supper?"

"Whatever we have. Pa left a chicken outside the lean-to. One of the old hens who hasn't been laying. He plucked it for me, and I'm supposed to fry it."

"Fried chicken?"

"Yes, ma'am."

"Do you know how to make fried chicken, Mary Alice?"

"Well...no. But there can't be much to it. You dress it, cut it, and fry it in lard."

Ruth let out a laugh. "There's a little more to it than that. Do you know how to dress the chicken?"

"I'm not real good at it. Last time I tried I cut my hand something awful." She held her hand out to Ruth. A scar sliced through her palm. "Pa usually comes in and does it for me if he has the time."

"Goodness, child. That must have been a nasty cut."

"It bled a lot. But Pa wrapped it up for me. Hurt something awful for several days."

"My goodness." *Be careful, Ruth. Don't get too involved here.* "Not to worry. I can dress the chicken this afternoon so your pa won't have to. Someday soon, when we have more time, I'll be happy to come over and teach you how to dress a chicken properly."

"Yes'm."

"Now, let's see." Chicken. Chicken pie. Had Mary Alice

and her father ever eaten chicken pie? "How about if I make you something special out of that chicken? And if you and your pa like it, I'll write down the recipe for you."

"I don't know..."

"It'll be fine. And you'll love it. I make the best chicken pie in the whole county."

"Chicken pie?" The child's eyes widened into saucers.

"Yes, chicken pie." Ruth smiled. "Does that sound good to you?"

"It surely does, ma'am. Why, we haven't had chicken pie since... Well, since my ma passed on."

"Then it's high time you had it again. Would you like to watch me make it?"

"Could I?"

"Of course. You do the dusting and sweeping, and I'll dress the chicken. By the time you're done, I'll be ready to make the pie."

"Oh, yes, ma'am!"

The joy in Mary Alice's eyes warmed Ruth. "Skedaddle, now, and get your work done. I'll call you when I'm ready to start the pie."

"Skedaddle?"

"Yes, it means 'go on.'" Ruth waved her hands.

"Oh, I know, ma'am. My pa says that. Says he learned it in the war. I've...never heard anyone else use it, is all."

"Why, yes, Mary Alice, it is from the Civil War. I read it in a book and started using it."

Garth Mackenzie had been in the war? He must be older than she thought. He didn't look much older than thirty or so. His eyes, though. They told a different story. Goodness, what those eyes must have seen.

She had no business, but she had to ask. "How old is your pa, Mary Alice?"

"He's thirty-six, ma'am."

Thirty-six. Fourteen years Ruth's senior. Strange that she cared.

"My ma was thirty when she died. She had the consumption."

"I'm very sorry you lost her, Mary Alice."

"My baby brother died first."

"Oh." Ruth touched trembling fingers to her lips. "I didn't know you had a brother."

"Yes. He was four, and he died first. Then ma."

"My goodness." Ruth's heart ached for the child. And for her father.

"We don't talk about them much."

"I understand." Ruth suddenly felt warm and uncomfortable. Not usually at a loss for words, she had no idea what to say. Her father would know. As a preacher, he was used to ministering to the grieving. She'd ask him at home tonight what she might do for this lonely little girl. For now, though, she had chicken pie to prepare.

"Mary Alice, go on and do your chores. Then we'll make the pie."

"Yes, ma'am."

Ruth's thoughts wandered to handsome Garth Mackenzie as she dressed the chicken and cut it into pieces. Losing a child and a wife—she couldn't imagine the pain. Her sister, Naomi, had lost her firstborn a year ago. It had devastated her, but she still had her husband and daughter. If she had lost her husband as well... Ruth shuddered to think of it. Naomi and her family had since moved to Minnesota. Ruth often wondered if her beautiful sister's face still paled with loss.

She sighed, went to the basin, and rinsed her hands. Taking two cups of flour from the pantry, she mixed in some lard and made a crust for her pie. As the dough rested, she chopped carrots and onions and sautéed them in a pan with some more lard and some flour. She'd found no sage or other herbs in the pantry, so the onion would be the only flavoring for the pie. She inhaled the spicy aroma. It would still be delicious.

★ ★ ★ ★

Garth stopped at the rain barrel outside the lean-to and scrubbed the grime from his hands and forearms. Perspiration stung his eyes. He'd worked hard today mending the roof on the barn. Damn place was falling down around him, it seemed. Always something to be fixed. As if he didn't have enough work trying to make a decent crop. No sons to help him with his work, either. And no wife to cook and clean for him. To hold him at night and take away the stress of the day. No soft flesh for him, only nightmares.

Inhaling deeply, he splashed some of the warm water on his face. Lord above, this day was hot. He inhaled again. What was that? Chicken? Onions? His mouth watered, and his stomach let out a rumble. Hungry, he was. Seemed he was always hungry. Mary Alice, bless her heart, wasn't much of a cook. Only seven when Elizabeth passed, she hadn't had the chance to learn much about cooking yet. Or housekeeping, for that matter.

He walked through the lean-to and into the small kitchen. Mary Alice was bent over the cookstove, pulling a steamy pan out of the oven.

"Careful, child. You'll burn yourself."

"I'm fine, Pa." She looked up at him, her pretty eyes beaming. "Surprise for supper. Don't it smell good?"

Garth eyed the steaming concoction, tan gravy bubbling out of the golden crust, and inhaled once more. It sure as shootin' did smell good. Damn good. "What is it, Mary Alice?"

"It's chicken pie, of course."

"Where in tarnation did you learn to cook chicken pie?"

"Well..." The child hedged.

"Where, Mary Alice?"

"I didn't, actually. Miss Blackburn came by."

Garth tensed at the mention of the pretty teacher. "What was she doing here?"

"She was worried 'cause I hadn't been in school."

"None of her damn business whether you're in school, girl."

"She's the teacher."

"Still none of her business. So she taught you how to make chicken pie, did she? Thought her job was readin' and writin'. And cypherin'."

"She didn't teach me. She...uh...she made the pie. Said if we liked it she'd write down the recipe and I could make it again for you."

"She was in my kitchen makin' supper?" Damn woman had a lot of gall. He looked around. The room was spotless. "Did she clean, too?"

"Well..."

"Answer me, girl."

"Y-Yes. She cleaned the kitchen. But I did the laundry and tidied the front room."

"I ought to throw that pie out for the pigs."

"Pa, please!"

His stomach growled, louder this time, and from the wide-eyed look on Mary Alice's face, he knew she'd heard it.

"You're hungry, aren't you, girl?"

"Yes."

"You want to eat this pie."

"Yes. And the cornbread, too."

Cornbread? Damnation. "What else did she do?"

"Just that. Well...and the loaf that's rising. For our breakfast tomorrow. I'm supposed to put it in the oven after dinner and let it bake until it's golden brown on top and sounds hollow when I flick my fingernail against the crust."

Garth glanced at the loaf next to the stove. Though covered, clearly it was rising high. Fluffy bread like Lizzie used to make. How long had it been since he'd had a decent slice of bread?

So they'd eat Miss Blackburn's creations. Mary Alice deserved a good meal. She worked hard for him, for the farm, and got little in return.

Yep, he'd eat this savory-smelling chicken pie and the sweet-smelling cornbread. Even the wheat bread in the morning. Not for himself, of course. For Mary Alice.

Tomorrow he'd pay a call to Miss Ruth Blackburn.

CHAPTER THREE

The crimson river meandered down the pale neck of the dying man. Raspy moans, shallow inhalations. Blood trickled against the dull edge of Garth's blade. When he finally eased it out of the man's flesh, his hands were covered with the scarlet stickiness.

He let the dead body fall away, and it hit the cold dirt with a thud. Garth dropped the blade next to his victim and examined his hand from every angle. Difficult to see in the murky darkness, but still it was a hand that had killed the enemy. A hand that had now killed a friend.

Wetness drenched his neck. He reached toward the moisture with his other hand. Red, oozing. His own throat had been slit. No! No!

★ ★ ★ ★

Garth sat up in bed, his heart thundering. He slowly reached for his throat. Always did. So many times the nightmare had disturbed his sleep. Yet when he awoke, he always checked his neck.

At least he'd stopped yelling in his sleep. That had scared Mary Alice something awful. Back when Lizzie was alive, she'd felt his agitation and awakened him before he screamed. Once she was gone, though, the bellowing had begun. After a few nights of waking up to Mary Alice shaking him, her petrified little face glowing in the moonlight streaming through his window, he'd willed himself to wake before the yelling started.

If only he could will away the nightmares altogether.

He turned in his bed and gazed out his window. Sunrise. Time to get up anyway. He had morning chores, and then a teacher to visit.

★ ★ ★ ★

Land sakes, the schoolhouse was stifling, even today, when a cool morning breeze was blowing. Ruth's morning drive had been pleasant. The crisp wind had drifted over her body like a sweet embrace.

She set her reticule on her desk and then walked back outside to raise the flag. Once done, she sat down on the wooden steps and breathed deeply. Might as well enjoy the breeze outside while it lasted. Her students wouldn't arrive for another hour, and by then the temperature would be rising. She leaned back against the solid brick building and closed her eyes. Ah, morning. Her favorite time of the day. Especially in Dakota spring heat. Only two more weeks of school.

Ruth looked forward to summer. Church picnic socials, sneaking to the swimming hole adjacent to her pa's land, lazy walks in the evening after the sun had set. No papers to mark. She smiled. If only a nice man—would it be too much to ask that he be taller than she?—would come courting.

"Miss Blackburn?"

She opened her eyes with a jolt. Garth Mackenzie, in all his raw male glory, stood at the bottom of the steps. Where on earth had he come from? She hadn't heard him drive up.

"Goodness, Mr. Mackenzie, you scared the daylights out

of me. May I help you with something?"

"As a matter of fact, ma'am, you can."

Ruth stood and straightened her brown calico skirt. Lord above, he was a fine looking man. His blond curls were moist against his chiseled cheeks. He'd bathed this morning no doubt, most likely in a cool creek on his land. She warmed in spite of the waning dawn breeze. Inhaling, she cleared her throat. "What might that be?"

He didn't come closer. "I'll thank you to leave the care of my house and my child to me in the future."

Glory, he couldn't be angry that she'd fixed his supper last evening, could he? Why, she'd done him and Mary Alice a favor. Probably the first decent meal they'd had in months. Years, even.

"I'm afraid I don't understand your meaning, sir."

"I'm certain that you do, ma'am." Still he did not walk up the steps. "You had no business barging into my home and doing Mary Alice's chores for her. Her work is her responsibility."

Ruth's dander rose. Icy prickles bit the back of her neck. Responsibility? The nerve of him. "Mr. Mackenzie, your daughter is eleven years old. I understand she has responsibilities, but my goodness, it's not a crime to avail herself of some help when it's offered."

"The house and cookin' are her responsibility."

"And she is *your* responsibility, sir. A responsibility that— I'm sorry to say—you've been neglecting."

"Excuse me?"

"I don't stutter, sir. You heard me."

Now, he did take the steps—slowly and calmly. As each step brought him closer, her body tingled with awareness. She steadied herself, determined to keep calm and not let his nearness intimidate her.

If only she could stop the inner trembling.

When he reached the top step, he stood only inches from her. She drew in a deep breath.

"It's customary for a gentleman to remove his hat when conversing with a lady, Mr. Mackenzie."

"For corn's sake."

His husky voice speared into her, chilling her skin underneath her dress and petticoats. But he did remove his hat.

"It's also customary to offer a word of gratitude when a neighbor shows you a kindness."

"Now what the hell are you talkin' about?"

"That language is not welcome in my schoolhouse."

"We're not in the schoolhouse, missy."

"We're right outside the door, and you may refer to me as Miss Blackburn or ma'am. Not missy."

Mackenzie blew out a breath and shook his head. "I mean it, *ma'am*. Stay out of my business."

He placed his hat firmly on his head and turned to leave. A waft of spicy male scent drifted over Ruth. Clean and woodsy, fresh and manly. She exhaled, clearing her mind. So he smelled good. He wasn't the first man to ever smell good.

"Tell me, Mr. Mackenzie," she said to his retreating back, "did you enjoy the chicken pie?"

★ ★ ★ ★

Did he enjoy the chicken pie? The words pounded into Garth's ears. Best damned chicken pie he'd ever tasted. Better than Lizzie's. Even better than his ma's. How was it some man hadn't snatched up Miss Ruth Blackburn? The lady was wasting her talents in a schoolhouse. She should be cooking for a family, keeping a husband's bed warm at night.

The thought sliced through his belly as he turned around and faced her solid stance. She sure was pretty. Those eyes sparkled as vibrantly up close as he'd imagined, with dark lashes as long as he'd seen. And that slender body. Damnation, she was the perfect length to press against him in all the right places. When his groin tightened, he erased the image from his mind.

Enticing though she was, Ruth Blackburn hadn't had any business coming into his home, taking over his daughter's chores. And she sure as hell didn't have any business telling him he was neglecting his daughter.

He ought to tell her he'd fed the damned pie to his pigs. He was a lot of things, but he was no liar. Grudgingly, he opened his mouth to speak. "Yes, we liked the pie."

Her pretty pink lips curved into a saucy grin. There went his groin again.

"I'm pleased you enjoyed it. Truly I am."

Garth sucked in a breath. Her smile was something out of heaven itself. "We are obliged, ma'am."

"Now that wasn't so difficult, was it?"

Difficult? He'd had to force the words from his throat. He couldn't recall the last time he'd uttered them. Of course, he hadn't had reason to. Nothing had happened in the recent past that was worthy of his thanks. Luckily, he didn't have to answer, because she started talking again. Confound it, the woman liked the sound of her own voice.

"Will I see Mary Alice in school today?"

"Mary Alice is done with school for the year. She's needed at the farm."

"Oh. I see. Well, why don't you come in for a moment, then. I'll write down a few things to keep her busy over the summer. I don't want her falling behind when school starts up again in the fall."

Before he could reply, she turned and whisked into the schoolhouse. He had no choice but to follow.

By the time he reached her desk, she had donned a pair of gold-rimmed spectacles and was scribbling notes on a piece of linen stationery. Expensive linen stationery. A gift from a suitor? Of course, it had to be. A schoolteacher couldn't afford such a luxury, and neither could Garth. Good thing he didn't plan on courting a woman any time soon.

She stood and handed him the cream-colored paper. "I've written down some work Mary Alice should do in her speller and reader. I've also taken the liberty of recommending a few books she might like. I have them all in my personal library, so she's welcome to borrow them any time."

Garth perused the list. Charles Dickens. Jules Verne. Louisa May Alcott. Who were these people?

"You'll see I've recommended *Little Men*. I'm assuming she's already read *Little Women*. My fourth reader class read it earlier this year. But since Mary Alice is fairly new to my classroom, she may not have read it yet. In which case, she should read *Little Women* before *Little Men*. Dickens may be a little difficult for her yet, but she's a fine reader, Mr. Mackenzie. You should encourage her gift. All other learning is dependent on reading, and she has a true aptitude for it."

Mary Alice liked to read? And she was good at it? News to him. Of course, the only book he had at home was the Bible, and he never opened that one. It was Lizzie's.

"I hope you don't think I'm sticking my nose in where it

doesn't belong, Mr. Mackenzie, but I'm worried about Mary Alice. You know she nearly fainted the other day, and yesterday when I stopped by your house—"

"It's the heat," Garth said.

"Of course, the heat will add to almost anything, but I truly feel she's overworked."

"Now just one minute—"

"I know her mother is gone. I'm so very sorry about that, sir. And I know the work needs to get done. I grew up on a farm, and my pa's a preacher, so much of the work fell to my ma, my sister, and me. I'm no stranger to hard work. But Mary Alice is still a child. She needs time to play. And she really shouldn't neglect her studies. She's so bright."

Tarnation, this woman liked to talk. Who the hell did she think she was? Telling him how to raise his child. She was still squawking like a prairie chicken, mostly about his failures as a father.

In a blaze of angry passion, he shut her up the only way he could think of with his body heating as it was.

He gripped her shoulders, pulled her to his chest, and crushed his mouth to hers.

CHAPTER FOUR

"Mister—mmmmmmpphhhh..." Ruth's words stopped as lips—full, firm, male lips—pressed against hers.

They slid, they nibbled, and then they settled on hers, and a growling, soft and low in his throat, hummed against her mouth.

Goodness, she should put a stop to this unseemly conduct. And in her schoolroom, no less. Her hands wandered to his chest to push him away. But when the moist tip of his tongue traced the seam of her lips—such a new and inviting sensation—she dropped her arms to her sides and went limp against his hard body.

What to do? Part her lips? She knew how men liked to kiss. She'd heard enough about it from her married friends, but she'd never experienced the pleasure. What if she did it wrong?

What if she did it with the wrong man?

Garth Mackenzie was attractive. Handsome as any man. And God love him, he was tall. So tall and masculine and beautiful.

But he wasn't exactly a *nice* man. He didn't seem to respect her or her position. Didn't take the greatest care of his child...

Ah, but his lips, so urgent against hers. Those little moans, those tiny nips.

She wanted to kiss him.

With a shallow breath through her nose, she parted her lips. His tongue glided into her mouth and his exotic vanilla spice flavor trickled into her. Smooth, masculine, and oh so very delicious.

She inhaled again, another shallow puff, and his raw aroma permeated her body. More spice, a hint of tobacco, and the fresh scent of the open prairie.

Ruth shuddered, her lips numb. She didn't know how to kiss him, how to respond, but he didn't seem to mind. He growled against her mouth and deepened his assault.

He slid his large calloused hands up her arms, heating her skin through the fabric of her dress. He trailed over her shoulders to her neck, where he cupped her nape and drew her even closer into his embrace. He swept his other hand over her cheek to her spectacles. He removed them without disturbing the kiss.

Where did he put them? Ruth didn't care at the moment. She was lost. Lost in the sweet urgency of his mouth against hers.

Her thoughts muddled, and vibrant images of him lying next to her emerged. His body, unclothed, pleasuring hers. A soft sigh escaped her, and he responded with a gentle groan.

His hand left her nape, and glided his fingers down her arms to her hands. He clasped them both firmly. A shiver raced up her spine, spread icy heat throughout her arms, her torso, and landed as an uncontrollable flutter between her legs.

Her hands trembled as Mr. Mackenzie—Garth—placed them on his shoulders. He removed his lips from hers and pressed a wet kiss to her cheek.

"Touch me," he whispered. "Please."

Touch him? Oh, she wanted to. She wanted to touch him everywhere. Where to start? How did a woman do this sort of thing? Perspiration—from the stifling schoolhouse or from the heat Garth ignited in her body, she wasn't sure—beaded on her forehead and rivered down the curves of her neck. Shaking, she extended one hand to his cheek. His golden stubble scraped against her fingers. He turned, then, and placed a gentle moist kiss to her palm. A spike of energy hit her in the gut.

"Oh..." she murmured.

His gaze drew her. Those bronze eyes had darkened and seemed to smolder as he looked at her.

"Your eyes," he said. "The color of midnight." He brushed his lips over hers, a feathery caress. "So lovely."

His mouth slid onto hers again, and she opened to him this time. She wanted his kisses. His embrace. She felt whole. Whole as she'd never felt before.

Boldly, she slid her tongue past his full lips, and he rewarded her with another rumbling groan. She caressed both his cheeks and then his hard, muscular shoulders through the broadcloth of his work shirt.

Her nipples beaded against her bodice, straining, aching. A fierce desire speared through her—a desire to explore everything unknown with this man.

The kiss went on and on, for how long, Ruth didn't know. He nibbled across her upper lip, her lower, kissed her nose, her cheeks, the sensitive flesh of her neck. But always he returned to her mouth and pleasured her with his smooth and silky tongue. Ruth melted into the warmth of his mouth on hers, of his chest against hers. The hard male part of him pressed against her belly. He pulled her closer, kissed her deeper, ravished her with lips, teeth, tongue.

Nothing existed except her and Garth and this kiss.

Somewhere in the edge of her awareness, a voice crept into her mind. Two voices. Then three.

The children, out playing in the schoolyard. They'd remain out until she rang the bell.

The bell. School.

Ruth ripped her mouth from Garth's and touched her lips.

"Oh, my! What on earth have I done?" Her voice pitched and sounded foreign.

She eyed the handsome man before her, his gaze scalding on her skin. His firm lips were swollen and red. She imagined hers were as well.

The cad still had his hat on, though it had jarred some and sat at an odd angle on the back of his head. She vaguely recalled fingering the rough felt as she'd struggled to get closer to him.

Closer to a man who was a stranger to her.

A man she wasn't sure she even liked all that well.

Goodness, what had gotten into her?

She'd never been courted, never been kissed, and the first time a man showed her any attention, what had she done? Behaved like a common hussy.

She cleared her throat, determined to regain her dignity. "Mr. Mackenzie, it is time for school and I must ring the bell. If you will excuse me, please. Be sure to tell Mary Alice she can"—Lord above, her heart was racing—"stop by my pa's farm anytime for the books. If I'm not home, my ma can get them for her."

"Ruth—"

"Miss Blackburn, please."

"Aw, tarnation." His face reddened. "Miss Blackburn. I..." He shook his head. "I just want to say that I'm sorry—"

"There is no need to apologize, Mr. Mackenzie. I... participated willingly in this little...er...dalliance. I hope you don't think any less of me for my lack of self-control. I assure you it won't happen again." She spied her spectacles sitting on the desk and replaced them on the bridge of her nose. "Now I must ring the bell. If you'll excuse me, sir."

Her body tingling, she rushed past Garth—such a masculine name for such a masculine man, goodness—and out the doorway to tug on the bell cord. The clanging of the school bell echoed across the yard and the children clamored into the schoolhouse, taking their places.

"Where's Mary Alice, Mr. Mackenzie?" a voice piped from behind her.

Ruth turned to see Garth stopped in front of Laura Brighton's desk. The empty place next to Laura belonged to Mary Alice.

"She won't be back to school, girl," Garth said, adjusting his hat.

"I'm having a birthday party next week," Laura said. "I'd like Mary Alice to come."

"Mary Alice don't have time for parties, child."

Garth, gaze straight ahead, strolled past Ruth and out of the schoolhouse.

No time for parties, indeed. What an insolent man, keeping his daughter from the fun of being a little girl.

How had she succumbed to his charms? She let out a scoff. Charms? The man didn't have any. She'd succumbed to his kisses, pure and simple. The drive of lust fueled by his physical attractiveness.

Never again.

Time for school. Preparing for the day ahead, she inhaled a deep breath.

Of spice, tobacco, and Garth Mackenzie.

★ ★ ★ ★

The drive home was sweltering. Ruth swiped her hand across her sweaty forehead as she urged her mare, Miranda, forward. The poor horse was thirsty.

Getting through the day had been a chore. Her mind wandered, and she hadn't been able to focus on the students' lessons. Finally, unable to concentrate, she'd sent them home a half hour early—a "reward" for their good behavior. Something she'd never done. Didn't even believe in. The school day was the school day, and that was that.

But not today. The memories of Garth Mackenzie's kiss, of his touch, had flooded her mind. Still flooded her mind. Her pulse had hammered all day. She took in a steadying breath.

A steadying breath hadn't helped in the schoolhouse. Why should it help now?

It didn't.

As she rounded a bend leading to her father's farm, a black buggy came toward her. Doc Potter's buggy. Her tummy lurched. Was everything all right at home?

"Afternoon, Miss Ruth," Doc Potter said, stopping alongside her buckboard.

Ruth halted Miranda. "Goodness, Doc, is something the matter with my ma? My pa?"

"Oh, no, ma'am. I was just paying a call." He smiled.

Relieved, Ruth released a breath. "I'm glad to hear that. I was a tad worried when I saw you."

"No need to be. All's fine. Good day." He urged his team forward.

Ruth arrived home, tended Miranda, and then strolled into the little house. Her mother was kneading on the wooden table in the small kitchen.

"Afternoon, dear."

"Ma, what was Doc Potter doing here this afternoon? I saw him on my way home and he nearly scared me silly. I thought something had happened to you or Pa."

"Nothing like that, I assure you." Her mother wiped her floured hands on her apron and smiled at Ruth. She pulled out a chair from under the table. "Sit down with me for a minute. I'll tell you."

"Where's Pa?"

"In the fields. He'll be in for supper later." Molly Blackburn sat down across from Ruth. "I have some wonderful news."

"Oh?"

"Doc Potter came to talk to Pa."

"About what?"

"About you, Ruth." Her mother's eyes sparkled. "He wants to court you."

Ruth barely stopped her jaw from dropping to the floor. Court her? After all this time, a man wanted to court her?

"Ma, he's too short."

"Goodness, Ruth. If you're determined to wait for a man taller than you, I'm afraid you'll be waiting a while."

"Pa's taller than I am. So is Naomi's Bobby." And so was Garth Mackenzie, but that was neither here nor there.

"Ben Potter is a nice looking man, and my goodness he's not a dwarf. He's average-sized. He's warm and intelligent, and he's a doctor, Ruth. He can offer you a good life. A life filled with luxuries your pa and I weren't able to give you and your sister."

"Hogwash, Ma."

"Watch your mouth, young lady!"

"I apologize. But really, he may be a doctor, but he's a doctor here in Dugan. He gets paid in chickens and rotten apples. He lives over the general store, for goodness' sake. I'm sure he can support a wife and family, but life with him would be far from luxurious."

"So it's luxury you want?"

"No." Ruth stood and paced three steps across the small kitchen. "Stop twisting my words around. I was responding to your claim that Doc could give me luxuries that you and Pa couldn't. You know I don't care about any of that stuff. I never have."

"Well, then, I don't see the issue, Ruth. I should think you'd be happy a man finally came courting."

Ruth sighed. That's what it always came down to. She wrenched her hands in the folds of her skirt. "You and pa can finally be rid of your old maid daughter, is that it?"

"Goodness, of course not. But you're a beautiful girl, Ruth. You're the only one who doesn't see it."

Ruth sat back down and clumped her elbows on the table. "I'd say most of the men in town don't see it, Ma, or they'd have come around before now."

"Most of the men in town are intimidated by you. And why wouldn't they be? Not only are you beautiful, but you're easily the most intelligent person in this town. That's been clear since you could talk. Everyone knows it. You can out think anyone here, and you're not afraid to give your opinion." She sighed. "And some are no doubt bothered by your height."

"You're tall. Naomi's tall." Ruth looked to the ceiling. "Why did I have to be the one who grew to freakish proportions?"

"You're five-feet-eleven, Ruth. Hardly a freak of nature. I'm five-feet-nine, and so is Naomi."

"Those two inches make all the difference, Ma."

"It's not your height that has kept men away, dear. It's their own insecurities. You're brilliant. And opinionated. And beautiful."

Ruth met her mother's blue gaze. "I'm not beautiful, Ma, and I wish you'd quit saying that. Naomi is beautiful. I'm plain. Average. A *C*."

"That is simply untrue. You're just as physically appealing as your sister, but in a different way. Your sister has your father's eyes. Those are a blessing. I'll grant you that. But your eyes are no less attractive. They're just like my mother's—such a dark blue they appear almost black at times. They're lovely."

Lovely? She'd never thought so. But Garth had said her eyes were lovely. Her skin warmed. Land sakes, this Dakota heat was unbearable.

"Doc Potter is an intelligent man," her mother continued. "Medical school is difficult, impossible for many. But not for him. So there's no reason why your intelligence would intimidate him. In fact, he most likely finds it attractive. A man secure in his own intelligence won't be threatened by another's. Even if she is a woman."

"There's still the issue that I tower over him."

"You hardly tower over him. You're an inch or two taller, that's all."

Lord above, her mother was right. Ruth should be pleased such a fine man wanted to court her. Ben Potter had dark hair and eyes, an infectious smile. Yes, he was handsome. She couldn't deny that. Always smiling, the doc. Why didn't he court one of the frilly younger girls? All of whom were in his height range. Any one of them would be thrilled to accept his suit.

"The doc has asked to escort you home from church on Sunday," Ma continued, "by way of Hattie's."

The restaurant? New to the town, Hattie's sat in an exalted spot less than a block from the church building. Ruth hadn't set foot in the eatery. Why spend money on such a frivolity when Ma's meals were as good as any she'd eaten in her life?

"That's silly, Ma. Why don't we just invite him over here after church?"

"He's been here for dinner before," Ma said. "I think he'd like the chance to converse with you alone, dear."

"We've conversed alone on numerous occasions. Why, just the other day I spoke to him about one of my students. She nearly fainted in the schoolhouse."

Her mother smiled. "I think he'd like to talk to you about other things, Ruth. Not your job or his. Get to know you on a more personal level."

Lord above. A personal level. Her fingers, seemingly of their own accord, trailed across her bottom lip. Personal level? She'd never spoken to any man on a personal level. But her encounter with Garth Mackenzie this morning had gone way beyond personal. Tiny shivers raced along her skin.

Shivers. Shivers she hadn't felt since she was an adolescent and she'd fancied herself in love with her older schoolmate, Byron Harris, who'd only had eyes for Naomi. Naomi didn't return his feelings, and Byron eventually married another and left Dugan.

Ruth hadn't felt those shivers since.

Until now. Truth be told, the current shivers made Byron's seem like mere goose bumps from the cold air. Not what was prickling along her body now, no sir.

These were frissons of excitement. Of fear. Of longing.

Of pure raw need.

And not due to Ben Potter. The good doc had never made her feel hot and cold at the same time.

Land sakes, this little house was hotter than blazes.

The soft caress of Garth Mackenzie's lips against hers invaded her thoughts, but she brushed it away.

Best make do with what she had. A lesson learned long ago as a preacher's daughter, and a lesson she'd be well advised to put to use now.

"Fine, Ma. I will accompany Doc Potter to Hattie's on Sunday."

And she'd try like the dickens not to wish he were Garth Mackenzie.

CHAPTER FIVE

Ruth felt conspicuous. All eyes were upon her. What was the preacher's spinster daughter doing dining with the town doctor at Hattie's?

That's what they were all thinking. She knew it.

Well, not all. Only seven other people graced the small dining room. Ruth had often wondered if a restaurant would make it in Dugan. Most of the townspeople she knew weren't likely to spend their hard-earned money for a luxurious meal.

Luxurious it was, too. A fried steak that took up nearly her whole plate, served with string beans, mashed potatoes, and buttered cornbread. The cornbread was flavored with white sugar, too. Delectable.

Doc Potter was easy to converse with. At least he used to be. They'd conversed many times before. But something was different now. A tension, tight as a bow string, hung in the air almost visibly between them.

He asked questions about her childhood, and she responded in kind, and then asked the same of him. He'd grown up in Iowa, the son of a shopkeeper. He was thirty years old.

Such a nice man.

Why couldn't she get those shivers?

"Miss Blackburn," he said, "I'd like permission to use your first name."

Gracious. "I suppose that would be all right, Doc."

"Thank you...Ruth. Please call me Ben."

"Of course, Ben." Lord above, it sounded all wrong.

"May I call on you some evening this week?"

"Well, Doc...er, I mean Ben...this is the last week of school. I'm likely to be quite tuckered in the evenings."

"Oh." He looked down.

She'd disappointed him. Drat. She'd said the wrong thing. Why wasn't she better at this? Some women were born to coquettishness. Not her.

"But you could still call, I suppose. I'd enjoy a walk around the farm. It will be...refreshing after a long day in that hot schoolhouse."

His mahogany eyes brightened. "I'd enjoy that very much, Ruth. How about Wednesday evening?"

She nodded. "That would be fine."

"Excellent. I'll look forward to it."

An aproned serving girl whisked their plates away. Ruth had left half of her meat. She normally had the appetite of a starving adolescent boy, but eating in front of a man—a man who was interested in courting her—unnerved her.

"Piece of pie or cake for either of you?" the girl asked.

"Ruth?" Doc looked at her expectantly.

"Goodness, no. I couldn't eat another bite."

"Then I'll pass as well," Doc said.

"Not on my account. Have a dessert if you'd like."

"I'm adequately sated," he said, "though a cup of tea would be nice."

"You, ma'am?" the girl asked.

"Uh...yes, of course. Tea would be lovely."

The tea was strong and delicious. Darjeeling, Ben called it. From India. Much smoother than the tea Ma served at home. When they had finished, he escorted her out of the restaurant and back to the church where his team and black buggy waited.

Glory, Ruth had never ridden in a buggy before. Doc helped her up into the comfortable cushioned seats. It was a half hour ride to her pa's farm. Though comfort wouldn't be an issue, Ruth worried about finding another half hour's worth of conversation topics.

Well, sake's alive, he'd invited her out. Why not let him find a suitable subject to talk about? She let out a shaky breath.

Ben talked a little about his experience at university as they drove along the beaten road to Pa's farm. The man had led an interesting life, and Ruth found herself listening with rapt attention, until he stopped talking and thick tension rose between them.

"Ruth."

"Yes?"

"I suppose..." His words faded, and he moved the reins to one hand and laid the other on top of hers. "I suppose you understand why I asked to see you today. And why I'd like to go walking with you this week."

"Well, of course, Doc...er, Ben. Ma spoke to me."

Doc cleared his throat. Crimson rose along his neck to his cheeks. Ruth turned and looked straight ahead at the bounding prairie.

"You see, I've come to admire you a great deal, and I'd like for us to get to know each other, with the eventual goal being marriage."

Ruth's mouth dropped below her chin, and she turned to regard Doc's profile. Marriage? After one outing he spoke of marriage? What did one say to such a proposal?

Before she could reply, Doc's Adam's apple bobbed with a gulp. "Well, I feel we are compatible intellectually. And physically."

She jolted. "Physically? What on earth do you mean?"

"Well...we would...produce children of optimal size and intelligence."

Size? *Land sakes.* Ruth's dander prickled the back of her neck. She reined it in. "I'm very flattered, but—"

"I'm not asking for an answer today," Doc said.

He squeezed her hand lightly. Funny, no sparks. Yet she sizzled at the slightest brush of Garth Mackenzie's hand.

"I certainly wouldn't presume to give you an answer today."

Doc opened his mouth, but before he could speak, the thudding gallop of a horse's hooves rambled up behind them.

Ruth stiffened against the cushioned back of the buggy seat. "Doc, what is it?" Her breath hitched as she imagined a masked outlaw. She doubted Doc was armed.

"I don't know." He urged the horses into a gallop, when a chilling voice rent through the air.

"Doc! Stop! Please!"

Doc halted the buggy, and a horse galloped up next to them, manned by a very large, very frazzled Garth Mackenzie.

"Thank God," he said. "I need you. It's Mary Alice."

Ruth's heart plummeted. "What's wrong with Mary Alice?"

"She fainted again. I can't wake her. Please, Doc, you've got to come."

"Of course, we'll follow you."

Garth galloped into the distance and Doc followed. Ruth braced her feet against the floor of the buggy and grasped the side to keep from bouncing into Doc's lap.

"I apologize for this inconvenience, Ruth," Doc said over

the thundering hooves.

"Gracious, this isn't an inconvenience. This is your job. I hope I can be of some assistance."

Ruth's belly churned with worry for Mary Alice. Perhaps this would be the wakeup call Garth Mackenzie needed. He couldn't work that poor girl to death. She prayed silently the rest of the way to the small ranch.

When they arrived, Doc didn't help her down from the buggy. No matter, he had his patient on his mind. She understood. She readied to climb down herself when Garth Mackenzie appeared at her side, offering his hand. Her jaw dropped open and she sucked in a shallow breath.

She took his outstretched hand, and a tingle shot through her. She looked up and met his dark and worried gaze.

"I'm glad you're here, Miss Blackburn," he said. "You'll be a comfort to Mary Alice."

"Of course I'll do what I can, Mr. Mackenzie," she said. "What happened?"

"I..." He seemed to stumble for words. "I have to take care of my horse, and then Doc's. Just go on in and I'll explain later."

"Mr. Mackenzie, the horses will be fine for a few minutes. You need to explain the situation to Doc so he knows what he's dealing with."

His eyes glazed over, as if he were looking through her. "Horses. I have to attend the horses."

"Goodness. All right." Ruth smoothed her mussed skirts and headed for the house, praying again for the child who had come to mean more to her than a student should.

She hurried into the small home and found Doc in a tiny bedroom off the front room—which was in disarray again— bending over a pale Mary Alice.

"Doc?"

"She's come to, Ruth." He pressed a moistened cloth to her forehead. "Fill the basin with cool water for her."

Ruth breathed a thick sigh of relief. She'd awakened. "Yes, of course. Right away."

She grabbed the basin and hurried out the back way through the lean-to. The rain barrel was nearly empty. Where was the pump? Was there a pump? She scanned her surroundings. To her left, she saw Garth exit a stable and begin walking toward the house. She ran to him.

"Mr. Mackenzie, I need fresh water for Mary Alice. Where is your well?"

His glossy eyes looked through her again. "Don't have one. We fetch water from the little creek yonder." He pointed.

"Thank you. Do tell Doc I'll be back as soon as I can."

She turned, but he gripped her arm, almost knocking the basin out of her grasp.

"Ruth."

She looked up, and his eyes burned into hers. He wasn't looking through her this time. "Yes?"

"Mary Alice?"

Ruth smiled her biggest smile. "She's awake. Go on into her. I'll get the water."

Was that a return smile? His lips edged upward ever so slightly. Then he turned toward the house, his pace increasing in speed.

As Ruth returned from the creek, she wished she had grabbed a pail for the water. It sloshed over the sides of the basin to the point she wasn't sure any would be left by the time she reached Mary Alice. She did her best to walk slowly and carefully, but her concern took over and she nearly ran.

HELEN HARDT

When she entered the small bedroom, Mary Alice was sitting up in bed. Doc sat next to her, and Garth paced at the foot of the bed.

"I hope I didn't take too long, Doc. Here's the water." She set the basin on a bureau.

"Thank you, Ruth," Doc said.

"How is Mary Alice?" she asked.

"I was just telling Mr. Mackenzie, her heartbeat is strong and she appears well hydrated. No fever. There doesn't seem to be any reason for her swoon."

"Oh? Perhaps she's a bit overworked?"

Garth scowled at that remark, but she held her ground. The man needed to stop insisting the child spend her life doing chores.

"She may be a little fatigued," Doc said. "But still, she seems healthy enough." He looked to Garth. "This child needs to stay in bed for a few days. No chores. No nothing."

"But you just said there's nothing wrong with her," Garth said.

"I said there's nothing wrong with her that I can see. But something caused this faint, Mr. Mackenzie. Doctors don't always have all the answers. That's why it's called the practice of medicine."

"For corn's sake," Garth said, shaking his head. "I always knew you all were just a bunch of quacks."

"Mr. Mackenzie!" Ruth stepped toward him. "Doc came all the way out here to treat your child. He interrupted our"—she warmed, and then cleared her throat—"outing. You might show him a bit more respect."

"Calm down, Ruth," Doc said. "I'm used to skeptics. It's part of my business."

Garth's handsome face reddened. Had she actually shamed him?

"Beg pardon, Doc," he said. "I haven't had the best... experience with so-called doctors."

Before Doc responded, a pounding echoed from the front door. "What on earth?" Ruth turned and looked over her shoulder. "I'll see what this is about. You two stay with Mary Alice."

She crossed the front room, opened the door, and looked into the frightened face of Oliver Hobbs.

"Miss Blackburn—" His voice shook. "Is Doc here?"

"Why, yes, he is, Mr. Hobbs."

"Thank God. Jon Sanderson said he saw him headin' out this way. I need him. The baby's comin'."

"Gracious! Come in, and I'll get the doc."

Ruth hurried back to Mary Alice's room. "Doc, Mr. Hobbs is here. Louise has gone into labor."

Doc stood. "All right. I've done all I can do here for now. Bed rest for a few days. I'll be back to check on her tomorrow or the next day."

"Let me get your payment," Garth said.

Doc held up a hand. "Later, Mr. Mackenzie. I have to go to Mrs. Hobbs. These things sometimes progress quickly. You just never know." He turned to Ruth. "I'm sorry. You'll have to come with me. I can't take the time to see you home."

"I'll see her home," Garth said.

"I'd be much obliged, Mr. Mackenzie," Doc said, "but you shouldn't leave your daughter alone."

"You're right," Garth said, shaking his head. "Not sure what I was thinkin'."

"Doc, don't worry about me," Ruth said. "I'm happy to

stay here and sit with Mary Alice. I'll make sure she gets a good supper. Once things are under control at the Hobbs place, if you could send Oliver to tell my parents where I am, I'd appreciate it. I don't want them to worry."

"Will do. Keep the child hydrated. She should be fine. But you know where I am if you need me."

Ruth nodded. She sat down on the edge of the bed, took the cloth from Mary Alice's forehead, and wiped her clammy face. "Are you feeling better, dear?"

"Yes, ma'am. Just a little weak, is all."

"Well, that's nothing to take lightly. You're to stay in bed. In fact"—she gestured toward Garth—"it wouldn't be a bad idea for your father to rest, either."

"Nonsense," Garth said. "I don't rest during the day. Work to be done." As if on cue, he opened his mouth into a giant yawn.

Ruth couldn't help but let out a laugh. "Yes, I see you've been working yourself as hard as you've been working your daughter, sir." She stood and faced him at the foot of the bed. "Off to bed with you, too. If you want to take care of Mary Alice, you need to take care of yourself. She needs your strength, Mr. Mackenzie."

"For corn's sake."

He shook his head, and his blond locks tumbled into his eyes. Ruth resisted the urge to sift her fingers through them and push them back.

"For corn's sake nothing," she said, trying to ignore the tingles racing over her flesh as she touched his arm and nudged him out of the room. "I will be here, and I'm perfectly capable of looking after Mary Alice. I'll see that you both have a hearty meal for supper. So you see, there's nothing to worry about."

"You don't need to cook for us."

"I am your neighbor, sir, and the neighborly thing to do is to help where I'm needed."

He shuffled across the front room and yawned again. "I got things to do, Ruth."

Land sakes, he was a stubborn man. And so handsome he made her skin heat. The image of his lips pressing against hers flashed through her mind. She'd been so concerned with Mary Alice, she hadn't let the kiss they'd shared enter her thoughts. But now, knowing the child was not in danger, and in the presence of his pure maleness, her stomach twisted and her nipples beaded against her bodice. She exhaled and tried to shrug the sensation off. "It's the Lord's day, Mr. Mackenzie. He rested on this day and so can you. Now go."

He seemed to relent then, and Ruth gazed into his brilliant bronze eyes and saw fatigue. The poor man looked like he hadn't slept well in days.

"Mary Alice," he whispered.

"I'll take care of her," she said quietly. "Please, you need rest."

He nodded and ambled toward the bedroom on the other side of the front room.

Ruth returned to Mary Alice and fed her a dipper of cool water. Satisfied the child was resting comfortably, she went to work straightening the front room. How could one man and one child make such a mess? Really, how much effort was it to take a used tin cup to the kitchen and rinse it?

Once the room was in order, Ruth sat down in a wooden rocking chair. What to make for supper? She doubted there was another plucked chicken waiting outside the lean-to.

She sighed and readied herself to check the contents of

the pantry when her ears prickled.

A low growl—agonizing, guttural, *human*—spilled from Garth Mackenzie's bedroom.

CHAPTER SIX

"Don't say a fuckin' word. I swear to God I'll slit your throat."

"I-It hurts. I—"

"I said not a word!" Garth pressed his blade against the pale skin of his friend's throat. The Rebel's bullet had lodged in Matthew's stomach. Garth held his friend on his lap like an infant, his dull knife poised at Matthew's Adam's apple. If Matthew screamed in pain, he'd give away their position to the Rebs.

Above them, Rebel boots crunched against the ground.

"Where are you, you Yankee rubbish?"

The icy voice slithered over Garth like a snake.

"We know you're hurtin'. Y'all can't hold out forever."

Garth trembled, his skin a mass of chills. His fingers shook against Matthew's throat. He wasn't ready to die. Had to get back. Back to marry Lizzie. He looked at his friend struggling to hold on, to not bellow out in agony. Matthew had a woman at home. He'd already married her. He had a child, too. A baby girl he'd never met.

Would never meet.

Blood poured from Matthew's stomach, soaking his blues with sticky vermillion. Garth didn't try to staunch the flow. He couldn't risk removing the blade from his friend's neck. If Matthew yelled, they'd both be dead.

"Garth, please." Matthew's voice slurred into a nearly

unrecognizable gurgle.

"Quiet!"

"Just...kill me. Kill me now, and save yourself."

"I said be quiet, damn it!" Garth's whisper left his mouth in a breathy fog. "Not another peep outta you, you hear me?"

Soothing hands slid across the back of his neck. Warm, enticing. He fought the desire to turn into their welcoming embrace.

"Wake up, Garth, it's only a nightmare."

No. No. Can't leave Matthew. Can't—

★ ★ ★ ★

"Mr. Mackenzie, for goodness' sake. Wake up. You're having a nightmare."

Caressing hands. Angelic voice. Not Lizzie, though. Different. But good. Oh so good.

Without opening his eyes, he reached toward that voice, gripped delicate shoulders, and pulled the soft feminine body atop him.

He inhaled—a touch of lemon and sweet soft woman. Not Lizzie. Lizzie was dead. This was Ruth. Beautiful, incredible, *alive* Ruth. Ruth whose midnight eyes held him captive.

He opened his own eyes then, and hers were wide as dinner plates. Her full pink lips parted and her throat bobbed. She was going to speak. To tell him to stop, no doubt. Before she could, he pulled her mouth to his.

His tongue slid easily between her parted lips. She tasted of new summer, of lemon shortbread, of home and hearth. He sighed and deepened the kiss. She'd kiss him back, wouldn't she? She had before. She'd kissed like a temptress, and her image, her fragrance, her softness, had haunted him since.

Ah, yes. Her silken tongue met his. Perfect. The perfect kiss. For an unmarried lady, she had amazing instinct. She knew how to kiss him just the way he liked—lots of little sucks along his lips and just the right amount of tongue. Nope, he wouldn't need to teach her how to kiss him. Goddamn, he didn't want to stop. He could easily kiss her all night long. So beautiful, and so responsive. Such kisses were made for chasing away his demons.

When she began to pull away, he trailed moist kisses along her cheek to her ear. "Hold me. Please, Ruthie."

"Oh..." The soft sigh from her lips drifted over his cheek in a feathery caress.

"Keep the bad dreams away." He took her mouth again. The kiss wasn't soft this time. Wasn't gentle. He plundered her mouth with a possessive hunger, as though she were his woman. God, he wanted her. Wanted to sink inside her. Lose himself in that luscious body and stay there until all the pain had been driven away. His cock strained against his canvas britches, and he pushed upward, rubbing it against her.

Ruth ripped her mouth from his as he thrust. "Oh, my!"

"That's me. Me wanting you. Tell me. Do you want me?"

"Mr. Mackenzie, please—"

"I can take you to heaven. God, I want to go to heaven with you." He maneuvered her to her side and fumbled with the buttons of her bodice. One by one, they fell open and revealed the creamy skin of her neck and chest. Sweet Jesus. She wasn't wearing a corset. He smiled and cupped one breast, thumbing her beaded nipple through the thin fabric of her chemise.

Ruth sucked in a breath, but a sweet sigh escaped. She liked what he was doing. His heart bloomed. She liked it a lot.

Such a long time since he'd had a woman. Such a long time since he'd wanted one. But God, he wanted Ruth Blackburn. Wanted her with a fierceness he'd never known.

He slid down the bed until his mouth was level with her nipple, and he tongued it through the thin material.

"Garth!" Her whisper was urgent.

He met her midnight eyes. "You didn't like that?"

"I...gracious me. This is...wrong."

"Nothing that feels good is wrong, Ruthie. Please. Let me."

Before she answered, he pulled the silky chemise downward and one perfectly rounded breast fell into his hand. The nipple was reddish brown—earthy and gorgeous—and had he had a gun to his head at that very moment, he wasn't sure he could have stopped his lips from claiming it.

She was as delicious as he'd imagined, and again, so responsive. She writhed against him, and husky little moans drifted through the small room. He sucked her slowly at first, tiny licks and kisses, and then, when she pushed toward him and ground her thigh against his arousal, he clamped his lips on the sweet nipple and sucked hard.

"Heavens!" she whispered.

"Mmm," he said against her warm flesh.

"Garth..."

He let the nipple go and kissed the creamy swell of her breast. He looked up into her nearly black eyes.

"I...I can't..."

"I want you so much." His tone was imploring. God, when had he become so needy and pathetic? "Let me love you. Please."

"I...I..." Her husky voice thrummed into him.

"What, honey? What?"

"I...we're not properly wed, Mr. Mackenzie. It's...it's wrong."

Wed? Hell and damnation, he'd wed her this instant if it meant he could make love to her. He wanted her that much. But despite the fact that he was no gentleman—could never be a gentleman, given his past—he wouldn't take anything from a woman that wasn't given willingly. He opened his mouth to say as much, but Mary Alice's voice cut through the tension in the air.

"Pa!"

He jerked away, his mind and body still full of Ruth. He inhaled. Burning grass. Smoke. *Damn it, smoke.*

"Ruth, did you leave a fire in the fireplace?"

Ruth, her cheeks a delectable pink, hastily worked on her buttons. "In this heat? Of course not."

"What in tarnation..." He stood and ran to Mary Alice's bedroom. She was sitting up in bed.

"Child, are you all right?"

"Y-Yes, Pa. But I smell smoke."

"I do too. Stay here.

Garth ran through the kitchen and out the lean-to. A billowing black cloud dusted the horizon. *A prairie fire.* And his place was farthest on the outskirts of Dugan. *It was headed straight for his home.* For his livelihood. For his child. For Ruth.

Goddamned Dakota heat. Hadn't had any rain in weeks, and the winter had been mild. Little snow. Dry prairie plus heat plus afternoon heat lightning—well, he didn't need the schoolteacher in his bedroom to figure this out.

The schoolteacher in his bedroom.

He rushed back into the house. Ruth was walking into the

kitchen, her cute nose wrinkled.

She nodded to him. "Fire?"

He closed his eyes, and then opened them. "On the prairie. Comin' this way. I need you to take Mary Alice out of here."

"But Doc said she's to stay in bed."

"Damnation, woman! I said there's fire comin'! Take my child and keep her safe!"

Ruth shook her head and reached a shaky hand toward him. "I'm so sorry. Of course I'll take her. I'm not sure what I was thinking." She paused. "What will you do?"

"Do what I can to keep my place safe from the flames. I need to drive the fire away from the house, toward the creek. If I lose this farm—" He couldn't finish. If he lost the farm, he'd lose everything. He'd have no means to support the only child he had left.

Ruth extended her arm and cupped his cheek. Her touch was scalding, and his whole body responded.

"Garth, do what you must. But please come back safely. Mary Alice needs you."

He nodded. True enough. Mary Alice needed him. But did Ruth? Somehow he wanted her to need him. "Take my buckboard and team. Go to your pa's." He paused. "Better yet, take her to town. Get a room at the hotel. I'll reimburse you. You'll be safer there than at another farm. I'll come for you when I can."

"I'll send anyone I meet along the way to help you," Ruth said. Her midnight eyes glistened with tears about to fall.

Garth's heart lurched. Funny, he'd felt more in the week since he'd met this woman than he'd felt in years.

"Don't cry. I'll...be fine. I've been through worse."

If she only knew...

"Once I get to town, I'll tell the menfolk, too. They'll help, Garth. Dugan is a good town."

Damn, he wanted to pull her to him for a wet kiss. But he only nodded and walked out through the lean-to.

★ ★ ★ ★

Sitting on the wooden plank seat of Garth's buckboard, her derriere bumping with each thud of hooves, Ruth hurried the horses along. Mary Alice sat silently next to her, her lips trembling. A shiny tear emerged from one bronze eye and trickled down her cheek.

"Don't fret, Mary Alice," Ruth said. "Once we get to town, we'll send all the menfolk out to help your pa. He'll get that fire away from your house. Don't you worry."

"I...I don't care about the house. Or anything. I just need Pa. He's...all I have left."

"Gracious." Ruth steadied her breath. "Your pa will be fine." Resisting the urge to look behind her at the smoky clouds, she cleared her throat. "What are your horses' names, dear?"

"The spotted brown one is Hector and the tan one is Josephine."

"What lovely names."

"Hector was Pa's brother. He died in the war."

"Oh, my." How much loss was one man supposed to take? "And Josephine?"

"I named her after Jo from *Little Women*."

"Oh, so you have read that story." Ruth smiled.

"Yes, ma'am. About a year ago. A lady at a boardinghouse we stayed at lent it to me. Pa was doing some work for her. The horse's name was Gingersnap when we got her. I guess 'cause she's kinda the color of gingerbread. Pa said we could change their names since horses don't know the difference anyway."

"No doubt he's probably right. I think Hector and Josephine are perfect names."

The child's lips turned into a shy smile. Good, Ruth had succeeded in getting Mary Alice's mind off the fire. For a few moments, anyway.

Ruth shivered under the sweltering sun as her nerves skittered. So far, she hadn't passed a single person to send to help Garth. The hour was nearing suppertime, and it was Sunday. Of course no one was about. But surely someone would smell the stench of the smoke.

A half hour later they rode into town. Ruth stopped the team in front of the small hotel, tied them to the hitching post quickly, and hurried Mary Alice inside.

"Miss Blackburn, good evening," Fred Blake, the clerk, said.

"I'm so glad you're here. I need some help. Fire is headed toward the Mackenzie farm. Garth is out there alone. Is there anyone available to go help him?"

"I'm afraid I can't leave the hotel, ma'am. But I think Manny's over at the store. I'm not sure anyone else is around. The men don't usually play checkers on Sundays. And Doc Potter's gone."

"He's at the Hobbs place. Louise is having the baby. Where *is* everyone?"

"This is the dinner hour, ma'am."

"For heaven's sake, Mr. Mackenzie needs help! Where are all the men in this town? Can't you sound an alarm or something?"

"You know we don't have any such thing."

"Well, we will by the next town meeting, if I have anything to say about it. I suppose I will go pounding on doors tonight. I need a room for the night, for the child and me. Supper, too." She turned to Mary Alice. "You take the key Mr. Blake gives you and go up to the room. I'm going to try to find some men to help your pa."

Mary Alice's face whitened even further. Moisture pooled in her pretty eyes. "Ma'am?"

"Sweetheart, I have to find some people to help your pa. You'll be fine. I promise. Can you be brave for me? I know what a brave girl you are. You've been through so much. I need you to find your courage right now, Mary Alice. I will be back for you soon. I promise you that." She hugged the girl to her breast.

Mary Alice nodded. "Yes. I will be brave."

Ruth kissed the top of her blond head. "I know you will. As soon as I know your pa has the help he needs, I'll be back."

She hurried out the hotel and over to the mercantile to rouse Manny Stiles. Then she'd head to Hattie's and interrupt those having Sunday supper in town. After that, she'd knock on private doors. Sunday supper be damned.

Garth Mackenzie, I swear to you. You are not in this alone.

CHAPTER SEVEN

Garth's eyes stung from the smoke. Rivers of sweat trickled over his face and neck. He lowered another armful of burlap sacks into the little creek, saturated them, and headed back toward the fire ring he was building. With a lot of luck, the fire ring would chase the fire toward the creek. Hell, he needed more than luck. He needed a goddamned miracle.

"Mackenzie!"

Garth turned. A man ran toward him. Manny Stiles, the storekeeper. Hooves thundered in the background. More were coming.

"You headin' it off?" Manny said.

"Tryin'"

"I brought sacks," Manny said. "Bill Rossi's right behind me. The Dooley brothers too. Miss Blackburn ousted them right out of Hattie's Restaurant. Last I saw, she was runnin' around town like a madwoman knockin' on doors. You'll have all the help you need to stop that durned fire."

Ruth. She'd said she'd send help. Bless her sweet selfless heart.

"By the time I rode outta town, I could smell the smoke, just faintly. It's gettin' closer."

"Closer all the time," Garth said. "We need to stop talkin' now."

Manny nodded. "Here comes Bill now."

Garth, Manny, Bill, and half a dozen others worked for

the next hour, soaking sacks and adding to the fire ring. The flames blazed closer, the smoke made their eyes water, but still they worked. As the evening air turned slightly cooler, the fire died down, but only slightly.

"Good Lord," Garth said under his breath as he humped back and forth to the creek for water and sacks. "Please. Something's gotta give. I can't lose this farm. Please."

★ ★ ★ ★

Ruth lay awake. Beside her in the large hotel bed, Mary Alice slept soundly. The child had eaten dinner, though Ruth had forced her. But at least she'd eaten, and for that Ruth was grateful. She'd taken a long bath and then fallen asleep in tears, worried for her father.

At least she slept. She needed it, and her soft snores were a comfort to Ruth.

But only a slight comfort.

She'd sent a town boy to put a notice on the schoolhouse door that classes were canceled for the next day, and then out to her family's farm to let them know where she was. Perhaps Pa had gone to help Garth. As the preacher of the town, he'd no doubt do what he could. Lead slammed into her belly. Sometimes, when all hope faded, the only thing her father could do was pray.

Sleep did not come. Horrible images of Garth's farm burned to the ground plagued her mind. Worse, Garth himself, like a tintype only in color, his face and body scorched and scarred from the fire. Ruth clasped her hands together and prayed for his safety. Silly repetitions of words already said. But what else could she do?

A soft rapping at the door interrupted her thoughts, and Ruth jerked upward and nearly tumbled out of bed. Gaining her footing, she walked quickly across the wooden floor. What time must it be? She had no idea. *Please, please don't let it be bad news.*

"Yes?" she said through the door.

"It's me, Ruthie."

Garth! Without thinking, she ripped the door open and launched herself against his hard body, nearly toppling him over.

"Gracious, I'm sorry," she said, pulling away. "You must be exhausted."

He held her fast, didn't let her go.

"The farm?" she said against his chest.

"Everything's all right." His voice was hoarse, no doubt from inhaling the smoke. "Just when it looked like all was lost, a wind came up and blew the fire past the property and into the creek."

"Oh, thank God." Ruth inhaled a sharp breath of smoke and prairie.

"Mary Alice?"

"She's fine. Asleep. She ate dinner and had a bath. She's terribly worried about you, though. Perhaps we should wake her."

"No. Let the child sleep. She needs it. Just bring her home in the mornin'. I paid for your room. I'll go back home."

"You'll do no such thing. What time is it anyway?"

"Around midnight."

"You're completely tuckered. Come in here. There's a basin of water. We can at least clean you up a little. Then you take the room adjoining this one. It's empty."

173

"I already woke Fred up to get in here. I can't wake him again to get a room."

"Pshaw. It's his job. You had to let us know you were all right."

"My animals—"

"Will be fine until morning."

"They breathed in a lot of smoke."

"As did you. And they'll recover just like you will. Land sakes, you're about the most stubborn man this side of the Mississippi." She urged him into the room and onto a chair. Mary Alice still snored softly on the bed. "Just sit tight for a moment. I'll go down and get the key to the room for you."

"Not dressed like that, you won't." Garth stood. "I'll get it."

"Oh!" Ruth clamped her fingers to her lips. She had taken off her dress to go to bed and wore only her chemise and petticoats. She'd been so eager for news she hadn't given a thought to her state of dishabille. "What you must think of me, letting you in when I'm—"

He smiled. *Garth Mackenzie smiled at her.* His shiny white teeth contrasted starkly with his soot-covered face. Pale moonlight streamed in through the window, illuminating him.

"You look like an angel from heaven. But I won't let you go downstairs like that."

"I assure you I'll be dressed appropriately when you get back, Mr. Mackenzie."

He winked at her. *Winked.*

"I'd rather you weren't." He walked out the door and closed it softly behind him.

Ruth's heart hammered and her nipples poked through the gauzy fabric of her chemise. How scandalous to be dressed this way when he returned. His bronze gaze would rake over her body and heat her skin. Perhaps he'd pull her into his arms and kiss her again. Maybe cup her breast as he had earlier. Suck on her hard nipple. The sensation had been something out of heaven itself. Every nerve in her body had responded. Tingles had shot through her and landed between her legs, in the private place that was throbbing now at the mere thought.

She shook her head rapidly, trying to shake away the images and feelings. She grabbed her dress that was draped over the foot of the bed. She stepped into it, when another soft knocking jarred her. Tiptoeing to the door, she said, "Yes?"

Behind her, the soft click of a door. She turned to see Garth standing in the doorway between the two rooms.

"I hurried," he whispered, "so you wouldn't have time to change."

The heat of a blush seared Ruth's cheeks and neck, and she clenched the fabric of her dress tightly.

Garth walked to her slowly, took her hands and unclenched them. The calico dress pooled at her feet.

"I wish I could kiss you."

"I—"

"But I won't. I'm filthy as a pig right now."

"I suppose it's too late to have a bath sent up for you," Ruth said, her voice shaking. She hoped Garth didn't notice.

"Afraid so."

"No matter. Go into your room so we don't wake Mary Alice. I'll bring the basin of water." She gripped the porcelain basin and lifted it, but Garth took it from her, his fingers brushing hers. A tremble surged through her. Had he not taken the basin, she would have dropped it.

Though she knew it a bad idea, she followed Garth into

his room. She closed the door, but only so they wouldn't wake Mary Alice.

Garth set the basin on the bureau and lit a table lamp, and soon the room was aglow in soft light.

He turned to Ruth and walked toward her. Standing in front of her, he fingered a lock of her hair.

"You look pretty like this, with your hair down, falling over your shoulders and down your back."

Ruth looked away, unable to meet his gaze. "Mr. Mackenzie—"

"Garth. Please.

"I can't—"

"You did this afternoon. You used my first name."

"It was inappropriate." Ruth concentrated on a knot in the wood floor under her bare foot. "I shouldn't have."

"Are you in love with the doctor, Ruthie?"

"In love?" She looked up.

His bronze eyes burned. "Did he give you that fancy writin' paper?"

Ruth furrowed her brow. "You're talking nonsense. What writing paper?"

"That you used at the schoolhouse. To write down the books for Mary Alice."

"Oh." Her linen stationery. "That was a Christmas gift from the children. They all pitched in a few pennies."

He closed his eyes. Was that relief on his face?

"So you're not in love with Doc?"

"Gracious, I've never been in love. The doctor and I are friends, nothing more." Discomfort prickled at her. Doc Potter wanted more, she knew. But she didn't feel that way for him. Her heart didn't flutter like a bird's wing. Her skin didn't feel hot and cold at the same time. No, not for Doc Potter. Only for the man whose gaze seared hers at this moment.

"Why were you riding with him this afternoon?"

Ruth didn't reply. She turned to the bureau and wet a cloth in the water from the basin. "Enough of this now. Sit down, and let's get you cleaned up as best we can."

She wrung the cloth and turned to Garth, who had sat down in a wooden chair. Her nipples poked through her chemise and she warmed, but didn't turn away. He saw them, she knew.

She liked that he saw them. God help her, she wanted him to see them. Wanted him to kiss them, nibble them.

She inhaled sharply and touched the wet cloth to Garth's chiseled cheek. The heat of his skin burned her fingers through the cool cloth. So overheated from fighting the fire all night. She dragged the cloth down his cheek, across his jaw line. Smudges of gray covered the cloth from just one swipe. She rinsed it in the basin and began again.

"I'm sorry the water's not warmer."

"Cool is fine. I've had all the heat I can stand for a while."

"Oh, yes, of course. What I meant was, warmer water would cleanse you better. As would a touch of soap. Let me just get a little from the other room. There's some left from Mary Alice's bath earlier."

Ruth turned toward the doorway, but Garth's soiled hand gripped her forearm. "Please."

"Please what?"

"Please. Just stay here. With me."

"Mr. Mackenzie, I'm just going to get the soap—"

"I don't need any damned soap." His voice was soft, but stern. "I need you. Here. With me. Please." Gently he slid his hand to hers, which still held the cloth, and returned both to his stubbled cheek.

Ruth's hand shook as she slowly trailed the wet cloth over the angles of his face, wiping away the dirt and grime. Twice she rinsed the cloth and returned. She moistened the gilded strands at his hairline and pushed them out of his eyes. When his golden skin was buffed to a shine, she rinsed the cloth again and took his hands into hers.

"Gracious, you're a sight," she said.

"So are you. A lovely sight."

Her cheeks warmed. Did he truly think her lovely? She rubbed the soot from Garth's strong hands. His fingers were long and thick, with perfect square nails and tiny golden hairs growing from the knuckles. Good, capable hands. Hands that worked from sunup to sundown. Hands that had cupped her cheek, her nape, her breast. Hands that knew how to please a woman.

Ruth's nipples surged against her chemise, and she let out a shallow breath. "There, that's better." She set the cloth next to the basin. In the soft glow of the lamplight, Garth's male beauty gleamed. Except for one smudge on his chin marring his perfection. "Goodness, I missed a spot." She grabbed the cloth again and wiped the smear away. He touched his hand to hers, moving with her as she continued to wipe around his jaw line. He pushed her hand downward, and she followed his lead, cleansing his neck and then the upper plane of his chest. Golden hair peeked out where two buttons of his shirt were open.

"Ah, Ruthie"—his hoarse whisper caressed her cheek—"I wish I could bathe proper."

"I know. You must be very uncomfortable. But this will

have to do for tonight."

"You don't understand."

"Of course I do. Being covered in soot can't be much fun."

"Hell, dirt don't bother me," Garth said. "I'm used to it. But I'm too filthy to hold you."

"Oh, my." Her heart fluttered so hard against her breast she thought for certain Garth could see it through her chemise.

"I think I'd give my right arm to make love to you right now, honey. But I'm so darn weary I'd probably fall straight to sleep, and that wouldn't be any good for you."

Ruth jerked away. The cloth dropped into Garth's lap as she backed toward the door that joined the two rooms. Heat consumed her body. Her nipples felt like hard glass marbles, and something burst low in her stomach. Fire rippled between her legs.

She opened her mouth to speak, but no words formed.

Garth stood and edged toward her very slowly. "I didn't mean to frighten you."

"Such bold words, Mr. Mackenzie—"

"Garth, honey. Please."

"I don't know what to say to you. We hardly know one another. I-I'm doing you and Mary Alice a favor. Nothing more."

"I won't touch you, Ruth," he said, his bronze eyes burning, "unless you want me to."

"Mary Alice—"

"Is asleep. You've taken good care of her. I'm grateful."

Ruth gasped. He was grateful? "Did you just say..."

"Thank you. I said thank you."

"She's a lovely child. I'm happy to help."

"Is it only Mary Alice you want to help?"

"I'm a preacher's daughter. I've been raised to help where I'm needed."

"I thought maybe..."

"Maybe what?"

"That is, I was hoping that you might be helping Mary Alice because you...cared a tiny bit for"—he cleared his throat—"me."

"I hardly know you—"

"Confound it, would you stop saying that, woman?" He lunged toward her, gripped her shoulders, and kissed her hard.

Tendrils of heated passion coiled between Ruth's legs. Garth's powerful bulge pushed into her lower belly and she gasped, yet couldn't stop herself from rubbing into the hardness. Her mind whirled with uncertainty, but her body knew what to do. Knew just how to grind into his masculine potency so that the pulse between her thighs intensified, blazed, and a rush of desire clawed at her from somewhere within.

His mouth ravaged hers. No gentle kiss this time. This was deep. Raw. Possessive.

Ruth went limp against his strength. His clothes would soil her chemise and petticoats, but she didn't care. All that mattered in this moment was kissing Garth. Bringing her body closer to his.

Sweet Lord, the temptation. Such a beautiful strong man, and he wanted her. Plain Ruth Blackburn. Spinster schoolteacher.

Garth ripped his mouth from hers, sucked in a breath, and sprinkled wet kisses across both her cheeks. "My God, I'd do just about anything to have you right now. I'll marry you if that's what you want. I swear it, Ruthie. I swear it."

Her knees buckled under her, but he held her steady. Had

she heard correctly? He wanted to marry her?

"Garth, I—"

He plunged his tongue into her mouth again as he thrust his arousal against her. Oh, the sweet sensation. His fingers crept down her arm, leaving a trail of pleasant chills in their path. He grasped her derriere and squeezed, and then crept under the waistband of her petticoats. His bare fingers against the flesh of her buttocks inflamed her to new heights. Improper though it was, she wanted his touch. Craved it.

"Oh!"

His warm hand slid to the front and entwined in her brown curls. He cupped her, and then slid a finger into her private heat.

"Wet, Ruthie." His hoarse voice hummed against her trembling lips. "God, so wet."

Icy fear speared her gut. This was wrong. So wrong. So why did she want it so much?

Fear won out over need, and Ruth pulled away, her breath heaving in rapid pants.

"Damn, honey, I'm sorry."

"It's...it's..." Her mind jumbled, unable to form what she wanted to say. Needed to say.

Her heart thumped. Her whole body quivered. The wet place between her legs felt hot, swollen.

Empty. Sweet Lord, so empty and aching. A void only Garth could fill.

Yes, he wanted to fill her. Wanted to lie with her. He'd said so, through both words and actions. Even said he'd marry her to have her.

Images of naked bodies swirled through her head. She wanted him. That she could never deny. Her body would betray her lies anyway.

Still, a problem existed. One she couldn't overlook.

He hadn't said anything about love.

CHAPTER EIGHT

He'd gone too far. Ruth's pretty face paled with fear. She backed against the adjoining door, her hands flat against the panel, her knuckles white with tension, as though she wanted to melt into the wood. Her tousled mahogany waves fell around her shoulders in disarray. Her chemise was crumpled and her petticoats twisted from his maneuverings. Criminy, he hadn't meant to scare her. Hadn't meant to do anything, truth be told. He was filthy and bone weary. Though his cock thought otherwise, he was in no shape to make love to a woman.

Especially not this woman. He wanted her with a passion he hadn't felt in years, maybe not ever. He wanted the first time with Ruth to be perfect, which included him being freshly bathed and thoroughly awake and involved.

He forced himself not to walk toward her. Didn't even reach out. "Ruth. Forgive me."

Her lips trembled, but she nodded, her gaze arrowed to the plank floor.

"I'd never hurt you. I swear it."

She nodded again.

This time he took a few steps, until he was close enough to tilt her chin up to meet his gaze. Tears misted in her eyes.

Damn.

"Don't cry, honey. I'm so sorry."

She sniffed. "You didn't hurt me."

"Thank God." He leaned in to kiss her lips, but the look

of pure horror in her midnight eyes stopped him. Damnation, what had he done? What could he do to make this up to her?

He backed off and turned the crystal door knob. "Come on." He led her to the bed where Mary Alice slept. "Bedtime." He helped her lie down next to his daughter who still slept soundly. He covered her with the bedding and bent to give her a chaste kiss on her tear-stained cheek. He strode to the other side of the bed, kissed his daughter, and then returned to the adjoining room and closed the door.

He stripped off his soiled clothing and lay down on the bed stark naked, his erection still throbbing. Too exhausted even to sate himself, he closed his eyes and fell into slumber.

★ ★ ★ ★

Ruth opened her eyes to the first rays of sunrise. She sat up in bed and stretched. Mary Alice still slept soundly beside her. She nudged the little girl. "Mary Alice, it's morning. Time to get up."

The child let out a low snore and turned over. No matter. She could sleep a while longer.

Ruth's body tingled, still hyper aware from Garth's touch. She wiped the image from her mind and left the bed. After tidying the room a bit, she donned her dress and sat in front of the looking glass. She had no comb and brush, and her hair was a disheveled mess. She sighed. Oh, well, nothing to be done. She finger-combed it and plaited it in a loose braid.

She left the room quietly so as not to disturb Mary Alice. After a quick trip to the water closet, she walked downstairs to order some breakfast.

Back in the room, Mary Alice still hadn't stirred. The

adjoining door drew Ruth's gaze. Garth was behind that door, most likely still sleeping, his masculine body sprawled upon the bed.

She shook her head to clear it. Such thoughts had no place. She'd decided long ago not to marry for any reason other than love, and when no men had come courting, she'd resigned herself to spinsterhood. Now, suddenly, two men wanted her. One wanted to court her respectfully because the time had come for him to marry. Yes, he admired her intelligence. That much was clear, and she should be thankful. But he also wanted to breed size into his line. And size she had in abundance. She'd bear him strong, intelligent, *tall* sons.

The other cared nothing for her intelligence, at least as far as she knew. And he certainly didn't need her to bear him strong sons. Garth Mackenzie's seed could no doubt produce a strapping lad from the most frail and petite woman on earth.

No, he merely wanted to bed her. She still couldn't quite wrap her mind around the concept. The most beautiful man she'd ever laid eyes on wanted her in his bed. Plain Ruth Blackburn. Average. A *C*.

And he was willing to marry her to have her.

After twenty-two loveless years, she faced two offers of marriage.

One fairly honorable, at the same time a bit insulting. One not honorable at all, though the thought of occupying Garth Mackenzie's bed had its own allure.

One man offered her a life of intellectual stimulation. The other probably didn't even own a book, but he made her heart go pitter-pat and his kisses seared her soul.

Neither had offered her love.

She'd waited twenty-two years for a proposal of marriage. Was it time to give up on love?

The soft rapping on the door brought her dueling wits to an end, thank goodness. Too much to think about.

She opened the door, and a maid brought in a tray and set it on the little table next to the bureau.

"Breakfast, ma'am."

"Thank you." Ruth gave the woman a coin from her reticule, and then went to wake Mary Alice.

The little girl opened her eyes. "Pa?" she asked timidly.

"He's fine, sweetie. He's asleep in the next room, so we must be quiet so we don't wake him. He's had a rough night. But he saved the farm."

Mary Alice's lips curved into a sad smile. She didn't move.

"Aren't you going to get up? Breakfast is here, and you didn't eat much last night. You need a good meal."

"No. I don't want any, thank you. I'm...not feeling well."

Ruth touched her lips to the girl's forehead. She was cool to the touch.

"You don't seem to be feverish. Are you nauseated?"

"A little. My tummy hurts."

"You're probably just hungry, dear. You haven't been eating well." Ruth uncovered her gently. "Getting out of bed will make you feel better. I promise. Come on, now."

"No, I can't, Miss Blackburn. I don't want to get up. It hurts to get up. I just want to sleep today. Please."

Ruth's neck prickled. Something wasn't right. "I'll get your pa, Mary Alice."

"You don't have to wake him."

"If you're ill, I certainly do have to wake him. I'll be right back."

Ruth strode toward the adjoining door, opened it, and whisked into the other room. *Land sakes.* Rays of sunshine streamed through the open curtains and illuminated the strong muscular contours of Garth Mackenzie's naked body.

Golden and perfect, he lay across the bed, his arms hugging the white pillow and his blond locks splayed across the cotton sheeting. Pure masculinity. Thankfully, he was on his side, his legs tangled around the sheets, hiding his male member. Her gaze dropped to his taut buttocks, and then to his powerful legs dusted with golden hair.

But now wasn't the time to ogle his perfection. No. Mary Alice needed her pa.

She walked to the side of the bed and clamped her hand on his sleek shoulder. Like solid marble, only hot instead of cool to the touch. Not the time. "Garth!" Her whisper was urgent.

No response.

She shook his shoulder gently, and then not so gently. "Garth, wake up! I need you!"

His bronze eyes opened, and he jerked. "Ruthie? You all right?"

"Yes, I'm fine. But Mary Alice is ill. Please come quickly." She turned toward the door. "And for goodness' sake put your drawers on!"

★ ★ ★ ★

Garth stood in the corner of the room as Doc Potter and Ruth tended Mary Alice. What in tarnation was wrong with his child? He couldn't lose her. Just couldn't. How would he ever cope?

"Everything's normal," Doc said. "She's just fine. She'll be up and around in a few days."

"For God's sake," Garth said, "she's not in perfect health,

or she'd be out of bed eating her breakfast."

Doc cleared his throat. "I assure you she's fine, Mr. Mackenzie, she's just a little under the weather from..." The doc's neck turned scarlet.

Garth fisted his hands at his side. "What in the hell are you tryin' to say?"

"She's starting her courses, Mr. Mackenzie."

"Courses?"

"Yes, her womanly time."

"Confound it, I know what courses are. But she's only eleven."

"I'm twelve next month, Pa," Mary Alice said, her voice but a whisper. Her pale face had turned a rosy red.

"She's not too young. Do you know when her mother started?"

"Why in hell would I know that?" Damnation, he and Lizzie hadn't discussed such things. How was he supposed to deal with this? Courses, for God's sake.

"There's only a little blood right now," Doc continued, "which is why she didn't notice it herself yet. But it explains her swoons during the last few days. She's fatigued. She's cramping a little bit. When girls start young, it's harder on their bodies. But I assure you, it's completely normal and she'll be just fine."

"How long will it last?"

"Now that the bleeding has started, about five days. But the cramping and weakness sometimes begin several days before the bleeding. She'll probably grow out of that, but expect it for the next year or so."

"Oh, for corn's sake." Garth plunked down in a wooden chair, jarring his already aching body. "How often does it happen?"

Ruth stood from where she sat on the edge of the bed, her ruby lips pursed in a line. Now what had he done to piss her off?

"Mr. Mackenzie, may I speak to you in the other room?"

"No, you may speak right here in front of the doctor, Ruth. What is it?"

She stomped her foot, and her midnight eyes flashed. "In the other room," she said through clenched teeth.

"Fine, fine." He followed her through the adjoining door. "What, Ruthie?"

"I know you don't mean any harm, but you need to stop interrogating the doc. This is a traumatic time for a young girl, and she doesn't have her mother here to help her through it. You're embarrassing Mary Alice."

"Why should she be embarrassed?"

"Listen to yourself, Garth. Of course she's embarrassed! This isn't something a young girl discusses with her father, or with any man. Did your wife ever discuss it with you?"

"I don't—"

"Of course she didn't. I never discussed it with my pa, either. To answer your question, it happens once a month, so get used to it."

"Ruth, I—"

"Now let's get back in there, and—"

"Damn it, woman, can I get one word in here?"

She huffed. "What?"

"I know how often it happens. I was married, remember? What I meant was, how often does the swooning happen?"

"Oh." Her pretty cheeks turned pink.

Well, that would teach her to run off at the mouth.

"You'll have to ask Doc," she said. "I've never swooned

before."

His groin jumped. God, she was pretty, all red and embarrassed. Damn, he wanted to make *her* swoon. Wanted to kiss those red lips until they both fell down panting. But not with Doc and Mary Alice in the next room.

"Ruthie?"

"Hmm?"

"Would you talk to her for me? She might be more comfortable talking to a lady about...these things."

She smiled, lighting those gorgeous eyes. When had these britches become so darn tight?

"Of course I'll talk to her. I'd be happy to. You know I'll help with Mary Alice in any way I can. I adore that child. Now get in there. She needs to know she's the same little girl to you that she was yesterday."

"Well, of course she is. Why would she be any different?"

She stomped her foot again and her smile faded. "You exasperate me, Garth Mackenzie."

He sighed. "What have I done now?"

"Mary Alice *is* different. She feels different. So assure her you love her as you always have, and all will be fine."

"Of course I love her. She knows that."

"Go tell her then."

"That I love her?"

"Yes, that you love her. What do you think we've been talking about?" She balled her hands into fists and pounded his chest.

Just her touch nearly sent him over the edge. He held himself in check and followed her back to the other room where Doc was closing his black bag.

"I trust everything is in order?" Doc said.

"Yes, Doc," Ruth said. "I just explained a few things to Mr. Mackenzie."

"Mmm. Good. Will I see you later, Ruth?"

Her cheeks reddened. Lord, she was lovely. Garth never tired of looking at her.

"You may call any time, of course," she said.

Call any time? What the hell? A railroad spike hit him low in the gut.

Doc grabbed his bag and smiled at Ruth. "I'll do that. Thank you, Ruth." He shut the door behind him.

Garth opened his mouth to ask what in tarnation Doc was talking about, but Ruth spoke first.

"I'm going downstairs for a few minutes. Mr. Mackenzie, I believe you need to talk to Mary Alice."

"Ruth, I—"

"I'll be downstairs, sir, sitting in the parlor." Her smile lit her face, and she touched a lock of his hair that had fallen across his forehead. "You'll be fine."

She was gone.

Garth turned toward the bed. His little girl sat up, her back upright against the oak headboard, her face back to its pasty paleness. What could he say? He wasn't her mother, for God's sake.

"Are you feelin' better, child?"

"A little, Pa."

"Some water, maybe? Breakfast?"

"A cup of water would be nice. I'm not hungry for breakfast."

Garth fetched a cup of water from the basin and handed it to her. She took a few swallows and handed it back. He set it on the night table.

Now what?

He cleared his throat. "I've asked... That is, I've asked Miss Blackburn to talk to you about this new...uh...condition. She'll be able to help you more than I can."

She nodded.

"We'll...have her out to supper tomorrow evenin'. Does that sound good to you?"

"Yes, sir. I like Miss Blackburn. I'm happy to have her visit anytime."

"Yes. I..." He wanted to say he liked Miss Blackburn, too. That he'd thought of nothing but the pretty schoolteacher since he'd first laid eyes on her. But that wasn't for his daughter's ears.

Ruth had told him to tell Mary Alice he loved her. Of course he loved her. She was his child. He opened his mouth to say as much, but the words caught in the back of his throat.

Why couldn't he bring himself to utter those damned words? He'd never said them. Not since the war. Never to Lizzie. Never to his children.

He inhaled, held his breath for a few seconds, and opened his mouth to try again.

"Mary Alice, I..."

"Yes, Pa?"

"I..." *Damnation.* "I...hope you'll be feelin' better tomorrow so you can make a nice meal for Miss Blackburn's visit."

"She taught me to make her chicken pie. I think I can do it, Pa, if you'll dress me the chicken."

He nodded. "I can do that." He stood and looked around the sparse room. "If you're feelin' up to it, get up and get dressed now. We need to be gettin' home. I got lots to do around the farm. The animals need tendin', and there's clean up from the fire. Let's make haste."

CHAPTER NINE

Ruth normally enjoyed walking the homestead in late spring. The floral aroma of the wildflowers, the sweet scent of new grass, downy baby jackrabbits hopping about after their mothers—she loved the prairie. Always had.

But walking with Doc Potter felt all wrong. Ruth would rather be sitting down, where their height difference wasn't so blatantly obvious to the entire free world. He'd come calling this evening. Land alive, she'd told him he could. This morning, right in front of Garth Mackenzie. She had no one but herself to blame.

After a short visit in the front room with her parents, he'd suggested a walk, and she hadn't been able to come up with a reason to decline, especially not with her ma and pa scrutinizing her every move.

"May I take your hand, Ruth?"

An honorable request, one she should grant to a suitor. He didn't pull her into his embrace like Garth Mackenzie had. But should she encourage his suit when her heart lay elsewhere?

Goodness. Her heart did indeed lie elsewhere. She wasn't merely enamored with Garth Mackenzie's kisses. She was in love with the man.

Completely in heart-wrenching love with a man who'd offered her his body, his name, but not his heart.

How in the world had this happened? She barely knew him. Hadn't even liked him at first. Still thought he was gruff, callous, and didn't treat his daughter properly. His touch set her afire, that much was true. But then the wild flames had nearly torched his farm, nearly torched *him*, and Ruth hadn't been able to rest until she knew he was safe. She'd told herself it was Mary Alice who concerned her, not the child's father. But here it was, plain as day, as though she'd known it the first time she gazed into his troubled bronze eyes.

She loved him.

Could she marry him? Her heart would break a little each day knowing he didn't return her feelings.

She couldn't marry Doc, though. That much was clear. Such a commitment wouldn't be fair to either of them. She was in love with another.

"I'm sorry, Doc."

"For what? That I asked to hold your hand?"

"No, not that. But no, I...I don't think you should hold my hand."

"I understand. We don't know each other that well yet, and—"

She touched her finger to his lips. An intimate gesture to be sure, but she had to stop him.

"What in the name of God are you doing, Ruth Blackburn?"

She and Doc turned toward the deep timbre. Garth. She gasped and dropped her hand to her side.

"Where did you come from?"

"Your pa's. I came to see you. He said you were out walking."

"I assume he told you with whom?"

"No, he did not."

Doc cleared his throat and looked at his boots. "Mr.

Mackenzie, how is your daughter?"

"Fine. Just fine, thank you. What are you doing out here with Ruth?"

"Mr. Mackenzie," Ruth said, "I fail to see how that is any business of yours."

Doc looked up, his diminutive stature apparent in the shadow of such a magnificent creature as Garth Mackenzie. "We're on a walk. I am courting Miss Blackburn."

"This true, Ruthie?" Garth's maleness permeated the entire prairie. "Is he your beau?"

"Mr. Mackenzie—"

"Damn it, stop calling me that!" He gripped her shoulders and turned her. His chiseled face was taut, tense. His bronze eyes burned. "Is this who you want to be with?"

"Garth, don't hold me so tightly. Please."

He loosened his grip but did not let her go. "I asked you a question."

Doc stepped forward. He was clearly no match for Garth, but Ruth admired his fortitude.

"I need to ask you to leave, Mr. Mackenzie. Miss Blackburn and I—"

"Are done with whatever business you had tonight," Garth said. "I need to speak to Ruth."

Ruth forced her gaze from Garth's. She couldn't say what she had to say when those beautiful eyes were piercing into her. "I wish to finish my outing with the doctor. I will speak with you later."

Garth dropped his hands to his sides. Her flesh tingled where he had grasped her shoulders. Burned through her dress, her skin, all the way to her heart.

"No need to speak later. I came for Mary Alice. She

wants you to dine with us tomorrow evening. She has some... questions."

"Of course. I'm happy to speak with her. How about six o'clock?"

"Fine." His face noncommittal, he turned and walked back toward the house.

Ruth watched him, unable to turn back to Doc. Garth's strong back in retreat brought mist to her eyes. His blond locks curled around his neck under his black Stetson. His posterior, taut in his trousers, drew her gaze. She'd seen its beauty unclothed. Natural.

Oh, he was magnificent. Raw and untamed. And alone. So alone.

She loved him. She loved his daughter. He may not love her, but he sure needed her.

"Garth!" Her own voice startled her.

He turned, his bronze eyes sunken. He did not speak.

"I..." She took a deep breath. "I need to speak to Doc for a few moments. Would you please wait for me outside the house?"

He nodded and resumed his walk.

"I have the feeling I won't like what I'm about to hear, Ruth," Doc said.

"I'm truly sorry, Doc. I can no longer accept your suit."

"You're in love with Mackenzie."

She nodded. "I didn't mean for this to happen."

"I understand. I'll see you to the house."

Though her legs itched to run to Garth, Ruth allowed Doc to escort her quietly back to her father's house where Garth stood waiting next to his buckboard and team. Doc tipped his hat to both of them before heading away in his buggy.

Sudden chills rippled over Ruth's flesh despite the pleasantly warm evening. Her body trembled, and tiny flutters flew through her belly. Did he still want her?

"Well"—Garth's voice was still hoarse from the fire—"what did you want to talk to me about?"

Ruth swallowed, and then said boldly, "I've decided to accept your proposal."

His eyes widened. "My proposal?"

"Well...yes." Heat flooded her cheeks. "You said you'd marry me to...well, to have me."

"What about Doc Potter?"

"I ended that. I...that is..." Goodness, why did she have to do all the talking? For once, she had no idea what to say.

"You'll marry me?"

"Yes, Garth, I will. If you still want me."

He gripped her elbow and rushed her to the door. "Your pa's inside. He can marry us now."

"Now?" What on earth was he thinking? "Now is out of the question, for goodness' sake. You have to court me first, and then we'll—"

"I didn't offer to court you, woman. I offered to marry you. And I'll have you. Tonight."

Gracious, what had she done? No, he hadn't offered to court her, but she'd assumed... Lord above, first item on her agenda would be to teach her new husband some manners. Truth be told, courting did seem a bit ridiculous at this point. They'd shared so much already. She loved him, and she was ready to be with him. So ready.

Pa would never agree. Unless...

"Garth," she said, her voice shaking. "Let me speak to my mother and father. You stay out here. Please."

Before he could argue, she rushed into the house where her parents were sitting in the front room.

"Ruth, you look...dazed, dear," her mother said, smiling. "Must have been some nice walk with the young doctor."

Land sakes. The doctor. Well, she'd just set them straight. That's all there was to it.

"No, Ma. Doc Potter and I will no longer be seeing each other."

"Oh?" Her mother's eyebrows arched. "Why not?"

"Because—" She gulped, and her tummy did a somersault. "Because I'm going to marry Garth Mackenzie, that's why. He's outside, and we must marry tonight."

That got Pa's attention. "Tonight? Are you out of your mind, daughter?"

"No, Pa. It must be tonight." She cleared her throat, summoned her courage. "You see, he and I have had...intimate relations."

It wasn't exactly a lie. Though she and Garth had not engaged in the act itself, they had been intimate on more than one occasion.

Her mother stood, fire flashing in her blue eyes. "I raised you better than this, Ruth Ellen Blackburn."

"I want to marry him, Ma. I love him." That was no lie. No lie at all.

Pa stood, his violet eyes glaring. "Did he force himself on you?"

"No! Goodness no." Again, no lie. "I went with him willingly. I swear it."

Pa inhaled sharply and let it out in a slow stream. He reached for his service book on the mantel. "Bring him in, then."

"Charles," Ma said, touching his arm, "you can't mean you're in favor of this."

"I'm in favor of nothing, Molly, but the deed is done. Ruth's choice was made then. I'll not have my grandchild born out of wedlock."

CHAPTER TEN

Ruth canceled the last week of school. First she'd let her students out early that fateful day last week. Then she'd canceled today's classes because she'd been caring for Mary Alice all night. Now, after leaving a note on the schoolhouse that there would again be no more school due to Miss Blackburn's marriage to Mr. Garth Mackenzie, she sat next to her husband on his hard buckboard, bumping along to his home.

Their home.

"I'll bring you to your pa's tomorrow after breakfast," Garth said. "You can get your things packed up then."

She nodded. She hadn't taken anything with her. The ceremony had been mercifully brief, and though her father had shaken Garth's hand, his face had betrayed his anguish.

"Is there anything you need?" he asked.

"Need? What do you mean?"

"For tonight."

"Oh. Yes, I guess. I don't have anything to sleep in."

He chuckled gruffly. "You won't need anything to sleep in."

Her neck warmed and she fingered her collar. "I don't have much. Just my clothes, a few things in my hope chest. My books, of course. And Miranda."

"Miranda?"

"My mare."

Garth nodded. "That it?"

"Yes."

The team plodded on. Ruth stared at the dry open prairie. Dust clouds rose from the wheels as they rolled forward. Green prairie grass grew on either side of the broken trail to the Mackenzie farm. In the distance, Garth's house appeared and became progressively larger.

Progressively scarier. Ruth gripped her own thighs, and her fanny bounced against the plank seat. The aroma of stale smoke hung in the air. The fire.

"I'm sorry," Garth said. "The smell will fade in time."

"I know." She wrinkled her nose.

"Behind the barn, on the way to the creek, the grasses are singed black as night."

"They'll grow again," Ruth said.

"Don't know if my wheat will come up. Too early to tell."

Her heart opened to him. To her husband. She unclenched her thigh and laid her hand on his hard muscled one. "Everything will be fine, Garth."

He didn't turn to look at her, but his lips curved into a slight smile. Ruth released a breath. Yes, everything would be fine. One way or another.

It had to be.

★ ★ ★ ★

Mary Alice had been happy to hear the news. Joyous, in fact. Ruth felt sure the girl would be calling her "Ma" within a few weeks. Her heart warmed at the idea.

Safely tucked away, the young girl slept now. Ruth had spoken to her for a few minutes, and Mary Alice had assured Ruth she was feeling better. She looked better, too. Her color was returning, and she'd eaten today. Ruth said a short prayer of thanks as she watched the child's chest bob up and down in slumber.

Time to see to her husband.

Time for her wedding night.

Garth sat in the kitchen sipping a cup of coffee. "Mary Alice all right?"

Ruth smiled, hoping she hid her trembling lips. "She's fine. I think...this will be good for her. I mean, I'll try to be good for her. Be a good mother."

"I know you will." He scooted his chair out from the table and held out his arms. "Come sit with me?"

She stepped toward him and he drew her into his lap. "I can take care of you," he said. "I know this house, this farm, doesn't look like much, and then the fire... But I will provide for you and Mary Alice. And any other children we might have."

"I know that, Garth."

"You might have had more with Doc Potter."

"I didn't choose Doc Potter. I chose you."

His stubbled cheeks flushed a light pink. Ruth couldn't help smiling.

"You understand what comes next, don't you?"

"Of course. I'm not a child. I'm twenty-two years old."

"Sounds young to an old timer like me."

"You're thirty-six. You've hardly got a foot in the grave yet."

"How'd you know my age?"

"I asked Mary Alice. The day I came over and made you the chicken pie."

"You asked about me?" He smiled a lazy smile. A "feel good" smile.

Ruth's heart leaped. "Yes, I asked about you. You're an interesting person, Garth Mackenzie. You intrigued me from the start."

"You intrigued me too, Ruthie. You're so pretty, and so smart, and you just told me where to go, didn't you?"

"Well, somebody had to. Mary Alice was failing for no good reason. And now that I'm here, things will change. Tomorrow I'll get this place in tip top shape, and then we'll—"

He hushed her with his fingers on her lips. They burned hot.

"Tomorrow we'll figure this whole marriage out. I promise. But tonight I want to make love to my wife."

She nodded, her lips quivering. He stood, and his strong arms lifted her off her feet. He strode slowly through the front room to his—*their*—bedroom. Once there, he set Ruth on the bed, closed the door, and latched it. He sat down next to her and began working the buttons to her bodice.

His gaze penetrated hers. "I could drown in those midnight eyes of yours."

So hot, and then cold, and then hot again. Ruth shuddered as his fingers grazed her skin. When her bodice was loosened, he pulled the pins from her hair until it fell down her back in soft waves.

He kissed her neck as he pushed the fabric of her dress down her arms.

"Garth, I—" How could she tell him she was frightened? Not of him, but of disappointing him?

"Shh," he said. "I'll try not to hurt you."

"I know. I'm not worried about that. I mean, I know it will hurt at first. I just...I'm not sure how to please you."

"You will please me, Ruthie. I promise."

"But I don't know what you want."

"I'm not that hard to please, honey. Trust me."

He fumbled with her chemise and petticoats, and soon she lay against the cool cotton covers in nothing but her pantalets. Her nipples poked forward, two hard berries, and a strawberry flush glossed over what she could see of her body in the moonlight streaming through the open window.

Garth's bronze gaze singed her body. Tiny tingles raced along her skin, igniting sparks along the way, and culminated in the moist spot between her legs.

The spot her pantalets still covered, but wouldn't for much longer.

He didn't speak, just scalded her with his eyes and then his strong hands, as they swept from her cheeks over her shoulders, over the slope of her breasts, to her waist, her hips, where they eased the pantalets over her bottom, down her legs, and onto the floor.

He sucked in a breath. "God."

She closed her eyes. Did he not like what he saw? Had he decided she wasn't what he wanted after all? Beautiful she was not, and her figure was more lithe than womanly. What she wouldn't give, at this moment, to possess Naomi's feminine curves.

A flutter touched her eyelash. She opened her eyes slowly.

"Such long eyelashes." Garth caressed her cheek with his thumb. "As much as I love to see them resting against your cheek, I want you to keep your eyes open."

"W-Why?"

"So you can see me touching you. I want you to be a part of this. Don't close your eyes."

"I'm sorry. I don't know what to do. And when you said

'God,' I thought you didn't..."

"Didn't what?"

She steadied herself, but her voice still trembled. "Didn't like what you saw."

A soft rumble hummed in his throat. "I said 'God' because I do like what I see. You're very pretty, wife, and I want to kiss every inch of you."

That's a lot of inches, Ruth thought to herself. Her eyes closed again, seemingly of their own volition.

"Open, Ruthie. Open your eyes and look at me."

She complied, her nerves skittering, and met his burning gaze. Garth unbuttoned his shirt, and Ruth tensed, waiting for the sides of fabric to part like the Red Sea. When they did, she gulped at the pure masculine glory exposed. A mat of golden hair covered his hard chest, and two mahogany nipples eyed her. Ripples of solid muscle walled his stomach, and a golden pathway of hair arrowed to the waistband of his trousers, and to his arousal that bulged beneath them.

She'd never seen a male member, of course. Even this morning in the hotel, when he'd lain naked on his bed, his sheets and legs had covered that part of him. Though she'd be lying if she said she hadn't taken note of him, her concern at the time had been Mary Alice.

Now, though, she focused solely on Garth. Her husband. Land sakes, that sounded odd, even in thought. After a few years of accepting spinsterhood as her lot in life, suddenly she was married to the most beautiful man on earth.

A man who was unbuttoning his trousers at this very moment, readying to expose his full self to her. She forced her eyes to remain open.

Garth leaned down and removed his boots, pushed his

trousers and then his drawers over his hips.

Oh, my! It was big. But beautiful, in its way. Darker golden than the rest of him, it stood straight and proud. Her fingers itched to touch it. Why not? She'd never been one to shy away from a challenge. And he'd touched her down there last night, and would again. Soon, she hoped.

She extended her arm and let the tips of her fingers brush its tip.

Garth jerked away.

Ruth's tummy dropped. "Gracious, I'm sorry!"

"Don't be. I want you to touch me. Just not yet. I don't want this night to be over before it's begun."

What? She turned her head to hide the mist in her eyes. She knew she'd do something wrong. He'd probably be petitioning for an annulment tomorrow.

But such negative thoughts fled when he lay down next to her and gathered her close. The heat of his skin sizzled against her. From their foreheads to their toes, they touched, bare skin to bare skin. A delicious sensation.

When he shifted gently, the tip of him grazed a place between her legs that shot a spark through her. Her breath hitched, and a spiral of rapture surged through her belly.

He took her lips then, while he still pressed against that lovely place, and she opened to him. A groan rumbled beneath his breath, and he thrust his tongue into her mouth with a sweet urgency that she returned. Ruth fingered his sleek shoulders, his strong arms, all the while reveling in his warm and silky mouth.

When he released her lips, a soft sigh escaped her. He rained kisses over her cheeks, her neck, groaning unintelligible words as he ventured lower, to her chest, to the mounds of her breasts. His firm lips slid over the rosy swells and then clamped around one nipple.

She remembered this—that wonderful licking and tugging that made her body quiver. His erection pushed against her thigh now as he lowered his body to suck her nipple. She arched into him, her secret place searching for his hardness. Such a void, longing to be filled.

Garth moved to the other nipple, and shivers raced through Ruth as he kissed the swollen nub while he plucked at the other with his strong fingers.

Such hunger, such longing! She wanted every part of him to touch every part of her. If she could crawl into his skin with him she would. She wished to become him, experience everything he could offer her, if only for one timeless moment.

"Oh, my." The whisper left her lips in a delicate sigh.

Garth smiled against the flesh of her breasts and then ventured lower, kissing her belly, her navel, the triangle of dark curls between her legs. A cushion of breeze fluttered through the window and floated over Ruth's moist nipples. She closed her eyes and shivered at the titillating awareness.

"Ah!" Her eyes shot open when a jolt of energy rushed through her. Between her legs, Garth's blond locks fell over her pale skin, tickling her. His firm lips were on her. Kissing her. Kissing that delicious place.

Unseemly, oh yes. But she couldn't have stopped him if her life depended on it. Rainbows of color pivoted around her, and she lifted her hipsoff the bed, pushed into Garth's face. Closer, had to get closer.

Empty. Aching. Garth. She needed Garth. She ran in her mind, hurtling toward something she couldn't name. Couldn't understand. Only knew she must get there. Must.

The explosion curled through her like a rippling tidal wave. Her own voice echoed throughout the room. "Garth! Oh, my! Garth, please!"

He licked her, soothed her, and when she floated downward, he kissed her. There. A sloppy, slurpy kiss, and then he looked up at her and smiled.

His chin and lips glistened with moisture. Slowly he inched forward, and his hardness brushed against her leg, her thigh, and nudged that glorious spot that now seemed even more sensitive.

With one smooth thrust, he pushed into her.

"Oh!" The word left her in a breathless gasp. A lance of pain shot into her. So big, so full. How would she ever get used to this?

But he whispered into her ear. Soothing words as his lips nibbled her lobe. "I'm sorry, honey. It won't ever hurt again. Just hold still. It'll pass."

She held still. Relished his warm body against hers. Slowly, her own body stretched, welcomed him. And she was home.

He seemed to sense her relaxation, and he began to move within her. Slowly at first, and then gradually increasing the speed of his thrusts.

He filled her emptiness with his body, and with each plunge, she rose higher and higher, until again the sparks threaded through her and she flew.

Garth's mouth clamped onto hers and he kissed her. More deeply than ever before as he continued to thrust. One arm curved under her thigh as he broke the kiss. "Your legs, honey. Wrap those long legs around me."

She did so, and when her hips rose, he thrust deeper.

Faster, harder, until with one final plunge he groaned into her mouth.

As she drifted back into her body once more, Garth inhaled a deep breath and turned onto his side, pulling her with him.

"You're so beautiful." He tunneled his fingers through her hair and brushed his lips against hers.

Ruth's eyes misted, and a tear trickled down her cheek.

"Don't cry." He caught the drop on the tip of his finger. "Please. Did I hurt you?"

"Oh, no." She sniffed and looked down at her lap. "It's not that. It's just...no one's ever said I'm beautiful before. Except for my ma."

Garth tilted her chin upward until she met his smoldering bronze gaze. "I can't believe that."

"It's true. I... My sister was the beautiful one. I was the smart one. Men didn't... Well, probably because of my height. And my intelligence."

"I love your height. You're perfect for me."

She couldn't help but smile. "Well, you are a large man, Garth Mackenzie."

"The first time I laid eyes on you, I imagined you as an Amazonian Princess. Then you opened your mouth and told me what you thought, and I nearly blew my top." He chuckled. "No woman has ever stood up to me like that. I can't say I liked it much, but damn, Ruthie, I liked you. Didn't want to, but I couldn't help myself. I couldn't get you out of my mind. You're strong, brave, smart, and beautiful. Just like a warrior princess."

He liked her. Her heart tapped at the sentiment. He didn't speak of love, but at least he liked her, held her in his esteem.

It was a start.

CHAPTER ELEVEN

Matthew's body was leaden. Nearly as large as Garth himself, Matthew was dead weight, even though he wasn't yet dead.

Blood spurted from his stomach, already soaking the blue of his uniform. The Rebels had scattered. Injured Union soldiers lay every few feet. Every couple of steps, a hand grasped Garth's ankle, a plea squeaked from a bloody mouth. "Help me. Please."

Garth steeled himself. He couldn't save them all. Could only save Matthew. Matthew—his closest friend, his confidante. His brother.

Garth dragged his friend clear of the injured. Behind a tree, he assessed the damage. It didn't look good. Every drop of crimson blood knifed into Garth as though he were the one who had been shot.

The one dying.

"Leave me," Matthew whispered.

"Never." Garth resisted the urge to haul Matthew over his shoulder and run. His wound couldn't take it. Instead, he continued to drag his friend while he scouted for a hiding place. Shots boomed around them. Garth's ears had long since gotten used to the ringing. The Rebs wouldn't stay scattered for long, and not enough men had survived from Garth's regiment to cover him and Matthew.

They had to hide, and they had to hide quickly.

The biting scent of gunpowder thickened the air. Garth inhaled, his throat raw. Though not injured, he was fatigued from fighting. He was bone weary. His legs numbed beneath him and gave out. He toppled to the hard dirt next to Matthew.

"Garth."

Matthew words were dense, sounded like he was speaking through a bubble. He let out a string of garbled directives that Garth couldn't translate. He stood and began again to drag his friend to safety.

If safety even existed.

The ground shook with a cannon's rumble. Shrill screams swelled through the heavy air until they were distorted into hollow howls.

Ghosts. Union-clad specters haunting this grave site. Because that's what it was—a grave site. No one existed to drag the rest of these men someplace else, to be mourned and buried next to loved ones.

He stumbled again but caught himself. Dusk fell, and Garth thanked whatever God might be out there. Now night would shroud them from the Rebs.

Matthew must have fainted. He made no sound, yet when Garth looked to his chest, it still rose and fell. He again whispered thanks. He didn't know how long he'd been walking when he found the hole. Or what he thought was a hole. More like an underground cave.

The Rebs would find them. Of that he had no doubt. He'd come to accept it after today, after watching too many Union soldiers fall. He'd been damned lucky to escape. But it was a bitter victory, and one that would be short-lived. When the Rebs caught him, he would die.

He wasn't going home.

Right now, he needed rest. Needed to see to Matthew's injuries. Perhaps he could do something for his friend. Perhaps...

He lowered his friend into the cave and then jumped down

next to him.

Pitch black. Within a few minutes, Garth's eyes adjusted to the dark. Matthew's light blue irises shone.

"You're awake."

Matthew's breath came in shallow pants. "G-Garth. H-Hurts."

"I know."

Matthew gripped Garth's shirt. "Hurts!" His voice echoed. "Do something. It hurts!"

"Damn it." Garth's survival instinct kicked in with a vengeance. "Be quiet," he whispered urgently.

"Can't. Hurts!"

Garth's skin prickled. "You've got to be quiet." He pulled his blade from its sheath at his belt and grabbed his friend. The sharp edge grazed Matthew's throat. "You will be quiet, Matthew, or I swear to God I'll slit your throat."

"Garth, Garth. It's all right. Wake up!"

"Damn it! I told you to be quiet!" He shook off the soothing touch. No time for that. Had to survive. Had to keep Matthew quiet or the Rebs would come.

★ ★ ★ ★

"Garth, please. Wake up. You're scaring me."

Garth jolted. His eyes shot open. Moonlight streamed through the window. A breeze drifted over his bare skin. Beside him, a warm woman gazed at him with worried blue eyes.

Ruthie.

His Ruthie.

What had he brought her into? God, he'd wanted her. Still wanted her. But he'd had no right to saddle her with his pathetic existence.

"Garth. You were dreaming again."

He nodded. No use denying it. She'd seen it before. "Every night."

"Even last night? At the hotel? I didn't hear you."

"I usually wake myself up before I yell. Learned to. My yelling in the middle of the night troubles Mary Alice."

She sat up next to him and kissed his cheek. A soft petal of a kiss. Enough to get his cock started, but now wasn't the time. Not while blood and killing still warred within his mind.

"Tell me the nightmare."

Four harmless words from the innocent mouth of his new wife. Of course, she had no way of knowing he'd never told another living soul the horrors that haunted his nights.

He shook his head. "I'm sorry I disturbed your sleep. If you'd be more comfortable, I'll sleep in the front room from now on."

"In the front room?" Ruth pulled the sheet up to cover her breasts.

Damn shame. They were lovely, indeed.

"Yes."

"I won't hear of any such thing. We're married, Garth Mackenzie. For better or worse. That means we share a bedroom, and a bed."

"I have this nightmare every night, Ruthie. Every night, do you understand? Every night since the war."

"Oh." She backed away a little.

He didn't blame her. War was evil. As a woman, she couldn't begin to comprehend what he'd seen, what he'd done. But she'd no doubt heard stories. Stories that made her blood curdle.

213

DAUGHTERS OF THE PRAIRIE

Her face softened then, and she smiled and touched his cheek. So innocent, but it burned straight to his groin.

"Please tell me. It might help."

"I've never told anyone, Ruth. I can't do that to you. It's ugly."

"I know. You forget I'm a scholar, Garth. I've studied the war. I haven't lived it, and I'm not so ignorant to think studying and living are the same thing. I know they're not. But I can handle it. I swear to you."

"I don't want you to have to."

"For better or worse, Garth. I spoke the same words you did."

"Doesn't matter."

"Oh." She caressed his cheek and then his upper lip with the soft pad of her thumb. "I understand, now. This is why you're...you."

"Pardon?"

"Why you're an island, Garth. You could be in a room full of people, and still you'd be alone."

An island. Alone. He opened his mouth to argue, but she started to talk again.

Well, he'd known that about her. She liked to talk. Didn't matter, anyway. She was right, and he damned well knew it. She was smart, his Ruthie. He wouldn't be able to hide from her.

"You're not alone anymore," she said. "I'm here, and I'm not going anywhere. I don't care what you did during the war. War is terrible. Men do things during war that they'd never think of doing otherwise. It's survival, pure and simple. It's human nature."

Would she understand? Truly? Could she comprehend

what Matthew's death had cost him? Garth wasn't sure, but nothing mattered anymore. Nothing except unburdening himself to his wife.

He took a deep breath, leaned back against the headboard, and closed his eyes.

"I killed, Ruthie."

Her warm body nestled against him. "Everyone kills during a war."

Though her voice soothed, her words did not. She didn't know.

"I killed a friend."

He braced himself for her repulsion. She'd back away. Run as fast as her long legs could carry her.

But she didn't. Her warmth still enveloped him, and when he opened his eyes, her own shone with concern.

"Tell me."

The story tumbled out of him. The battle, the blood, the air thick with the stench of fresh death. How Matthew, his best friend since childhood, had begged Garth to leave him behind. But Garth had dragged him through the mass of injured and dead to the underground cave. Only the darkness of night had cloaked them. Had the sun shone, the Rebels would have seen the opening to the cave.

"The Rebs were right above us. They'd come back to finish off any stragglers. Matthew was dying, in pain. His need to cry out was so thick, so strong, I could feel it. But I held my knife to his throat, and I told him if he screamed, I'd kill him."

Ruth didn't budge. Still held him tight. "Go on."

"He had told me to kill him before. Before I dragged him away. I couldn't do it. I..." Images of Matthew's face, pale and pasty, blood soaking his skin, blurred in his mind. "I thought I could save him. But I couldn't."

"He was too far gone, Garth. You couldn't do anything."

He swallowed. "I told him to keep quiet." The lump in his throat thickened. "But he didn't. He screamed, and I slit his throat. His blood poured over my hand, and he gurgled and snorted." The sounds ripped through Garth's head. "Then he died."

"Oh, Garth."

"Once the Rebs dispersed, I left him there."

She nodded against his shoulder, her silky hair tickling his flesh. He kissed the top of her head.

"I loved him like a brother. More so, even. We'd done everything together from the time we were five years old. I stood up for him at his wedding. But he wasn't there to stand up for mine. Wasn't there to hold his baby girl."

"It wasn't your fault, Garth."

"Not my fault? I killed during the war. Killed men who were husbands, fathers, brothers. I justified it in the name of principle. But my best friend... I sank that blade into his flesh, Ruth. To save my own hide!"

"He would have died anyway. And who says it's a crime that you wanted to live? That you wanted to get back to your life? I'd want the same thing. Any person would."

"I'm not sure it was worth it."

She pulled away slightly and burned angry midnight eyes into him. "Of course it was worth it. You're alive!"

"I came back half a person."

"You are *not* half a person, Garth Mackenzie. You're strong and passionate. You have a lovely little girl who adores you and needs you."

"I haven't done right by her."

"Well, you will from now on. You'll respect her, and teach her, and you'll love her as she deserves."

"I-I can't."

"Can't what?"

"Love her."

Ruth's eyes widened. Saucers of deep sea blue. "Of course you can love her."

"I never told her. Never told Lizzie or the boy."

"The boy? What was his name?"

Garth winced. It was easier to think of him as "the boy." "The doctors couldn't help him. Couldn't save him. Or Lizzie."

"That explains why you don't like doctors much. But Doc Potter is a good man. A good doctor."

Garth nodded. Perhaps Potter was all right. Perhaps a lot of things would be all right now. Now that he had Ruth. He closed his eyes and took a deep breath. "Jonathan Garth."

"A lovely name. I'm so sorry you lost him."

He shrugged his shoulders. "I'm used to it."

"You're not used to it. No one is. So stop telling yourself you are. You've been through a lot of loss in your short life. More than any soul deserves." She cupped his cheeks and forced his gaze onto hers. "Listen to me, Garth Mackenzie. *I love you.* Do you understand? I didn't plan to fall in love with you. I didn't much even like you at first. But I decided a long time ago to only marry for love. And I married you. I love you, and you are not alone."

Floodgates opened, and emotion, raw and pure, roared into Garth. His body trembled and he held Ruth against him—a rock in a swirling sea of commotion he'd kept buried far too long. His vision blurred, and wetness trickled from his eyes.

Tears.

She loved him. He wasn't a ruthless killer, a heartless monster to her. She saw a man. A man worthy of her love. This princess loved him.

Lordy, he loved her, too.

Her soothing words met his ears. "It's all right, Garth. It's all right."

"I love you, Ruth." The sentiment flowed out of him. "God, I love you so much."

She continued to hold him, and the demons crept away into the inky blackness of the night.

And somehow, in the depths of his being, he knew the nightmares would be fewer and farther between from now on.

★ ★ ★ ★

Garth ambled into the kitchen wearing trousers and an unbuttoned shirt. Tousled and raw, he oozed masculinity. Ruth's heart quickened at the sight. She'd never tire of his male beauty.

"Good morning." She reached for the empty plate Mary Alice, seated at the table, handed her. "Good?"

"The best breakfast I've had in a long time," Mary Alice said.

Ruth smiled and turned to Garth. "We thought we'd let you sleep a little longer today since you're probably still tuckered out from that fire."

"Morning, Pa." Mary Alice's rosy face beamed. She looked good. Good and healthy.

"Your breakfast will be ready in a jiffy," Ruth said to Garth.

She hurried to the cookstove, but he caught her arm and pulled her into a tight hug. He kissed her lips, and she gasped, looking toward Mary Alice. The girl was engaged with her cup of milk and didn't give them the time of day.

"I love you," he whispered.

Her skin bristled and she nuzzled his neck. "I love you too. Now sit. I'll get you something to eat."

He patted her bottom—oh, she could get used to those husbandly caresses—and sat down next to his daughter.

"Mary Alice."

Ruth couldn't help herself. She turned to watch their exchange. Bronze eyes so like Garth's own gazed up at him. "Yes, Pa?"

He smiled. "I love you."

Her eyes sparkled. "I love you too, Pa." She rose from her chair and timidly walked into his outstretched arms.

He kissed the top of her blond head.

She eased out of his embrace. "Got to do my chores."

"You take it easy today, sweetheart," he said.

"I feel fine. Much better. Honest."

"I'm glad."

She smiled a shy smile. Oh, she was going to be a beauty. They'd have all sorts of men coming to court her. Not a one would be good enough for her father, Ruth imagined. Her blond braids bobbed as she headed out the lean-to.

Ruth turned back to the stove. Within a few seconds, Garth's hard body pressed into her from behind. His erection nudged the cleft between her buttocks.

"Garth!" She turned into his embrace, her heart pumping wildly. "I'll burn your eggs."

"Got plenty of hens, honey. Plenty of eggs." He kissed her throat and she shivered. "You smell like yeast."

"I'm making bread, of course."

"Already making bread. Already taking care of me." He pushed a stray curl behind her ear. "What did I do to deserve you?" His bronze eyes smoldered.

She smiled into them. "You loved me."

"I do, honey. I never thought love would find me again. I swear to you, I'll love you until I draw my last breath."

Ruth couldn't help the tears that flowed. "I never thought love would find me either, Garth."

And she pressed her lips to his in a searing, loving kiss.

Song of the Raven

CHAPTER ONE

The Black Hills of Dakota Territory, 1890

Ella Morgan threw a few more wild blackberries into her basket, paused, and turned her head toward the hills.

The drumming. Again. Rhythmic beating that was both beautiful and terrifying. Her heart thumped along, matching the cadence.

She wiped her hands, raw from the thick spiny foliage, on her muslin apron and hurried back to the dirt trail. Tonight her family would have blackberries and cream for dessert. If old Sukie felt like giving milk. Ella winced at the thought of milking the cranky old cow with her sore fingers. But milk her she would. It was her chore. Her duty to her family.

The pounding of the drums faded as she neared her family's small cabin. She longed for the safety and security of their humble dwelling back in Minnesota, but Papa thought it important that he be here, in the Black Hills, to minister to the gold prospectors who risked going to hell because of their greed, their gluttony, and their lust. If he could convert some of the heathen red men while he was here, all the better.

Ella didn't give a hoot about those avaricious men. Let them have their gold, their liquor, their soiled doves. As for the red men? She wouldn't bother them. They should be allowed to live their own lives, have their own beliefs if they wanted.

None of it concerned her.

What did she care if a bunch of greedy gluttons wanted to scour for riches in the Black Hills? If they were hell bound, so be it. Let God punish them. Clearly they were beyond redemption anyway. Several in town had offered Ella fistfuls of gold for an hour with her. Alone. She hadn't told Mama or Papa. She couldn't. The fear of what might happen to her kind father should he attempt to avenge her honor sliced into her stomach like a butchering blade.

She wanted to go back to her friends. Back to Andrew, the boy she had known since toddlerhood and who she had planned to marry.

"I'm home, Mama," Ella said, opening the door to her family's cabin.

Her mother stood over the wood stove, stirring a cast iron pot of stew.

Ella inhaled the meaty fragrance. "Smells good. I got enough berries for a nice dessert."

"That's fine, dear. Have you milked Sukie yet?"

Ella rolled her eyes. "No. Not yet."

"You'd best get to it. The longer you make her wait, the nastier she'll get."

"Yes, I know." Ella absently rubbed her shin where the cow had kicked her two days before. "I'll do it now." She grabbed a tin milking pail from the shelf above the pump and sauntered to the barn.

Picking berries. Milking Sukie. Listening to her father preach. Fending off indecent proposals from the gold diggers. Was that all life had to offer an eighteen-year-old woman in the Black Hills?

Maybe not all eighteen-year-old women. But for Ella

Morgan, that's all there was. She sighed. She'd never be able to leave her home. Her parents needed her. They hadn't been the same since her older brother, David, had been kidnapped on the Kansas prairie fifteen years ago. Even her dream of marrying Andrew had been only that—a dream.

Her parents' dependence on her was her joy. And her sorrow. Her cross to bear.

She opened the barn door, dreading the sight of that fat old cow. She edged inside. The afternoon sun cast its luminous rays through the windows on the west side of the barn. Hay rustled in Sukie's stall.

"It's just me, Sukie. I've come to let you kick me and snort at me." She laughed to herself.

She walked toward Sukie but stopped when a low groan rumbled into her ears. "Sukie? Are you ill?"

She turned into the stall and gasped, dropping her pail with a clunk. A man sat on the ground, his back propped against the barn wall. Not just any man. An Indian clad in what appeared to be tan buckskin pants covered with hay. And moccasins. His chest was bare. Bronze and sculpted and bare. Ella's breath caught, and she looked away. She shouldn't stare at a man like that.

Her heart pounded. In fear? She wasn't certain.

"What are you doing here?" she asked.

He groaned again, and she returned her gaze to him. Blood seeped through the hay covering his left leg. "Oh! You're hurt. My goodness." What she thought might be fear vanished. Her heart churned with sympathy. She hated to see any living being suffer. She went to him and knelt down. "Can you understand me?"

"Yes." He panted, trembling. "I speak the white man's

tongue."

"Good, good. What happened? How did you come to be here?"

"A bear. Attacked me. My horse... I..." He closed his eyes and took a deep breath.

"Don't try to talk." Ella fidgeted with her skirts. What should she do now? "I'll get my father. He'll know what to do."

"No!" The man jerked forward and grimaced. "No white men. Please."

"But my father's a preacher. He won't harm you. I promise."

He reached for her and grabbed her forearm. His black eyes melded to hers. "No. Please. Promise."

Was it his tone that convinced her? The pleading in his big black eyes? The strange yet pleasant sensation of his hand on her arm? "I won't. I won't. Calm down. Let me take a look at your leg."

He nodded, and Ella whisked away the soiled hay. Sukie bawled. "Yes, I know you need milking, but you'll just have to wait."

"Milk...her," the Indian man said through clenched teeth.

"No, she can wait."

"Please." He hissed as he inhaled. "It is not right for an animal...to suffer."

"But it's all right for you to suffer?" Ella shook her head. "A fine thing."

"We have a duty...to the animals we keep. To care for them." He thunked his head against the barn wall, closed his eyes, and exhaled. "My wound can wait. Milk her."

"If you insist." How hard-headed could one man be? Clearly he wasn't acquainted with Sukie. Ella picked up her pail and positioned the milking stool, sat down, and grasped two of the swollen teats. The cow bawled again. "See?" Ella gestured her head toward the Indian. "She's not any happier now that I'm milking her. She just likes to whine." Ella squeezed, and a stream of milk swooshed into the pail.

"She...does not know any better. She is old, yes?"

"Nearly as old as I am, truth be told," Ella said, as more milk hissed into the pail.

"And how...old are you?" he rasped.

"Eighteen, a month ago today. You?"

"I have seen...twenty-five winters."

She looked up from the pail. The Indian's eyes were closed, and beads of sweat trickled down his forehead and cheeks. She whisked the bucket out from under Sukie and brought it to the Indian.

"Enough of this nonsense," she said. "The cow can wait. You need tending. Here"—she held the pail to his lips—"fresh milk. Drink."

"D-Don't want it."

"Did I ask you if you wanted it? No. I said drink. You need sustenance. When did you last eat?"

The Indian took a sip of the frothy milk. "This morning, before sunrise."

"And it's nearly suppertime now. Goodness. Take another."

The Indian drank several more sips. "Enough."

"For now," Ella said. "Let me see your leg." She began removing the sticky blood-soaked hay.

"You...do not fear me."

"You're hardly in a position to do me harm."

"But if you came upon me. In the wild..."

"Then I'd likely run away screaming." Ella said. "Is that

what you want to hear?" She gasped at the extent of his wound. Flaps of his beautiful bronze skin gave way to blood and muck. "What on earth did you do to anger that bear?"

"It was...a she-bear. Not her fault. She was protecting her cubs."

"And did you mean to cause her cubs harm?"

"Of course not. I would never—" He gasped when she moved his leg.

"I'm so sorry. I didn't mean to hurt you."

"It is nothing. I am fine."

"Not the bear's fault, you say?" Ella inspected the exposed flesh. "Seems to me we might be able to blame her just a little bit."

"No. She did not...know any better. Protecting her children, as any good mother would."

"But you would not have harmed her children."

"She...did not know that."

"I see. How did you get away from her?" Ella examined the wound further. The blood was already clotting. Thank goodness. The man was in no immediate danger.

"Ran."

"You outran a bear with a wound in your leg?"

"I believe she was more interested in her cubs than in me. And I run...fast. I am a warrior. Pain does not...stop me from doing what I must do."

"It's doing a pretty good job stopping you now, I'd say. And what of your horse?"

"Scared. Ran away."

"Hmph. Fine thing. Do you inspire no loyalty in your property?"

"My horse is not...my property. We don't own animals. Or

land. We—" He coughed, and his chest heaved.

"That's enough talking for now," Ella snapped. "I need to get this wound cleaned and bound. I'm not sure how..." She stood and looked around. "You can't stay in here. Papa will bring the horses in when he gets home, which could be any time now. Although I still think—"

"No. No white men."

"Goodness." *Think, Ella think.* What could she do with him? Whether she helped him or not, he couldn't stay here in the barn. Ella paced, tapping her finger to her temple. The old soddy! He'd be warm and dry there, and she could tend him until he could walk back to wherever he came from.

But how would she get him there? On the other hand, he had run from a bear. He could no doubt walk a couple hundred yards.

"Do you think you can move?" she asked. "There's a dugout on the property not far from here. You could stay there until you can travel back to your home."

"*Hau.* Yes. I will do what I must."

"My mother is in the cabin cooking supper. We must make haste. Come." She leaned down and offered her arm.

"I can...do it myself." He grunted as he attempted to rise.

"Have it your own way, then." She looked away as he continued his ascent. His handsome face twisted into a grimace. Ella couldn't bear his pain.

"I...go now," he said.

She turned toward him. He was standing. A little wobbly, but he was standing. "Do you need help?"

He shook his head.

"Follow me, then." Ella strode toward the door of the barn and peeked out. No sign of her mother or her father. She motioned to him and then cautiously walked out of the barn toward the old soddy. She walked briskly and hoped he kept up. She couldn't tell without looking back. The Indian was extraordinarily quiet for someone in pain. When they reached the dugout built into the side of a hill, she unlatched the wooden door and pulled it open.

She wrinkled her nose at the musty odor. The room was tiny, even compared to her family's small cabin, and had only one window. She'd need to find him a lantern or something. No, she realized. A lantern would draw attention to the soddy after dark. He'd have to make do with no light.

"Here we are," she said. "I'll bring you a blanket and tend to your wound after I finish supper. I'm sorry there isn't much I can do now."

"You have...done plenty. Many thanks." He sat down on the dirt floor, braced his back against the wall lined with straw, and grunted. "What are you called?"

"You mean my name?"

"Yes."

"Ella. Ella Morgan. You?"

"I am called *Mazaska Kagi Taka*."

The melodic sounds of his language, in his deep and husky voice, melted over Ella. "That's beautiful. Does it have a translation?"

"I am sorry. I do not...understand."

"What does it mean?"

"In white man's language, it means Silver Raven."

"Oh." Ella breathed. "That's lovely. How did it come to be your name?

"When I was born, I had very thick black hair. But in the back there was a"—he winced—"streak of silver. My mother called me Silver Raven."

"I didn't notice the silver streak."

"It is gone. My infant hair fell out and grew in again, without the silver. But the name...it stayed."

"I'm glad. It's a beautiful name."

"When a Lakota boy becomes a brave, he gets...a new name. I did not."

"Why?"

"I was—" He grimaced.

"You don't have to talk." Ella patted his forearm but then whisked her hand away. She should not be touching him in a friendly manner. What would her parents say?

"I am...fine. When I was a young brave, I played...what is the word?" His forehead wrinkled. "Jokes. I played jokes on my friends. The raven is known to be...clever...and filled with... mischief. So my name...stayed."

"What a nice story." Ella wiped his forehead with the edge of her apron. "But no more talking now. You need to rest, and I need to join my family for supper. Later I'll bring you some food and a blanket. And some water to clean your wound."

"Many thanks. Ella *Hopa. Lila Wiya Waste.*"

Ella started to ask what he said, but stopped. His eyes were closed and his breathing had become shallow. He had fallen asleep. No doubt the best thing for him. She smoothed his thick black hair, slick with sweat, away from his troubled face. "I'll return soon," she whispered, wondering why her heart was beating faster than normal.

★ ★ ★ ★

The Lakota drumming pounded in Raven's dreams. The roll,

the fast drum beat, thumped in his ears, in his veins. His eyes flashed open, his heart pulsating in time with the nocturnal drum.

Where was he?

Trickles of sweat meandered down his cheeks and his bare chest. His right leg throbbed. He gasped as he tried to move it. Yes. The bear. He had run, had found shelter in the small barn on a white man's homestead at the foot of the woods. Bits and pieces fogged his mind. The cranky cow. The woman. The beautiful woman with hair the color of the soft earth beneath him, her tresses pulled back in a long braid that fell below her waist. What would it look like unbound, cascading over her milky white shoulders and full breasts?

And her eyes. The color of the violets that grew in the foothills near his home. Violets at first bloom.

He had found her.

She had cared for him with her smooth white hands. His skin still burned from her touch.

Ella.

Her name was Ella.

Had she said she would return? Yes, he was certain. He ached to see her, to hear her voice.

Despite his pain, his cock stiffened under his soiled buckskins. He had never imagined being drawn to a white woman.

But he had found her.

He jerked when he heard a rustling at the door. When it opened and Ella appeared, his heart lurched. She carried a blanket and a basket made of straw.

"Good evening," she said, her voice chipper and pleasant as she set down the blanket and basket. "I'll return in a moment. I need to draw a pail of water from the well. For your wound." She walked briskly out the door, leaving him feeling empty inside.

Though the sun still shone, Raven could tell dusk was imminent. The thought of Ella out alone after dark concerned him. But this was her home. The women of his band were safe on their land after dark. His face furrowed into a frown. He did not trust the white man. Not even Ella's father, the preacher. He sat, tense, until she returned.

She set down the bucket of water, splashing some onto the soft dirt floor of the dugout. "Oops," she said. "Well, no harm done. It will dry." She rummaged in her basket, pulled out a tin cup, and dipped it into the pail of water.

"Now, first things first," she said, approaching him and holding the cup to his lips. "Drink."

The cold liquid tasted like nectar in his parched mouth. He downed all the water within seconds.

"More?"

He nodded, and she brought him another cupful and held it to his lips again. He didn't need her to hold the cup for him, yet he made no effort to discourage her. Her nearness soothed him.

When he had finished his second cup, Ella reached into her basket again and pulled out a few slices of brown bread. "I'm sorry. This is all I could manage. We had stew for supper, and I could hardly bring some of that out without my mother wondering what I was up to. As it was, I sneaked the bread into my apron during dinner. Oh!" She reached into her apron pocket. "I did manage to save you some of the blackberries I picked this afternoon." She giggled. "They stained my pocket horribly, I'm afraid. We couldn't eat them with cream. I never did finish milking Sukie, and most of what I got I fed to you." She pulled out a handful of crushed berries. "Here"—she held one to his mouth—"they're nice and ripe. Very sweet."

He ate the berry from her hand. The warm juice burst onto his tongue and trickled down his throat. Yes, sweet. All the sweeter because she had fed him.

"Another?" Her fingers, stained purple from the berries, touched his lips. They were warm and smooth, like the smoothest hide after tanning.

"Good." She grabbed his hand and dropped the remaining berries into it. "But you'll have to feed yourself now. I can't let your wound fester any longer. It needs cleaning." She turned to his thigh. "The bleeding has stopped, which is good. It doesn't appear to be too deep. But still we need to watch for infection." She reached into her basket and withdrew a pocketknife. "I'll need to cut the leg of your buckskins off. I'm sorry."

"It's...fine." The first words he had spoken since she entered the dugout.

He winced, hoping she knew how to use the knife. He knew little about white women, but he did know that they did not usually work with knives such as this one. Ella proved agile with the blade, however, and soon the leather of his buckskin sat crumpled in the corner of the dugout, his bare leg exposed.

Ella closed her eyes, clearly uncomfortable with his nakedness. Although his lower body was still mostly covered, his chest was bare. He silently thanked the Great Spirit the bear had not attacked him there.

Ella opened her eyes and let out a shallow sigh. She took a cloth out of her basket, wet it in the water, and gently cleansed his wound. The ache in his thigh had dulled, but the soft cloth stirred the sharp pain again. He sucked in a breath and groaned.

"I'm so sorry," Ella said. "I know it hurts. But I must cleanse it."

"I am...fine."

She looked at him and then darted her gaze away. "Eat your blackberries. It will give you something to focus on while I do this."

His stomach rumbled, and he stuffed the remaining blackberries into his mouth. Ella looked up as juice trickled down his chin.

"Goodness, there's no need to make a hog of yourself. I'll bring you more berries tomorrow." She finished cleaning the wound and covered it in a sharp-smelling salve.

"What is that?" he asked.

"Beeswax. With a little oil of peppermint. It will help stave off infection and keep the air out of the wound while it heals. I'm sorry if the smell bothers you."

"Does not...bother me. Just different."

"Yes, well, I suppose it is. What do you use for healing in your...culture?"

"Herbs and flowers. I do not know the white man names. My mother is...a medicine woman."

"Oh. Well, she likely knows more than I do. But this salve has healed many a wound in its day." Her gaze rose to his lips. She grabbed a fresh cloth from the basket, wet it, and gently cleansed his face of the sweat and grime that had built up since the attack. She chuckled when she came to his chin. "My, you're like a child with that purple chin. You do love your berries, don't you?"

"Just...hungry."

"Then eat your bread."

But he couldn't, not while she was touching him. She

picked up the salve and twirled her finger in the small tin.

"Your lips are parched. This will help." She touched her finger to his mouth and rubbed the salve into his lips.

His skin heated and he hardened instantly. Before he could stop himself, he grabbed her wrist and pressed his lips to her fingers in a soft kiss.

CHAPTER TWO

Ella's heart thumped as blood rushed through her veins. This was inappropriate behavior. Highly improper. Even Andrew had never taken such a liberty. Yet she couldn't bring herself to snatch her hand away. The feel of his lips, dry and cracked though they were, on her fingers calloused from homestead work enthralled her. Such a foreign, yet delicious, sensation.

She gasped as he kissed her fingers once more and then pushed her hand away. "I am sorry."

"I-It's—" She stopped to catch her breath. "It's...my fault really. I just thought... Your lips are so chapped. Dry from lack of water, I imagine. I..."

He reached toward her and touched his fingers to her cheek. "*Hopa*," he said. "*Lila Wiya Waste*."

The harmonious words struck a chord in Ella's memory. "You said that before. What does it mean?"

"*Hopa* means beautiful." His voice was hoarse, raspy. "*Lila Wiya Waste* means beautiful woman." He caressed the apple of her cheek with his thumb.

"Oh." Ella breathed. His hand on her face felt hot. So hot. "That's just...lovely, Silver Raven."

"Just...Raven. My friends call me Raven."

Even as dusk neared, his black eyes still sparkled with a smoldering intensity that disturbed yet pleased Ella. His hypnotic gaze blazed into hers, and she found herself leaning toward him. His mouth was so close to hers. Close enough to...

She jerked away with an almost violent motion. Her skin felt clammy. Prickly. Hot. Her heart throbbed against her breast. A strange flutter settled between her legs. What on earth was happening?

"I-I'm afraid I couldn't bring you a lantern. If you light it in the darkness, my father, or worse, someone else, might find you. I'm very sorry."

"I do not mind the dark," he said. "But I need..."

"What? What do you need?"

"Will you...cleanse my chest? Like you cleansed my face?"

His chest? He had gone quite mad, obviously. Yet his chest was covered with the same sweat and grime that had covered his face. He was no doubt uncomfortable. And she had made a commitment to care for him. She wanted to care for him, though she didn't know why.

She dipped the cloth she had used on his face back in the water and rinsed it, and then, hands shaking, brought it to his chest. For the first time since she'd found him in the barn, she allowed herself to gaze at his beautiful form. Bronze skin, hard planes and muscles. His warmth seeped through the moist cloth and onto her hand as she washed him.

He closed his eyes and sighed. "Mmm. Feels...nice."

Yes, Ella thought. It did feel nice. Too nice. Best to keep talking. "So tell me, Mr. Raven—"

"Just Raven."

"All right. Raven. How did you learn to speak English so well?"

"My father. And my brother."

"Oh?"

"My father learned it from his grandmother. And my

brother...he is a white eyes, like you."

"How can that be?" Ella washed his shoulders, unable to tear her gaze from their golden beauty.

"He...came to us when he was small. My father... What is the word? Adopted him into our family."

"Really?" Ella dropped her hand. "You took in a white boy?"

Raven opened his eyes, picked up Ella's hand, and placed the cloth back on his shoulder. His hand covered hers. He moved her hand and the cloth in tiny circles over his skin. His fingers were warm on hers. Warm, and so disturbing. Again, the unfamiliar flutter unsettled her.

"We would take in anyone who needed our help, no matter what their color," Raven said, closing his eyes.

"That was extremely"—her voice rasped and she cleared her throat—"hospitable of you."

"I don't know that word. But...we are not the savages you think we are."

Ella removed her hand from his chest. His fingers still covered hers. "I never said you were savages."

"Not you. Not Ella. Kind, beautiful Ella. *Ikta*. I mean white men. In general." He pulled her hand back onto his skin. "Many thanks, *ikta*. But it grows dark. You must go to your cabin."

"Yes, I will. Just let me get you tucked in."

"Go now. I fear for what might happen to you if it is dark."

"Don't be silly. This is my father's home. I've been out here many a night walking. No harm will come to me."

"I do not trust..."

"The white eyes. Yes, I know." Ella rinsed the cloth in the pail and wrung it out. "You don't need to worry about me. I'm perfectly capable of taking care of myself. Besides, I need to get you a fresh pail of water first."

"No."

"But you must drink during the night. I'll only be a moment."

"There is water left."

"But I rinsed the washcloth in it. New water will be much more refreshing."

"Then I will wait until morning."

"That is completely absurd." Ella stood and shook the dust out of her skirts. She grabbed the pail. "I shan't be long."

"Ella..."

His voice trailed off as she left the soddy and headed for the well.

Goodness! What a strange man. She knew every hill and valley on this homestead. She had taken moonlit walks along the edge of the woods on many a clear night. First dark was her favorite time of the day. Strolling along, veiled in the luminescence of the moon, she could immerse herself in her own thoughts and dreams and imagine, if only for a short time, that she could leave the stifling neediness of her mother and father and begin a life of her own.

She drew a fresh bucket of water and headed back to the dugout.

"See? Still in one piece." She drew a cupful of water from the pail and handed it to Raven.

He drank it quickly and held it out to her for more.

"Thirsty, aren't you? And you thought you'd go all night without fresh water." She smoothed her skirts and reached for the cotton blanket she'd brought earlier. "Lord knows you won't be chilly tonight." She wiped a loose strand of hair out of her eye, confused by the surge of heat when she touched him. "But in case you are..." She set the blanket down next to him. "Or if you'd rather, I can put it under you. Might be a sight more comfortable than the dirt."

"Do not mind the dirt." Raven opened his mouth in a gaping yawn.

"What a day you've had. You must be absolutely exhausted." Ella moved the pail closer to him. "Here you are, in case you get thirsty later. I...I'll be going now, I suppose. Do sleep well."

Raven yawned again and closed his eyes. "Please. Be safe, *itka*."

"Don't worry. I will. And I'll come as soon as possible in the morning. After I finish my chores." She let out a laugh. "Sukie will be good and cranky by then. Good night."

"Mmm. Night," Raven murmured, his eyes still shut. "I wish you could send me a signal. That you reached your home safely."

Ella's heart ached. He truly was worried about her. "Trust me, Raven." She reached out and smoothed his hair. Tangled though it was, its silkiness caught on her calloused fingers. "I'll be fine. Until tomorrow." She rose and left the dugout.

Heading toward her cabin, Ella whirled around and inhaled the fresh mountain air. She missed Minnesota, but she couldn't deny the Black Hills held a certain magic and mystery. The way the flowers bloomed in what appeared to be fairy rings. The way deciduous and evergreen trees grew side by side in the woods and foothills, as though east were truly meeting west. The sun had set, and the full moon rose and cast its glow over her family's small homestead. She strolled languidly and then reversed her path, deciding to take one of her favored walks. She inhaled again, and the fresh scent of pine tingled in her nose.

Yes, Minnesota was still home, but the Black Hills... They fascinated her. They could be a place of peace and beauty, a wonderful area to make a home for her family, if only the greedy and lecherous gold diggers weren't here.

In the faint distance, the drumming of the Indians thumped. Medium paced, it was a happy sound. Not the terrifying war-like beat she'd heard while picking berries. She wondered if Raven heard it. No doubt he was fast asleep by now.

Ella walked along the edge of the woods that framed her father's land and imagined how her life would be if only circumstances were different. She'd be in Minnesota, perhaps married by now.

But when she visualized her husband, it wasn't Andrew's coolly handsome visage she saw.

No.

It was a perfectly sculpted face, carved out of hauntingly beautiful bronze.

★ ★ ★ ★

"Raven has not returned." Wandering Bear faced his father, Standing Elk.

"Indeed. How long has he been gone?"

"He left at sun up, to trade with the white men and then to search out herbs for Summer Breeze."

"I see." Standing Elk raised his pipe to his lips. "My older son is brave. And resourceful. Wherever he is, I am sure he is safe."

"I fear for him. The white men, they fear what they do not understand. I have begged you, honored Father, to send me to trade with them. They will not see me as a threat because I am one of them."

"Bah! You are Lakota now. No more white eyes."

"Yes. I am Lakota. Your ways are mine. But still, I look like them."

"With hair below your waist?" Standing Elk guffawed. "I do not think so."

"I will cut my hair."

"No."

"But I am willing. It is the best way to see to our needs and keep our people safe at the same time."

Bear gazed into his father's stoic face, wrinkled by the passage of time. The young warrior remembered little of his time with the white men, but he did remember their fear. And their blood-thirsty ways. He worried every time Raven left camp to trade with them. But as he was the older son of Standing Elk, the duty fell to him.

"Singing Dove cried herself to sleep when he didn't return. And Summer Breeze still frets inside the lodge."

Standing Elk's gaze softened, slightly, at the mention of his daughter and his wife. "You are a good son to worry of your sister and mother. Had you come from my own loins, I would not be more proud."

"Dancing Doe came by earlier looking for Raven. She still hopes he will take her to wife."

"Your brother does not love Dancing Doe."

"I know."

"He will know when he finds the one for whom he was meant, as will you, my son. The spirit will guide you."

Bear nodded.

"Go to your tipi, Bear. Sleep. Raven can take care of himself."

"Yes, Father."

Bear walked with stealth to his lodge, his moccasins digging into the soft ground. He loved his brother, but did not understand why Raven would not take Dancing Doe. She was the prettiest maiden in the camp. If only she would look at Bear the way she looked at Raven.

But Dancing Doe was the least of Bear's concerns at the moment. Raven was in danger. He sensed it with every fiber of his being as he listened to the drums' dancing beat.

Tomorrow he would search for his brother.

CHAPTER THREE

Ella rose early, swept the cabin, and then went to the barn to milk Sukie, who was crankier than usual, no doubt from being left half full the previous evening. After the cow landed a swift kick to Ella's shin and toppled over the pail of milk, Ella swore under her breath and limped back to the cabin for some breakfast.

"No milk this morning, Mama," Ella said. "That darn cow tipped over the pail."

"Ella!" Naomi Morgan turned to face her daughter. "Do not use such language in this house."

Ella rolled her eyes once her pretty and willowy mother had bent back over the stove. "Sorry, Mama. But she's such a belligerent animal."

"She's old, but she's our only cow," Naomi said. "It's a miracle she hasn't dried up yet. She'll most likely never calf again at her age. Now sit down, dear. I have your breakfast."

Naomi set a bowl of oatmeal porridge on the table in front of Ella. She seasoned her cereal with some butter and maple sugar and wondered how she could get oats to Raven in the dugout.

"Do you have any soft bread this morning, Mama?"

"Yes, if you want it." Naomi set a plate of bread on the table.

"Thank you." Ella deposited a few slices into her apron

pocket once her mother's back was turned. She hastily finished her oats and tea.

Tea. Raven might appreciate some tea. But did Indians drink tea? Or coffee? Ella had no idea.

"Mama, where's Papa this morning?"

"He left early. To minister in town." Naomi sighed. "I do hate to say this, but I fear it's a lost cause, Ella."

"As do I." Ella held out her bowl. "I'm quite famished, Mama. Might I have some more porridge?"

Naomi filled her bowl. "Bread and two bowls of porridge? I thought you were done growing."

"Just hungry." Ella hedged. "Sukie took a lot out of me this morning. The little fiend kicked me."

"Oh, I'm sorry. Shall I have a look?"

"No. I'm used to it." Ella seasoned her oats and picked up her bowl. "It's a lovely morning. I do believe I'll enjoy the rest of my breakfast outside, if you don't mind."

"Enjoy it while you can," her mother said. "It will be frightfully cold here once winter comes."

"No colder than in Minnesota, I'm sure," Ella said.

She walked outside and headed toward the dugout, bowl of porridge in hand.

The sun shimmered in the cerulean sky. Ella gazed at a few puffy clouds that hovered over the Black Hills. A beautiful day. When she reached the door to the soddy, she hesitated. Should she knock? She glanced around, making sure she was unseen. Then she rapped on the wooden door. Once, twice, thrice. "It's me. Ella."

She entered. Raven sat as she had left him, his back plastered to the wall. His black eyes seared her.

"How are you this morning?" she asked.

"Better. I think."

"Do you need to—" Warmth crept onto her face. How did one bring up the subject of personal needs?

"I did. Earlier."

"Goodness!" Ella set down the bowl of oats. "You must take care to not be seen."

"I am Lakota. We are trained to...tread quietly. And invisibly."

"Well"—Ella picked up the pail, which was nearly dry—"I must fetch you some fresh water." She dropped the pail with a jerk. "I'm so sorry. I brought you breakfast." She retrieved the bowl of porridge from the dirt floor and handed it to him. "I hope you like oatmeal. I added some butter and sugar."

"You limp, *itka*," Raven said. "What is wrong?"

"Oh, that dratted cow, Sukie," Ella said. "She kicked me in the shin."

"May I look?"

Look at her leg? How could he suggest such an improper act? "I'm fine, really. Now eat. Please. I hope it's satisfactory for you."

"It will be fine. I thank you."

"You are most welcome. Now I shall see to your water."

"Please." His deep voice trickled over her like hot maple syrup. "Stay with me. While I eat."

"But you need water."

"It can wait. I would rather have your company, *itka*."

"You called me that yesterday. What does it mean?"

"*Itka* means bloom. Or blossom. I call you that because your eyes are the color of the violets on the hills, when they first bloom. At first bloom they are darker. Then they lighten in the sun."

"Oh, my." Ella breathed, willing herself not to faint dead away. Did all Indians have such a way with words? Embarrassed, she changed the subject. "I must have a look at your leg. You said you're feeling better?"

"Yes."

"Thank goodness. If you haven't developed a fever by now, you likely won't. You're quite lucky, you know. Most bear wounds are more severe."

"Yes. I know. I got away quickly. I only wish I could have saved my horse."

"Be glad you saved your own hide," Ella said, inspecting the wound. It was still raw, but looked no worse than before. "I see no reason why you can't return home tomorrow. Perhaps even tonight if you're feeling up to it." A pang of regret washed over Ella at her own words. If he left, she would not see him again.

"I will leave as soon as I am able. You need not be burdened with me any longer than necessary."

"Oh, I didn't mean—" Ella motioned to the bowl of cereal he still held. "You must eat." She looked away and began tidying the small room. "You are no bother. I am happy to look after you."

"I am glad, *itka*." She turned and watched him take a spoonful of oats into his mouth. He winced.

"Is something the matter?"

"It is...sweet."

"Of course it is. I told you I added sugar."

"I am not used to it so sweet." He took another bite. "It is good."

Ella smiled. "I'm glad you like it. I brought you a few pieces of bread, too. I'm sorry I have no milk. After she kicked me, the silly cow who you think is worthy of the utmost respect kicked over the pail of milk."

A raspy chuckle escaped Raven's throat.

"A fine thing, I'll say," Ella scolded. "What is so funny? Not only have I a terrible Charley Horse, but we've no milk for breakfast or lunch!"

"I do not laugh at you, *itka*," Raven said, "but at the cow. Please"—he patted the ground next to him—"sit with me."

He drew her like a magnet. "Ooph," she said, as she sat down on the dirt floor.

"What is wrong?"

"My shin. Where Sukie kicked me." Ella arranged her skirts so no skin on her legs showed. "I'm fine."

"It pains me that you hurt."

"Yes, well, it's part of life here in the hills, as I'm sure you know." Ella sighed and then smiled. Goodness, he was a handsome man. High cheekbones and a straight nose. Radiant long black hair. Though unkempt at the moment, she imagined it braided, entwined with feathers. He would be quite a sight in full warrior regalia. Her cheeks warmed and she looked away. "Did I bring you enough food?"

"Yes. Thank you."

"Good." She fidgeted with her apron pocket and began to rise. "I must see to your water."

Raven touched her arm. A burning spark sizzled underneath her skin where his fingers lay. "Please," he said. "Stay. I find your presence...soothing."

"Well. All right." Ella stilled, but did not attempt to remove his hand from her arm.

"Tell me, *itka*, do you have a"—Raven cleared his throat—"man that you wish to marry someday?"

What a question! The warmth in her cheeks turned to scalding. She tensed under his touch still on her arm. "There was a man in Minnesota. Andrew is his name. I always thought... But then Papa brought us here, to minister to the gold prospectors."

"Were you in love with this Andrew?"

Was she? She'd always assumed they'd marry. She'd looked forward to a home and children. She held him in high esteem and valued his friendship. But did she love him? "I don't know. I'm not sure." How had she never considered whether she'd loved him? She stiffened further. This conversation was inappropriate and extremely uncomfortable. But she couldn't help asking, "What about you? Do you have a wife?"

He shook his head. "The spirit has not yet led me to my wife. There is a maiden, Dancing Doe, who would like to be my wife. I care for her but..."

"You don't love her."

"No." His tone was firm, commanding. "I do not."

"Well, I don't quite understand how your people...marry, I guess. Not all marriages are based on love."

"But they should be," Raven said.

"Yes." Ella nodded. How had she intended to marry a man she wasn't sure she loved? She stared into the black orbs of Raven's eyes—beautiful onyx eyes fringed with long ebony lashes. "They definitely should be."

"My father, Standing Elk, is a very wise man. He says the Great Spirit will show you the mate of your soul, and you will know him or her instantly."

"Oh?" Ella shuddered, her voice cracking slightly. Perhaps he didn't notice. She hoped not. This topic had gotten far too personal. But deep down, she knew she wasn't nervous because of the impropriety of their conversational subject. No. Her stomach fluttered and twisted into knots because when she looked at Raven, she felt the wisdom of the Great Spirit guiding her. She eyed his hand, which still lay on her arm, and felt him tighten his grip.

"Will you come closer, *itka*?" he whispered.

She couldn't. She shouldn't. But she leaned toward him, his full mouth, not nearly so parched as yesterday, too tempting to resist.

"*Hopa. Lila Wiya Waste.*" He brushed his lips against hers.

Ella stiffened. She had never been kissed before. Andrew had never taken such a liberty. She should stop this. Now. But she had no desire—not even a fleeting one—to end such a beautiful moment.

Raven's lips were firm yet soft against hers. A chill rippled over her skin despite the summer heat, and the strange yet oddly pleasant flutter between her legs returned.

Raven brought his palm to her cheek, cupped it, and pressed his lips more firmly to hers. He flicked his tongue across her upper lip and then her lower.

"Will you open for me?" he whispered, his breath warm against her chin.

Icy heat speared through Ella's body. What was happening to her? "I-I don't know what you mean."

"Open your mouth."

"But...why?"

He chuckled, a soft rumble against her mouth. "So I can kiss you."

"But...you *are* kissing me."

"I want to show you a real kiss, *itka*."

"I...I don't understand what... What is going on?

Raven...I..." Ella stopped and leaned backward slightly to take a much needed breath. She panted, her chest heaving, her body quivering. "What are you doing to me?"

"Do not be afraid. I would never harm you." He raised his other hand to her face, cupped both her cheeks, and seared her with his gaze. "I want to kiss you because you are mine, Ella Morgan. I have finally found you. You are the mate of my spirit."

CHAPTER FOUR

Raven closed his eyes against the light streaming into the dugout as the door opened. His heart jumped at the thought of seeing Ella. But it was the fair face of Wandering Bear, his brother, that met his gaze.

"You are surprisingly easy to track, Raven," Bear said in Lakota.

Raven smiled. "You are just a very good tracker, Bear. The best in the camp. I expected you would show up soon."

"Are you hurt?"

Raven bent his leg and winced at the slight twinge. "A bear attacked me, but the wound was not deep. I was lucky to get away quickly. Unfortunately, Golden Feather is gone."

"Golden Feather returned to camp this morning. He is fine."

Raven sighed. His horse was safe. "I thank the Spirit."

Bear knelt beside him. "How did you come to be here?"

"I didn't realize I had wandered so far from camp looking for herbs. I found the barn on this land and I took refuge. My leg was bleeding."

Bear removed the fabric bandage and prodded the wound in the dimness of the soddy. The dull ache made him tremble.

"I am sorry," Bear said, replacing the bandage. "But it is not deep. Can you come home with me now?"

Raven fingered the fabric covering his wound. Go home?

Two days ago he'd have jumped at the suggestion. But not today. "I cannot. I will not leave this place."

"Why not?" Bear's golden eyes widened. "This is a white man's homestead. You are close to the town where the prospectors drink and gamble. You are not safe here."

"There is no danger for me here."

"I disagree, brother. You must leave at once."

"I cannot and I will not." Raven set his jaw. How could he make his brother understand? "There is a maiden here. She cared for me. I will not leave her."

Bear stood and paced the short distance to the door. "You are being stubborn."

"No." Raven rose. His thigh grumbled, but he met his brother's golden gaze. "I have found her, Bear. I have found the mate of my spirit."

Bear's facial muscles tightened. Even in the dim soddy, Raven noticed. Bear didn't understand. "A white woman? What about Dancing Doe?"

"Dancing Doe does not belong with me." Raven touched his brother's forearm. "She never did. She is yours, Bear, not mine."

Bear sighed. "She does not see it that way."

"She will, in time. She is young yet. She has not yet reached her eighteenth winter. She is yours. Do not give up."

"And you? You truly believe this white woman is yours?"

"I do not believe, Bear. I know. Her name is Ella. And she is mine. I feel it in my soul, in the breath of my body, in the beat of my heart. When I saw her, I came alive."

Bear smiled his crooked smile. "So the Raven has fallen. You're not playing the trickster, are you? This is the truth you speak?"

Raven let out a chuckle. "No trick, brother."

"And have you told her how you feel? That she is the mate of your spirit?"

"Yes."

"What did she say?"

Raven smiled, his heart lurched. Chills skittered over his skin. Pleasant chills he'd never experienced at the thought of Dancing Doe or any other maiden. Yet he couldn't help the soft laugh that escaped his throat. "She didn't say anything. She ran out of here as fast as a jackrabbit."

Bear spat out a throaty guffaw. "I see. Well, good luck, brother. If you are determined to stay here, there is nothing I can do." He brushed the dirt from the knees of his buckskins. "But I urge you to take care. These white men are a danger to you."

"Ella's father is a preacher."

"You are a heathen to him, then. He will not allow you near his daughter."

"He will have no say in the matter. She is mine, and I intend to have her."

"I see. What did you say her name was again?"

"Ella."

"Ella. Hmm." Bear lifted one eyebrow.

"What is it?"

"Nothing. I will return to camp and tell Summer Breeze and Singing Dove you are recuperating from an injury and you will be fine. I will not tell them I fear for your safety. Nor will I tell them of your white woman. Perhaps you will come to your senses and return home."

"I *will* return home. With my Ella."

Bear shook his head. "I am leaving a fresh pair of buckskins for you. You should burn the ones you're wearing. Plus they are hacked to bits. They are in my saddlebag, and I left Spotted Eagle hobbled not far from here. I will leave them at the door." Bear nodded and left the dugout.

Raven smiled. He had a battle to wage. A battle for his mate. His groin tightened at the image of her beautiful face, her silky sable hair. Yes, a battle. But he was a seasoned warrior. He had every intention of emerging the victor.

★ ★ ★ ★

Ella grunted as she lugged the pail of water toward the soddy. The thought of seeing Raven frightened her beyond measure. He ignited emotions within her she hadn't known existed. She would have stayed away indefinitely had she not felt guilt over leaving him for several hours without fresh water.

No. That was a lie. She crossed herself and asked quickly for forgiveness. She would not have stayed away indefinitely.

She couldn't.

Her hairbrush bulged in her apron pocket. What had possessed her to bring it along? He would never allow her to brush his hair.

So why did she want to so badly?

She hesitated before the door and then knocked softly. "Raven?"

"Come in, *itka*."

Her heart thudded as she pushed the door open. "I'm... sorry I let you go so long without a pail of water. I—" Her words caught in her throat.

"You can look at me, Ella. I will not harm you."

"I...I know that. It's just..."

The whoosh of Raven's sigh met her ears.

"I believe you fear what you do not understand," he said. "You are like all white eyes."

Ella snapped to attention and set the bucket down with a soft thunk on the dirt floor. "I am *not* like the white men who fear your kind, Raven. I can't believe you would say such a thing!" She paced in small circles. "I have always believed that everyone, no matter what his skin color, should be able to live his life as he sees fit. So long as it's a moral life, in the eyes of whatever god he chooses to worship."

"Calm down, *itka*. I meant no disrespect."

"Well, I should hope not." She stared long and hard at his bronze chest, her heart skipping, and then lowered her gaze to his legs. "You have new pants."

"Yes. My brother came by after you left this morning."

"But your injury. It needs to be... That is, I need to check it."

"I am healing quickly. I am lucky. My brother... He wanted me to leave with him."

"And why didn't you?"

"I told him I would not leave you."

"Oh, good Lord in heaven." Ella raised her hands to the ceiling. "This can never be, Raven. Don't you understand? You barely know me. I can assure you I'm not an easy woman to live with. You've seen how I let an old cow get to me."

"You are kind and compassionate. And beautiful." He chuckled. "I care not whether an old cow vexes you."

"I'm from a different world."

"As was my brother, and he is now Lakota."

"But he was younger, I assume, when he came to you. I—" She gasped when Raven braced himself against the hay covered wall and stood. "Goodness! You shouldn't be up."

"I have been up twice already today, Ella. I am a warrior. I am fine." He came toward her and enclosed her in his arms. She had forgotten how tall he was. Ella, like her mother, was tall for a woman, but Raven's chin rested on the top of her head.

"Tell me you want me to leave, *itka*, and I shall go." He lowered his head and pressed his lips to her neck.

Warmth speared through her, and she shuddered.

Ella's lips rested against Raven's hard bronze chest. She inhaled. His scent was crisp and male. Rugged, like the beautiful Black Hills themselves. Without thinking, she slid her lips into a pucker and kissed his bare skin.

"Ah, *itka*. That feels nice."

"Oh, my." She pushed against his chest. "I'm so sorry. My goodness, what you must think of me."

"I think only that you are mine, *tehila*," he said against her hair, "and that your soft lips on my skin was the sweetest sensation I have ever felt."

"Oh." She sighed and melted against his chest again.

"Tell me what you desire. Tell me, and it is yours, if within my power."

"Goodness. I don't have need of anything." She eased into him, and a hardness poked her belly. The hairbrush. Oh, how she wanted to brush his beautiful, long hair and then braid it. A silly girlish folly. He'd no doubt laugh at her. Yet he had told her he'd allow her anything she wanted.

"Raven?"

"Yes, *tehila*?"

"There is something I would like."

"Anything."

"May I—" She cleared her throat. "May I brush out your

hair for you?"

As she feared, he chuckled, but it was a friendly, loving little laugh. "If that is what you wish."

She pulled away from him. "I know it seems silly." She reached into her apron for her brush. "Oh!" Her apron pocket was quite a bit lower than the hardness she had felt against her stomach. Of course it was. She knew that. "Oh, my!" She gasped at the bulge in Raven's buckskin trousers and backed farther away.

"Do not fear me, Ella," Raven said, inching toward her. "And do not fear that part of me. I cannot control my desire for you, but I assure you I *can* control my actions. I told you I would never harm you, and I meant it." He smiled. "Now"—he took her hand that held the brush—"please. Brush my hair for me."

Ella's hands shook as she looked into his black eyes. They smoldered, as though catching on fire. Little sparks ignited across her skin.

"W-We'll have to sit back down. You're so tall."

"As you wish." Raven sat down slowly.

"Please. Be careful of your injury."

"I will. Do not worry."

Ella sat down behind him and gathered his tresses into her hands. "Such long hair. Nearly as long as mine."

"My brother's is even longer."

"Oh?"

"Yes. The longest of any warrior in our camp."

"He is the white one?"

"He is Lakota. But yes, he is white."

Ella whisked the brush through Raven's hair and caught a snag. "I'm sorry. You've been leaning against that straw wall for quite some time. There will be tangles."

"The tangles are from my encounter with the she-bear. My hair came loose from its braid and went...as you say...every which way. Be careful, though. If you brush an Indian's hair too hard, it falls out."

"Goodness, that doesn't make any sense at all! Perhaps I'd better not—"

Raven's full lips curved into a knowing smile.

"You're joking, aren't you? How silly of me to fall for it."

"Yes, I am only joking." His onyx eyes danced.

She smiled back. "Then this may hurt." She yanked on his hair just a little to tease him. "But I'll do a thorough job, Raven."

"You may do whatever you like to any part of me, *itka*."

"Your hair is beautiful. As black as the bird you were named for, and silky smooth." She tunneled her fingers through the locks, shocked by the intimacy with which she was touching him, yet unable to stop. She continued brushing until she had pulled through all the snarls. "I'll braid it for you now, if you'd like."

"I'd like."

She bound his hair into a tight braid that reached below the middle of his back, tore a thread from her apron, and tied it. "There we are. All finished." Ella stood and turned to face him. She gasped.

He had been handsome before, but now, his hair pulled behind him accentuating the high cheek bones of his chiseled face, he was beautiful. "Oh, my."

"Ella mine," he said. "May I brush your hair now?"

She nearly lost her footing. He wanted to brush her hair? She had never heard of such a thing. A man brushing a woman's hair. *Really.* "I...am not sure that would be proper."

"Why not? You just brushed mine. It would please me."

Her feet threatened to give way. Such strong feelings scared her. She wanted him to brush her hair. She wanted him to kiss her. To touch her body. Her bare body.

"Raven, I'm sorry." She walked briskly to the door of the soddy. "I must go now. I...I shall see you after supper. I'll bring your meal."

"Ella."

"I'm sorry," she whispered, and rushed out the door and shut it behind her. She leaned against the door, her pulse racing. Her body chilled, and then heated, and then chilled again, and the place between her legs throbbed in time with her heart. Images of his dark skin covering her swept through her mind. Heat, desire, confusion—what was occurring inside her?

"Ella." Raven's deep voice carried through the sod and the wood of the door. "I know you are still there. And I know you desire me as much as I desire you. Please do not fear the feelings. They are natural. As natural as the grass beneath your feet, the sun in the sky. I shall see you tonight, my *tehila*, my love."

CHAPTER FIVE

Raven paced around inside the soddy, his leg burning from the effort. It was nearly sunset and Ella had not come. What if something had happened to her? A weight settled in his stomach and his heartbeat thudded. He could not lose her, not now that he had finally found her.

But what if he could not convince her to go with him, to his home, his life?

He knew other warriors who had loved white women. They had stopped at nothing. Some had stolen their brides.

A ribbon of possessiveness threaded through him. So would he, if it came to that.

He hoped it would not come to that.

He jumped when the door opened and Ella appeared. Relief coursed through him in a warm tingle. He pulled her to his chest and smothered her in an embrace.

"Goodness, Raven. What has gotten into you?"

"You did not come. I feared for your safety."

"I'm fine." She set down the basket she carried. "Papa brought home guests for dinner, a couple of lost sheep, and I couldn't leave until they were gone."

"You brought sheep to your house for dinner?" Raven furrowed his brow. What did she mean?

"You silly goose," Ella said, her smile lighting up her face. "A lost sheep. A lost lamb. It means someone who needs help. For whatever reason. In the case of these two men, they sought

Papa out in town. They've become bored of the gold rush and are searching for something more...I don't know...meaningful." She chuckled. "Ripe for the picking, as Papa would say."

Raven was still puzzled. "Perhaps you are the jokester now, *tehila.*" He smiled. Her beauty mesmerized him. "Sheep for dinner. And I am a goose? And do you speak of fruit? What is ripe to be picked? I have spoken the language of the white man for half of my life, but you do not make any sense."

"Can I explain it all later? I'm sure you must be starving. Let me feed you."

"To be fed from your hand, *tehila,* would please me greatly."

"I wasn't speaking literally. Goodness." She pulled out a loaf of bread and a tin of blackberries. "I promised you more blackberries," she said, handing him the tin. "And I have a treat for you." She rummaged in the basket and pulled out a cloth. "It's chicken. My mother breaded it and fried it in the renderings from salt pork. It's delicious. You'll love it."

Raven unspread the cloth and regarded the pieces of meat. He inhaled. The scent was strange, but not unpleasant. "Many thanks. I shall enjoy it."

"I know you will."

"You will stay? While I eat?"

"Yes, I suppose I can. It's a beautiful night. Not a cloud in the sky. All the stars will be out."

"Do you wish to take one of your moonlit walks this evening?"

"Yes. I think I just might. It's too lovely a night to waste."

"Then I shall accompany you."

Ella cocked her head to one side, and the look on her beautiful face troubled him. Would she refuse his suit?

But her eyes softened. "I would like that, Raven. Very much."

He smiled, his loins surging, and sat down on the floor to eat his meal. The chicken had a pleasant flavor, but felt fatty in his mouth. He was used to game meat which had little fat and a tougher texture. This chicken had no doubt been raised by Ella's mother here on their little farm. Still, the crispy coating was interesting and tasted of black pepper and...was it sage? Yes, sage. Tasty.

"Raven?"

He set his chicken on the napkin and reached for his tin cup of water. "Yes?"

"How does a man..."

She turned her head, and a lovely shade of pink crept up her neck. How he longed to press his lips there, to stroke his tongue along her smooth skin, to memorize every peak and valley of her body.

She cleared her throat. "What I mean is, how does a man court a woman, in your culture?"

Raven grinned, his skin warmed. This question was a good sign from the Spirit. "Many different ways. My father, Standing Elk, blew on a whistle shaped like an elk to court my mother."

Her lips curved into a saucy grin. "Are you joking again?"

He smiled. "Not this time."

"Why then? Because his name is Standing Elk?"

"Partly. But more to draw on the potency of the elk bull, which is very powerful, to woo his love."

"And your mother? Did she...enjoy this ritual?"

"They became man and wife. Does that answer your question?"

"I suppose." Her hands fidgeted in her lap.

Raven wanted to grab them, cover them with kisses, and then lead them to his erection that ached inside his buckskins.

He winked. "Would you like me to blow an elk whistle for you?"

That got a chuckle from her lovely lips. "Goodness, no."

"What would please you then, *tehila*?"

"That's a new word. You've used it a few times. What does it mean?"

"It means mate." He leaned closer to her and inhaled her fresh floral scent. "Lover."

"Oh, my." Ella edged backward slightly.

"I mean it in a most affectionate way, Ella."

"Yes. Of course. I understand. It just...goodness, it's a warm night, isn't it?"

"Too warm to wrap ourselves in a blanket?" He gave her what he hoped was a lazy grin.

"What are you talking about now?"

"Another courting ritual. One we learned from the Cheyenne. Unmarried couples who want time alone together wrap themselves in a blanket and talk quietly."

"And?"

He arched his brows. "And...other things."

"Goodness."

Again, her blush ensnared him. "Have you never been courted, *tehila*?"

"Well...no. I guess not. Andrew and I, we talked of marrying, but we never...that is..."

"I understand. You did not love him, Ella."

"No." She shook her head. "You're right. I didn't."

His heart thundered. "You love me."

"Oh, Raven, I hardly know you."

"But you feel the connection the Spirit has forged upon us. We are mates, Ella. We cannot escape our fate."

Raven stood and held out his hand. His body throbbed in time with his heartbeat. Her soft, supple body would slide against his so easily, so perfectly. He burned with the urge to take her, to thrust into her and make her his. But first, a walk. A walk with his beautiful mate. "Come, *tehila*. The moon is bright and the stars shine. Walk with me."

"But your bread. Your blackberries."

"Can wait. Right now I wish to walk under the stars with my *tehila*."

★ ★ ★ ★

Raven was even more beautiful in the moonlight than in the sunlight, Ella thought, as she walked next to him, following the moonpath against the edge of the wooded foothills.

"Do you see those hills? To the west?" Raven's long finger pointed toward a crest of blackness, nearly invisible in the dark.

"Yes."

"They are sacred to my people. Warriors and braves climb the rocks to commune with the Spirit. Sometimes the Spirit will grant a vision."

"Have you ever made such a...pilgrimage?" Ella asked.

"Many times, but only two times has the Spirit granted me a vision."

"Would you tell me?"

"Of course. I have no secrets from you, *tehila*. The first time, I was young. Only ten winters had passed since my birth. I climbed the rocks and prayed to the Great Spirit. I was granted a vision of a bear cub, lost and wandering."

"Oh? What did it mean?"

"The next day, my brother came to us, starving and frightened. We call him Wandering Bear."

The devotion in Raven's eyes moved Ella. Clearly he loved his brother very much. "How very interesting. What of your other vision?"

"That was more recent, the day before the bear attacked me."

"Yes?"

"I climbed the hills, searching for answers about finding the mate of my spirit. My grandfather, the chief, and Dancing Doe's father wanted me to marry Dancing Doe. I did not feel she was mine. I felt—I *feel*—very strongly that she is for my brother, Wandering Bear. I asked the Great Spirit to grant me guidance finding my love. I had a vision of flowers growing on the side of the hills, underneath the tall pines. They were violets, at first bloom." Raven stopped walking and pulled Ella into his arms. "The next day, I found you. You, with eyes the color of violets at first bloom."

Ella's mouth dropped open as she stared into Raven's smoldering gaze. When he lowered his head and took her lips with his, she didn't resist.

The sensation of his tongue in her mouth was new and different. But not unpleasant. Oh, no, not at all. It was hot, so hot, and she tasted him. Raven. Slightly sweet, like cinnamon sprinkled over a tart apple. He explored her mouth, touching every crevice. When she tried to speak, to ask what to do, only wordless sounds, muffled by his mouth over hers, emerged.

If only she knew how to please him. She wanted to kiss

him back, to tangle her tongue with his. To grasp his strong shoulders and pull him ever closer until nothing could separate them.

Such impure thoughts! But she didn't chide herself, because only seconds later she couldn't think at all. She only felt. Felt with all her body, all her heart, all her soul, that she wanted Raven. Wanted to be with him. In every way a woman could be with a man. She boldly forced her tongue into his mouth.

He groaned and tightened his arms around her. Instinctively, she knew her actions pleased him. And she wanted to please him. In all her life, she had never wanted anything more.

She let her tongue wander over his teeth, caress the inside of his cheeks. When he pulled back, panting, she traced his full lips, first the upper and then the lower, and she reveled in his moans. She smiled against his mouth.

"Do I please you?" she whispered.

"Always, *tehila*." His breath caressed her cheek. "Always."

She sighed and turned her head to draw a much needed breath. To no avail, however. When Raven pressed a trail of wet kisses down the side of her neck, she lost her air once more.

"Will you let me show you," he whispered, "some of the wonders that exist between a man and a woman?"

"I-Isn't that what you're doing?" Ella barely recognized her own voice. It seemed lower, earthier.

"Yes, but there is more than kissing. I can take you to the stars and back. If you will allow me." He rained kisses over both her cheeks and then found a place below her ear and nibbled.

Ella's skin heated, yet she shivered. Such sweet contradiction. "I don't understand."

"Surely you know what occurs in the marriage bed?" Raven untied the string binding her braid and slowly tunneled his fingers through her thick locks.

The gentle tugging of her hair, the warmth of his hands on her scalp—all good, all touched her soul. "Y-Yes. Of course." She knew of the physical act. She inhaled deep. What a warm night!

Raven's chuckle tickled her neck. "Would you enjoy soaring into the sky with me, *tehila*? I could lead you to places you have never dreamed of, all without taking your maidenhead. Just say the word, and I will."

"Raven—" She swallowed, her heart pounding so hard against her breast she thought he must be able to hear it.

"*Techi' hhila*," he said. "I love you."

The words warmed Ella's heart. She longed to return the sentiment, but she'd known Raven how long? Two days? Yet such overwhelming emotion cascaded though her when she was with him. Emotion so thick, so powerful, she could almost see it sizzle between them.

"Yes, *tehila*. Ella. You are mine. I love you."

"Raven..."

"The soft moss beneath our feet will cushion us. The evergreens of the forest will shield us. And I will take you to the highest peak of the Black Hills."

He crushed his mouth to hers and kissed her. Ella responded dreamily, vaguely aware of Raven's long fingers untying her apron, unbuttoning the back of her sprigged calico work dress. In the back of her mind she formed a wayward thought that she was glad she hadn't donned her corset that morning. She rarely wore the restrictive garment anymore. What was the point, when all she did was work around the farm?

He brushed the soft fabric over her shoulders, and his swift intake of breath buzzed in her ear. She wore nothing under her dress but a sheer chemise. And drawers, of course, but he hadn't gotten that far yet.

Ella stiffened. Where had that last thought come from? Surely he wasn't thinking of removing her drawers and stockings.

As his rough fingers swept the translucent chemise from her shoulders, she looked into his black eyes, aware, and uncaring, that her bare breasts were exposed to his smoldering gaze. The tips of her nipples tightened. A desire for him to touch them surged through her.

"*Hopa*," Raven said. "So very beautiful." He fingered wisps of her thick hair, positioning the tresses around her shoulders and breasts. "The first time I saw you I wondered how you would look naked, with your hair unbound. I am not disappointed, *tehila*."

Warmth drizzled through her. He pulled her to his body, crushing her breasts to his bare chest. "This is how it should be between lovers. Nothing between us."

Ella gasped, and a high pitched squeak escaped her throat. The sensation of his chest against her soft breasts enthralled her. He was warm, and oh, so hard. Her nipples tightened further, until she was certain he could feel them poking into his muscle. Chills ran through her body, and the moist place between her legs pulsed. Nothing, Ella decided, had ever felt quite so good.

"Oh, Raven." Her voice was breathy, as though it came from above their bodies.

"Good, *tehila*?"

"I had no idea."

He chuckled softly. "This is only the beginning." He lowered her gently to the soft ground. "You are so very beautiful. So perfectly made by the Great Spirit. Skin the color of the moonlight that shines above us."

He ran his hand over her shoulder, over the hill of her breasts, cupping one. Ella inhaled sharply. His touch was foreign, yet she'd never felt anything quite so right.

"Raven?"

"Yes?"

"Will you touch me? On my..." Ella couldn't form the word.

"Anywhere you like." He flicked his thumb over a nipple.

She arched upward, moaning.

"There? You want me to touch you there?"

"Yes. Please."

Raven kneaded both breasts together and ran his thumbs in circles over her nipples. Ella shuddered, her entire body prickling with awareness and pleasure. When he plucked a nipple between his fingers and tugged, she groaned and nearly shot upward. The sensation traveled over her body and landed between her legs.

"Raven! I feel so—"

"Shh, *tehila*. Let me pleasure you." He smoothed a finger through the valley between her breasts. "Would you like me to kiss you here?"

Kiss her? On her breasts? "That's not where you kiss."

He laughed, a slow, deep rumble. "Why not? I kiss your cheeks, your neck, your sweet lips. Why not the rest of you?"

"But...there?"

"There is only the beginning, *tehila*. I wish to kiss you

everywhere. But I'll start with these."

"Raven, I don't know..." *Yes, please. Kiss them.*

"You like my hands there, do you not?"

She sighed, trying to catch her breath."

"My mouth there will please you, Ella. I promise."

He lowered his head and brushed his lips lightly over the skin above her nipple. She quivered, rolling her head back against the soft mossy ground and closing her eyes. The sleek warmth of his tongue claimed her, and when he grazed over a hard nipple, her body jerked and her eyes opened. A blazing flame flickered under her nipple and traveled outward, igniting her entire body. He continued licking. She moaned, and just when she thought she couldn't take any more of this torturous pleasure, he latched onto a tender bud and sucked.

Any rational part of her brain that was left fled. The soft tugs of his lips on her nipple catapulted her into a frenzied dreamworld. From some faraway place, her own voice cried his name, begged him to continue, to tug harder, to make her his. And even farther in the distance, the Indian drums thumped rapidly, in pace with her heart.

"*Tehila.*"

A voice. Raven's voice.

"Ella."

Her eyes fluttered open, and she gazed into a blur. She blinked, trying to focus. Raven. His black eyes seared into hers. Why had he stopped kissing her?

"Please," she said. "Don't stop."

"But I must. Or I will not be able to. I fear I have overestimated my control."

"But you said you'd kiss me everywhere. And if other places feel as good as...as that did..."

"They will feel better. But I cannot."

"Raven." She breathed, inhaling, exhaling, her heart thudding. If he didn't put his lips back on her, she feared she might die an untimely death. "*Please.*"

"You test my strength." He brushed her cheek in a soft kiss. "I will try to please you."

Thank God. Ella closed her eyes. The swish of soft fabric tickled her thighs as Raven removed first her dress and chemise and then her drawers, shoes, and stockings. The soft night breeze caressed her bare skin.

Bare skin? Goodness, what had she been thinking? Her eyes flew open. Raven's head bobbed between her legs. When had she spread them? This was most unseemly. She opened her mouth to protest, but gasped as his tongue touched her. *There.*

He looked up. "*Tehila?*"

What did one say? What *could* one say? He was looking at her secret place. He was *kissing* it. "Raven."

"You are so beautiful, Ella. Every part of you. Do not be afraid."

"I-I'm not afraid."

"You wanted me to kiss you everywhere."

"Yes, but I didn't think you meant—"

His chuckle reverberated against her folds, sending chills throughout her body. "Do you wish me to stop?"

He lapped at her again and she nearly flew off the ground. No, her mind demanded. No. *Do not stop.*

"N-No, Raven. I...it feels...so..." She groaned as he licked her again. Sensation danced within her. Fear. Pleasure. Want. Need.

She felt, more than heard, the soft words he murmured

into her core. "Beautiful... Wet... So lovely..." Then words she couldn't understand. And then his lips clamped onto a spot that made her convulse with a joy so rapturous, so pure, she thought she had soared out of her skin and into the heavens themselves.

From the ground she heard herself sobbing his name, and from somewhere deep within her body, she felt him breach that most private part of her with his finger, moving it in slow circles inside her until she flew even higher.

After moments of mindless bliss, she opened her eyes and found Raven's face next to hers.

"My beautiful Ella," he said. "I must take you back now. To your cabin. If I do not, I will take your maidenhood."

"M-My maidenhood?" Ella squirmed, still feeling the glow of her flight to the stars. Yet she knew there was more to share with Raven. And she wanted it. She wanted it all.

"Yes, my love. I want to come inside your body. Make you mine. But I cannot. Not until you consent to be my wife."

"Y-Your wife?"

"Yes. I will not take what is not mine."

"B-But, Raven. I want you to. I-I need you to." Ella looked into the black eyes of this beautiful man who seemed to recognize her soul. He was hers. Her destiny. Why hadn't she seen it before? "I will be your wife, Raven. I want nothing more."

"*Tehila*," he groaned, and then locked his mouth onto hers in a searing kiss.

Ella kissed him back with a passion she had only now uncovered. The passion of a woman in love. He tasted different, tangy, and she warmed as she realized she tasted the nectar of her own body. He fumbled on top of her, removed his buckskins, and within seconds his hardness probed for entrance.

"*Tehila*," he whispered, kissing her ear. "Are you certain?"

"Yes, Raven. Please."

"When I take your maidenhead, you will feel pain. This part of me is...larger than the finger I used before. But *tehila*, I will not be able to stop. Do you understand?"

"Yes. I know it's painful the first time. I...I want to be yours. In every way I can be."

He spoke several words in his own language, and then plunged into her body with one swift thrust.

Ella gasped at the intrusion. A tear of pain knifed through her, but then she felt only a fullness. It was strange, yet somehow comforting. In a foreign way, she felt complete.

"Ella." Raven's voice was hoarse, as though he'd caught the fever. "Ella."

"Raven?"

"I...I must. May I?" He panted against her neck.

"May you what, Raven?"

"Are you? Are you...in pain?"

"No. It...it hurt at first, but now I feel mostly full."

He murmured in his own language again and then said, "I will move inside of you now."

"Yes. All right."

He pulled his hardness out of her and plunged it back inside. She gasped, not from pain, but from the fresh intrusion of his body into hers. He pulled out and thrust again, touching her, completing her. She gasped each time, and the whole of the sensation—his hard chest brushing the tips of her nipples, his lips nibbling on her neck, the hot skin of his thighs caressing hers, her body hugging his in the most intimate of ways—flooded her with an emotion so powerful, so fierce, she couldn't keep from crying out in joy.

As she sobbed into his hard shoulder, her body climbed the peak once more and she ran toward the precipice. "Raven!" Her voice flew toward the Black Hills. "Raven!"

"Yes, Ella. Come with me. Come!"

And together they soared to the stars.

CHAPTER SIX

Ella lay in Raven's arms, her head snuggled into his shoulder. Though rationally she knew she shouldn't have lain with him outside of wedlock, she couldn't bring herself to regret the action. Against the warmth of his hard body she felt complete in a purely spiritual way. "Is it always this way?"

"No." He smoothed his hands over the contours of her back, her buttocks. "Only between true mates of the spirit."

"But, how do you know?"

"I have—" He cleared his throat. "With widows in my band. Men have needs."

"Oh." A stab of jealousy pierced Ella's gut.

"I was fulfilling a physical need only, *tehila*. Now that I have you, I can fulfill the physical, the emotional, and the spiritual. There is nothing in the world more beautiful."

"Raven, I fear I cannot... That is, when you came into me..." Ella sighed. So much emotion flooded her and she had no idea how to put it into words.

"What did you feel, *tehila*?"

"I felt...complete, Raven. Complete in the most wonderful of ways." A tear trickled out of her eye, down her cheek, and spilled onto Raven's hard shoulder.

"It will always be that way for us. We complete each other. And when we are not joined, a small part of us will always ache for it."

"I think..." Ella let out a soft giggle. Her body felt on fire—

swollen, ripe, and on fire. "I think I'm aching for it already, Raven."

His husky laugh feathered through her hair. "As am I. But you are sore. You must heal before I take you again."

"Why?"

"A maiden must heal after her first time. It is natural and normal. For now, I want you to put your clothing back on. The breeze has gotten a bit cooler, and I don't want you to catch a chill."

"In the summer? I couldn't possibly."

Raven tightened his arms around her. "For me, *tehila*."

"Goodness. All right." She sat up and glanced around for her clothing. "You'll have to button me." She pulled on her stockings and drawers, then her chemise. When her head popped through the neck opening of her calico, Raven was already behind her, fastening her. After he had helped her, he donned his buckskins and moccasins, pulled her to his body once more, and embraced her.

"You are everything to me, Ella," he whispered into her hair, his breath tickling her. "Everything."

She warmed, and smiled against his chest, slick with perspiration. Her heart felt complete. Oh, so complete. "Raven?"

"Hmm?"

"What will we do now?"

"You will come live with me. With my people. I will care for you and for our children."

"Leave my family?" What would Mama and Papa do without her? She was all they had. "And have children? Goodness."

"What? You do not wish for children?"

"Well, of course, I would love children." She imagined a little boy with bronze skin and black eyes. A beautiful baby boy. Oh, yes, she definitely wanted children. "I just hadn't thought about it. But yes, Raven. I would love to have your children."

"We will live with my people, high in the Black Hills, where the ravens and hawks soar."

"How lovely."

Raven turned Ella in his arms, positioned her back against his chest, and pulled her close. "The waning moon sits high in the sky, *tehila*." He pointed. "You can see the summit of the highest peak."

Ella nodded, taking in the breathtaking beauty of the shadowed mountains in the moonlight.

"That is where the thunderbird lives."

"The thunderbird?"

"Yes, he flashes lightning from his eyes, and with each flap of his wings, the thunder booms."

"You're joking again." She swatted his forearm lightly.

"No. It's a story my people tell their children."

"That's silly, Raven." She laughed. "A storm is just a storm."

"Perhaps." He kissed the top of her head. "But my people have passed stories of the thunderbird down for centuries. Still, young children are warned not to go too near the peak of the highest mountain."

Ella shivered in Raven's arms. Silly, to fear a mythical creature. Perhaps her shivers were not due to the thunderbird, after all.

Raven's husky laugh blew into her hair. "I will protect you from the thunderbird."

She giggled. She knew he would protect her from

everything. "Where is your camp?"

"Do you know the creek that runs through these woods?" He gestured, and she nodded. "It runs downstream. If you follow it upstream for several hours, it will lead you to a clearing in the dense evergreens. It is there my tribe makes its home."

Ella closed her eyes and imagined living with Raven, making a home with him in the Black Hills, raising his beautiful children.

"Raven..."

"Yes?"

"Why are the Black Hills so important to your people? To you?"

"Why do you ask this?"

"Well, I know little of how our government works, but I do know that the Black Hills were given to your tribes, weren't they?"

"No one can give us any of this land, *tehila*. It is not ours to take, nor yours to give. But yes, you are correct. Your government decided to let us keep the hills. Until your army decided there was gold here."

"Yes, yes, I know all about that, and I'm sorry. The prospectors are a greedy bunch, Raven. I didn't want to come here, but my father felt it necessary. If he only knew..." Ella trembled, remembering the vile men who had offered her money.

"If he only knew what, Ella?"

"Never mind."

"What is it?" He tightened against her. "We have no secrets now, wife."

Ella's lips curved upward at the word "wife." She didn't

want to tell him about the men in town. It made her feel...dirty. But he was right. They had no secrets now. "Several men in town, prospectors, have offered me gold."

"For what?"

"For..."

Raven's arms tensed around her. "You are to stay away from that town. Venture nowhere from now on without me at your side. You are mine to protect now, Ella," he rasped in her ear. "No other man shall touch you."

Ella gasped. "I don't want any other man."

His arms loosened. "Forgive me. I did not mean to hold you so tightly. But the thought of one of those... Putting his hands on you..."

Ella turned in his arms. His handsome face was twisted in anguish.

"Nothing happened, Raven. You were the first."

"I know, *tehila*." He kissed her neck. "I know." He lifted her chin to meet his gaze. "You asked why the Black Hills are so important to us. I will tell you. They are a reminder of the power of the Great Spirit and the insignificance of everything else. The hills are a symbol of the beauty and strength of the Great Spirit." He lowered his mouth to hers. "But they pale in comparison to you."

The kiss was not gentle. He claimed her, dared any other man to touch her. She became his with that one kiss, almost more so than when he'd made love to her. She reveled in his passion, his possessiveness. She melted into his mouth, into his body, into his soul, and gave all of herself to him, knowing, without a doubt, that he was her destiny.

And then, from somewhere outside the shield of love that housed her and Raven, a shotgun barrel clicked.

CHAPTER SEVEN

"Get your filthy red hands off my daughter!"

Ella stiffened. Her father. She tore her lips from Raven's and turned in his arms. A veil of moonlight illuminated the creases of her father's handsome face. Her heart quickened. "P-Papa?"

"Move away from him, Ella."

"Papa, please."

"Move away from him, so I can send him to his maker."

Raven's arms tightened around her body. "Papa, you're not a killer. And there's no reason—"

"Ella, I'm not playing around here. Has he hurt you?"

"Of course not. Papa, he—"

"Move away from him, so I can put a bullet through his brain."

The icy tone of her father's voice sliced into Ella's marrow. Her father was against violence. Against killing. What had gotten into him?

"You bastards won't take another one of my children," Robert Morgan said.

She had never heard her father use such language. Take another of his children? What did he mean?

"Now take your hands off her!" He raised the shotgun.

"Papa, no!" Ella leaned back into Raven's hard chest. "Y-You can't. I love him!"

"What?" He let the gun falter slightly but then steadied

his hand.

"Raven," Ella said, her voice shaking, "I-I've never seen my father like this. I want you to go."

"Not without you." Raven's body was stiff. Unwavering.

"If you love me—"

"If I love you, which I do, I will not leave you."

"Please." He had to listen. Had to go. She couldn't bear the thought of her father hurting the man who was the other half of her soul.

"You heard her, redskin. Get the hell out of here before I blow your guts out the back of your head." Her father took aim once more.

"Not without my wife."

Ella couldn't see Raven's face, but she knew he spoke through clenched teeth.

"Your wife? Are you daft?"

"*My wife.*" Her lover's deep voice cut through the night air in a feral rasp.

"I haven't officiated at any wedding." He nodded to Ella. "Come on, girl. Go to the house."

"Only if you promise not to hurt him, Papa."

"*Tehila—*"

"Shh. Raven, please." She trembled against his solid frame. He was so steady. So sure. "Papa, I'll come with you. Just please don't hurt him."

"Ella, you're trying my patience."

"Please." Her heart thundered. Protect Raven, her body hummed. Nothing else mattered. "I'll never ask you for another thing. Just let him go."

"I go nowhere without my wife." Again, his tone bit through the words with a primal rage. So different from the loving tone when he spoke to her.

"Raven," Ella said, as she slid her fingers over his taut forearms holding her, "we'll figure this out. But for now, please. Just go."

He sighed against her hair, and the loose strands tickled her neck. "If it is what you wish."

"Yes." Ella swallowed as her eyes misted. "It's what I wish."

"Very well. But he will not keep me from you forever."

Within seconds, Raven had disappeared into the thick woods. He made no sound. He was just gone. Only the musky, leathery scent of him remained. Ella inhaled, trying to trap the fragrance inside her to keep him with her.

"Ella." Her father spoke sternly, steadily. He said nothing more as she followed him to the cabin.

★ ★ ★ ★

Ella's body thumped against her mother's as the wagon wheels jostled along in the darkness. Naomi wrapped Ella in her arms, whispering soothing words as Ella sobbed. Her tummy clenched, her body trembled. Raven. She needed Raven.

"Shh, dear. Please."

"Why, Mama? Why?"

"You know why."

Ella hiccupped and wiped her nose on her mother's shoulder. "No, I don't."

"He's an Indian, Ella."

"He's the man I love," she said, her voice hoarse and nasal from crying.

Naomi sighed, her breath stirring a few wisps of Ella's

HELEN HARDT

hair. "I know."

"M-Mama?"

Naomi grasped Ella's shoulders and pushed her gently away. "We need to talk." She cleared her throat. "How did you meet this Indian, Ella? And when?"

Ella closed her eyes. There was no point in lying to her mother. "A few days ago. He was injured by a bear and he sought refuge in the barn. I came across him while milking Sukie."

"And?"

"And I helped him to the old soddy and cared for his injury, which luckily was not serious."

"So you think you love him after only days?"

"I don't think, Mama." Love, sadness, loss—emotion so thick she thought she could cut it with a knife—threaded through her body. "I *know*. He is everything to me."

"And he loves you?"

"Yes."

"How can you be so sure, Ella?"

"Because he told me so. And because I feel it in the very marrow of my bones. Because he's an honorable man. He wouldn't lie to me."

"You know so much of his honor after spending such little time with him?"

"Yes."

"Lord above." Naomi buried her head in her hands for a few second and then looked again at Ella. "Your father... He..." Her mother's pretty face wrinkled with worry.

For her? For her father? Ella wasn't certain. "What is it?"

"He wasn't himself last night."

"I know." Ella nodded. "He used words I've never heard from his lips. And he threatened to kill Raven—that's his name.

I've never seen such rage from him. I never knew him to be a prejudiced man, Mama. But such hate emanated from him. It frightened me."

"Ella, you were barely three when your brother was taken from us. There are things you don't know. Your father...he wasn't always a preacher."

"He wasn't?" Ella's skin chilled. Why did she feel she was about to find out something about her father she didn't want to know?

"No. He was—" Naomi inhaled sharply. "Well, you already know he's nearly thirteen years older than I am." She cleared her throat. "He was a bounty hunter when I met him."

"A bounty hunter? Papa? Pious, peaceful Papa?" She gasped. Her belly churned. Though he hadn't been all that pious and peaceful while he was holding Raven at gunpoint.

"Yes. But I won his heart and convinced him to give it up. So he bought a small farm, and your brother was born within a year of our marriage. Two years later, you arrived."

"You and Papa never talk about David."

"No. Your father issued an edict shortly after David was taken. We were never to mention him."

"Why? How did you cope?"

"I threw myself into raising you. And your father turned to God."

"So that's when he became a preacher."

"Yes. And it has served him well. He found peace in the Lord's teachings and in helping others. But last night, when he saw you..."

Ella regarded her mother's face. Such a beauty, she must have been. Still was. But her violet eyes—so like Ella's own—were troubled. Ella trembled with the need to know the truth.

"But why, Mama? I know it must have been strange to see me with an Indian, but Papa has ministered to the Indians. He has ministered to the downtrodden. To the evil, even. Why, then, did he react so harshly?"

"It brought back memories for him, child. Memories long buried. You see, your brother was taken by Indians."

Ella gasped and touched her fingers to her lips. Lips that had so recently kissed the man she loved. "Are you certain?"

"It is what your father believes," Naomi said. "The night David was taken, a band of Lakota Sioux were in the area. We were traveling through Kansas, on the edge of Indian territory. David was gone when we awoke."

"Then you don't know for sure if the Indians took him."

"No. But there was no reasoning with your father. He was convinced—is still convinced—that they took his son."

"I'm sorry, but that's nonsense. Without proof—"

"There are other reasons he hates Indians, Ella," Naomi said softly.

"Why, then? Tell me. Help me understand why he treated Raven so."

Naomi shook her head. "I cannot. It's not my story to tell."

"I suppose I can't force you to speak to me. Clearly I'm just a child to you. But at least tell me this. If he has such valid reasons for hating Indians, how has he been able to minister to them all these years?"

"Indians were kind to him once. Kind to me. So your father moved forward. He learned forgiveness."

"He wasn't very forgiving this eve."

"No." Naomi shook her head. "Seeing you with an Indian brought losing David back to him."

Ella nodded. "He said he wouldn't lose another child to

them. Now I know what he meant."

"Yes. Seeing you in the arms of that Indian—"

"He's not *that Indian*." Ella whipped her hands to her hips. "His name is Silver Raven, and he is good, and kind, and gentle. And he happens to be the man I love."

Naomi smiled. "All the fire I used to possess. I see myself in you, Ella. So many times I stood before my father, and before yours, hands on my hips, shooting daggers from my eyes. I admire your spirit."

"My spirit? You have your own spirit," Ella said. "What happened to it?"

She sighed. "Losing David took its toll on me as well. When you have a child of your own, you'll understand."

The look on her mother's face was pure torment, and Ella felt it in the depths of her soul. She truly did not understand her father's wrath, her father's pain. But her mother did.

Naomi continued, "Have you thought this through? What it will mean to marry one who is not your own kind?"

"He's a person. A man of honor. And he is definitely my kind."

"He will take you away from us."

"Any man would take me away from you. You can't depend on me forever, Mama. I know I helped ease the pain of David's disappearance. I'm sorry you lost him. I truly am. But that was fifteen years ago. Don't I deserve happiness?"

"Of course you do." Naomi smiled and pulled Ella into her embrace, kissing her softly on the cheek. "Your father and I, we've been selfish, trying to keep you with us. I would never deny you the happiness and love that he and I share. You deserve all that and more. I just never thought you'd find it with an Indian."

HELEN HARDT

"Did you think you'd find it with a bounty hunter?"

Naomi pulled away from her daughter and her face softened, and Ella knew her words had touched her mother.

"He will come for me."

"Your father knows. That's why we're moving on in the middle of the night."

"He'll come for me anyway. He'll find me. And if he doesn't, I will go to him."

Ella turned away from her mother and curled into the straw bedding. Silent tears fell from her cheeks as her father's wagon took her farther and farther from the man she loved.

CHAPTER EIGHT

Ella awoke when the wagon jolted to a stop. She crawled to the end of the wagon and glanced out of the canvas cover. The orange rays of the sun peeked over the horizon.

"Naomi, Ella." Her father's gruff voice poked through the wagon cover. "The horses need a breather and a drink. Take care of your necessities."

Naomi rustled behind Ella. "You heard your father," she said. "Let's take care of things." Within a few minutes, Naomi had exited the wagon.

"Bobby," Ella heard her mother say, "you've been awake for nearly twenty-four hours. You must rest. Why don't you—"

"No." Her father's tone was soft, yet sharp. "Those redskins are born trackers. Our only chance is to keep one step ahead of them."

"She says she loves him, Bobby."

"She's eighteen. What does she know of love?"

"Did those words really come out of your mouth?" Her mother's tone dripped with acid. "I was barely nineteen when I married you, and I assure you, I was most definitely in love."

"I wasn't an Indian."

"No. You weren't. You were a bounty hunter and a fugitive. You had kidnapped me, remember? My parents weren't thrilled, but I would have none of it. I fought for you, Bobby. I begged and pleaded with my father until he asked you not to leave me because he wanted my happiness. What makes you think Ella is any different?"

"Ella's place is with her family."

"How could you have forgotten what it feels like to be young and in love?" Her mother sniffed and her voice lowered. "You remember, don't you, how we couldn't keep our hands off each other, how we felt alive only when we were together?"

Ella warmed. This was a private conversation between her parents.

No. Not between her parents. Between a husband and wife. Yet she couldn't stop listening.

Silence lingered as her mother paused. Then, "How we *still* feel, Bobby, when we let ourselves."

More silence. In her mind's eye, Ella pictured the look of resignation on her mother's pretty but worn face. She heard only fragments of conversation after that. "Keep her... Own life... Indian..."

Then her father's roar. "I will not give up another child to those heathens!"

Ella's heart lurched, but she kept perfectly still.

Within a few moments, her mother's head peeked into the wagon. "Come now, Ella. You can wash in the creek and I'll fix us some bread and jam for breakfast. Papa says we will be off within the hour."

Ella slumped her shoulders and crawled out of the wagon.

Her mother sat on a crate, lighting a fire over some stray twigs. "That way."

She followed her mother's gesture to a babbling creek about two hundred yards away. Her skin prickled. She didn't know her father at all, really. In a mere day, he'd become a stranger to her. What had happened to the man who had tossed her in the air when she was a child? Who had laughed with her when she was happy, embraced her when she was sad? Her eyes misted with unshed tears.

Where was he now? This stranger who was her father. She looked over her shoulder. If he was gone, taking care of his morning ablutions, perhaps she could...

"Quickly, Ella." His voice came from behind her. Had he appeared out of thin air? "We need to move on soon."

She turned, nodded curtly to him, and then sat down at the creek bank and rubbed her hands and face with the sandy grit. A few birds chirped in the trees above, and the rustling of wildlife whispered across the morning air.

Yet quiet consumed Ella.

What was different? What was missing?

As she splashed the cool water over her face, she knew.

The drums had silenced.

★ ★ ★ ★

"I have found her, Father. The mate of my spirit."

Standing Elk's eyes raked over Raven, and not for the first time, he felt as though his father could see inside his soul.

"Your brother told me. It is she who kept you from us the past days."

"Yes."

"Tell me then, Silver Raven, why is she not with you now?"

Raven took the plate of food his mother offered to him and nodded his thanks. He had walked during the night to return to his camp. His leg stung, his body was weary, but his mind raced. His heart cried for his mate. "Her father found us together last night. He threatened to kill me. She asked me to leave so he would not harm me."

"And you did."

"Yes. I would do anything she asked of me."

Standing Elk's lined face tightened, his black eyes burned. "And you plan to make this white woman your wife?"

"She is already my wife."

The older man looked above Raven's head. "I see."

"Bear and I will go for her. Tonight."

Standing Elk nodded, and Raven pursed his lips into a line. There was nothing more to be said.

★ ★ ★ ★

Raven jumped onto Golden Feather and let go with his war cry, the shrill vibration tightening his vocal cords. Next to him, Bear echoed the call. They kicked their horses and galloped from the camp. A knife of possessive lust speared through Raven as he led Bear down the creek. The moon, now waning, shone above them lighting their path. His heart ached with emptiness. Soon she would be with him again.

When they reached Ella's cabin, the hour of midnight had passed. They hobbled their horses near the soddy and walked quietly to the house.

"Keep watch," Raven said in Lakota. "I will return with her."

"Be careful, brother," Bear said. "If what you say happened is true, this man will not let her go without a fight."

Raven patted the blade at his side. "I am ready for a fight if need be."

Bear nodded, and Raven crept to the door of the cabin. As he had suspected, it was latched. He drew out his blade and cut through the wood. Moving with stealth, he entered a small sitting room. Another door led to a bedroom.

"*Tehila?*" he whispered.

The room was empty. He walked through the small room to another door that housed only a bedstead and bureau. He inhaled. Lavender. And wildflowers. The mere scent of her tightened his groin. Ella. This was Ella's room.

But where was she?

He sat down on the bed and buried his face in the feather pillow. The concentration of her sweet aroma constricted his throat.

"Bear!"

Within seconds, his brother stood in the doorway.

"They are gone." Raven's heart thudded and his stomach threatened to empty. "Her father has taken her from me."

"We'll find her, Raven," Bear said. "Together we can track anyone."

Raven nodded and rose from the bed. He willed his bowels to settle. Had he ever felt such fear? In the face of the she-bear? During his warrior training?

No. The fear of losing his mate overpowered everything else. He had to find her.

"They did not take much with them. Perhaps they plan to return someday."

Bear shook his head. "I don't know, brother. Come, let's look for the trail."

Raven followed his brother out of the cabin and to the barn where Sukie had been let loose to graze. "They did not take their cow."

Bear stalked around the barn, observing the earth under his feet. "Whoever took her knows how to cover his tracks. It will be difficult to pick up the trail."

"Difficult? Her father is a preacher, Bear."

"A preacher who knows how to make himself invisible." Bear knelt to the ground and fingered the dirt.

"You don't think—" Raven stopped, his mind a mass of emotion. Ella's violet eyes, her cherry lips, her innocent kisses...

"What?"

A jolt brought Raven back. "What if someone else took her?" His heart pounded. "What if she's in danger?"

"Use your head, brother," Bear said. "If she had been kidnapped, would the kidnapper have let the cow loose so she wouldn't starve?"

"You are right. I wasn't thinking." He needed to be thinking.

"I understand. You worry about your woman. But keep your head. You will need it." Bear stood. "Let's go."

Raven silently vowed not to let his heart rule his mind. "We must find her."

"We will, Raven, we will. I promise you I will not let you down."

Raven stared into Bear's golden eyes, so different from his own, yet so alike in their fierce determination.

They would find Ella. And when they did, Raven would never let her out of his sight again.

CHAPTER NINE

The jostling of the wagon stirred Ella's stomach. It was night again. They had been traveling for over twenty-four hours. Her father must be exhausted, but still he persevered. At some point he'd have to sleep, wouldn't he? And then she'd run to Raven.

She sighed, the straw from her bedding prickling her back. Run to Raven. How could she? She had no idea where she was, or how far they'd traveled, or what direction they were going. Her throat tightened, but no more tears came. Perhaps she had cried them all away.

Beside her, her mother slept fitfully, soft snores escaping her lips. When the wagon stopped, Ella jolted. She heard her father's deep voice speaking to the horses. What was happening?

When she heard her father's footsteps coming toward the back of the wagon, she closed her eyes, forcing her breath to come in shallow, even puffs, feigning sleep.

The wagon jarred and blankets rustled as Ella listened to her father lie down next to her mother. He cleared his throat.

"She's asleep, Bobby," Ella's mother said softly. "Come to me. Rest your head."

"Can't." her father said. "Can't let them…take her."

"Shh. It's all right. Sleep, my love."

The love and devotion in her mother's voice soothed Ella.

Her parents loved each other. Needed each other. Had been through...well, hell...together. They were soulmates. Mates of the spirit, as she and Raven were. Her mother understood.

One day, so would her father.

When both her parents' breathing had evened, Ella quietly stole out of the wagon.

★ ★ ★ ★

"I do not understand," Bear said to Raven, as they ate a small rabbit they had caught, skinned, and roasted over a campfire. "No wagon tracks, no horse droppings. It is like they disappeared. How is it that a preacher is so good at covering his tracks?"

"Luck, perhaps." Raven gnawed on the meat, eating only for sustenance. Though he normally enjoyed rabbit, he found no joy in this one. The taste did not soothe him. A thought niggled at him. Ella's father. He was not what he seemed on the surface.

"We will find her, Raven."

Raven nodded. He had no wish to harm Ella's father.

But he would if he had to.

★ ★ ★ ★

Ella's legs felt like jelly under her as she forced them to keep moving through the dark, dense woods. Why hadn't Raven come for her? Something must have happened to keep him away. Something terrible. He hadn't been on a horse the previous night. What if another bear had attacked him? His leg still wasn't completely healed. Ella shook, her mind a jumbled mass of fear, anger, passion. She stopped to rest and sat down on a bed of downy moss. Moss so like the patch where she and Raven had made love. She lay down and closed her eyes, and the darkness took her.

"Looky here, Jasper."

Ella jerked awake at the male voice. The light of a lantern shone in her eyes and she blinked. Before her stood a balding man dressed in a dirty shirt and trousers. His lips curved upward to reveal rotted teeth.

Icy tentacles of fear gripped her. "Wh-What do you want?"

"Oh, I think a little of your sweetness might quench our thirst, eh, Jasper?"

Another man strode toward her. This one was tall and lanky and stank to high heaven. Had he wrestled a skunk? "Whatta ya got there, Irv?"

"Found myself a sleepin' beauty." Irv brought his head closer and his rancid breath nearly made Ella lose what little was in her stomach. "Spread your legs, darlin'."

Ella winced. Her heart thundered against her breast. Surely he didn't mean...

"I mean to have a little o' you. It's been a long hard day, and Jasper and me, well, we ain't any richer than we were a coupla months ago. Cain't afford the whores in town. I reckon you'll give us a little for free."

Ella shuddered. They were bigger and stronger than she was. She could never fight them off. "Please..." Her voice came out hoarse and squeaky.

"She's sayin' please." Jasper came nearer. "I think she wants ya."

"No." Ella shook her head. "Please, don't hurt me. My father... My...my husband." Raven's face flashed into her mind.

Where was he? Why wasn't he here to protect her?

"You know, Irv, this chit looks a tad familiar to me. She's that preacher's girl, I think."

Irv breathed on her again, and Ella heaved. Nausea overwhelmed her. Her belly cramped and she heaved again. Nothing came up.

Jasper guffawed. "Seems you make her sick, Irv."

"You're right. She is the preacher's brat." Irv bent and ran his tongue over Ella's cheek.

Ella grimaced and her bowels churned.

"You cain't take her," Jasper said. "You'll go to hell fer sure."

Irv let out a chortle. "Think I'm goin' already. So what's the harm in takin' a little honey before I go?"

"Well." Jasper spat a wad of saliva onto the moss.

The mixture of phlegm and tobacco landed next to Ella. She heaved again.

"I guess you got yerself a point there."

Ella thought quickly. Papa had always said she could sell spectacles to a blind man. Here was her chance. "You're wrong," she said. "You *can* go to heaven. All you have to do is ask for forgiveness and live a righteous life hereafter."

"You're lyin' through your teeth, little lady," Irv said. "There ain't no way God'll ever forgive my reckless life."

"You're wrong. I swear it." She fidgeted. This had to work. *It had to.* "My father's a preacher. I should know."

"She has a point, Irv," Jasper said.

"See? He believes me."

"Hmm." Irv lifted his brow. "All I need to do to get to heaven is ask for forgiveness. Lead a righteous life?"

"Yes. I swear it. God will forgive you. You have my word."

Please, Ella begged silently. *Please let them believe me and leave me alone. Raven. Oh, Raven, where are you?*

"That's darn nice to know, little lady," Irv said, and then spat. "And I think I might just believe you after all."

"I'm glad." Ella breathed a sigh of relief.

"Just one thing though." An evil smile spread over his pockmarked face. "I reckon he'll forgive me tomorrow as well as today. So that means I can taste a little of you before I begin this here new righteous life o' mine."

"Now you're talkin'," Jasper said. "I never thought of it that way."

"That's why I'm the brains o' this operation," Irv said. He tore Ella's dress down the front, revealing her breasts through her chemise.

"No. Please." Ella hated to beg, but she had no choice. She couldn't bear the thought of these men's dirty hands on her body. She gathered all her strength, but couldn't move against both of them. "Y-You're wrong. Now that you know the truth of God, he will punish you if you don't start your righteous life. He...he'll send you to h-hell. Tonight. I swear it!"

Irv's evil laugh slithered over Ell,a and she heaved again. This time the remains of her dinner appeared, covering Jasper's phlegm.

"Damn, Irv," Jasper said, "Guess we can't kiss her now."

"Hell, I reckon she still tastes better than I do." Irv let out a raspy chuckle. "And get a load o' those." He grabbed Ella's breast.

She screamed as Irv closed his mouth over hers.

She squirmed as he forced his tongue past her lips. She retched, writhing to get away from him. His clammy hands traveled downward and lifted her skirts. When his fingers grazed her thigh, her body shook violently. She tried to scream, but his mouth still covered hers.

In the near distance, a high-pitched shriek ribboned through the night air. A strangely melodic sound.

Within seconds, a voice from heaven itself.

"Get your hands off my wife."

CHAPTER TEN

The whizz of an arrow pierced the air, and the weight of Irv's sweaty body fell upon her. In an instant, the man was flung off her, landing twenty feet in the distance.

Ella looked up at Raven. Wonderful, beautiful Raven! Her heart soared. He had come!

Another man—was that her father?—held Jasper at bay.

She shook her head, trying to clear the fog. It wasn't her father. But it was a white man. Dressed like an Indian.

Raven knelt beside her. "Ella. *Tehila*. Are you hurt?"

"N-No. He didn't..." Her throat constricted. Fog thickened her thoughts. Those men. Those dirty horrible men had almost... Tears moistened her eyes. "But he tried. And I wasn't...I wasn't strong enough. If you hadn't come..." She looked into his black eyes. His kind, worried eyes. "Wh-Why didn't you come for me? I-I thought another bear had attacked you. I was trying to come to you."

"Ah, *tehila*. I am so sorry." Raven scooped her into his arms and held her tight against his bare chest. "If anything had happened to you..."

She choked out a sob. "I-I'm all right." She reached for his cheek and stroked it. He was so beautiful in the moonlight. Her own personal savior and hero.

"I came for you the next night, but you were gone. We tried to track your father, but could not. Finally, early this morning, Bear was able to track you. I knew you had left your father."

"He stayed awake for over twenty-four hours. I got away as soon as I could."

"You should have stayed with him. He would have protected you."

"No." She stood up but nearly lost her footing. Her mind raced through the haze. "I don't want his protection. I want yours. I—" Her feet gave way, and she stumbled against Raven's hard chest. "I don't understand why I can't get my mind and body to work."

"Because you're frightened, *tehila*. Those men tried to force themselves upon you. You have reason to feel the way you do."

"Is... Does..." Ella's insides quivered at what she needed to ask. What she needed to know about Raven's people.

"What is it?"

"Do the men of your tribe...do they...take women like that?"

Raven held her body from his, though still held her steady. His chiseled jaw twitched. Only slightly, but Ella noticed.

"Did your father tell you that?"

"Goodness, no! He never speaks ill of anyone. Or at least, he never used to. It's just...I've heard..."

Raven's hold gentled a bit, and he sighed. "Some of my kind do. As do some of your kind. And I'm sorry that you now have personal experience of that."

She shuddered, and he drew her to him again. "I'm taking you home."

"To my cabin?"

"No. To my camp. You are my wife, Ella."

Warmth coursed through her. *His wife.* "But we haven't been married yet."

"We are married in the ways of my people. We have been since we joined our bodies. That is all that matters."

Ella didn't argue. She had no desire to. Being safe and secure in Raven's arms was all that mattered.

"Raven?"

"Yes?"

"Who's that man?" She nodded toward the white man dressed like an Indian. He had bound Jasper's legs, arms, and mouth and tied him to a tree.

"That is my brother, Wandering Bear." He turned his head toward the tree where Jasper was tied. "Bear. Come and meet my Ella."

The white man stalked forward slowly, his eyes narrowing. "Good day."

"Well...good day to you, too, Mister...Bear."

He cleared his throat. "Just Bear is fine, new sister."

"Of course, and you may call me Ella." She held out her hand. "It's very nice to meet you. Raven has told me a lot about you."

"As he has told me about you."

Ella stared at the handsome white face. His hair was long—longer than Raven's, like he had told her—and fell nearly to his knees in a thick chestnut braid. Strange that she'd mistaken him for her father earlier, through the fog that had coated her mind. They were about the same height and build, and their eyes were similar, though Bear's were lighter brown, almost gold. But there the similarities ended. He might look white, but clearly he was Indian through and through. He had a savage look to his handsome face, his golden eyes. A look she had never seen on her father's visage—until recently.

Ella turned back to Raven. "You should know, Raven, my

father will come for me. He"—she cleared her throat—"knows how to track. H-He used to be a bounty hunter."

"Ah, that explains much," Raven said, nodding. "Bear is the best tracker in our tribe, and even he could not track your father. It was you we tracked, once you escaped."

"Escaped? You make it sound like he imprisoned me."

"Didn't he?"

"Oh, no." The urge to defend her father overwhelmed Ella. "It wasn't like that. My father and mother, they've been through a lot. A lot I didn't know about. A lot I still don't know. You see, their son, my older brother, was kidnapped by Indians. Long ago. I was barely three at the time. I don't remember David at all. I know I should feel something for him. But how can I feel for someone I don't remember? It's...very sad."

"I am sorry for your parents' loss, *tehila*, as well as for yours. I do not agree with those of my people who take what is not theirs to take."

"Don't you?" She couldn't help grinning. "Didn't you go to my cabin to take me?"

"That's different. You are mine to take"—his eyes blazed—"*wife*."

He embraced her, brushed his lips over her neck. When he raised his head, he said, "I am sorry you lost your brother. I do not know what I would do without mine. Or my sister, Singing Dove."

"Don't worry about me. I told you I don't remember David. But my parents do, and they feel the loss greatly. That's why they're so protective of me. I'm all they have left, and now you're going to take me away from them."

"You do not wish to go with me?"

"Oh, yes, of course I wish to go with you. It's my heart's

desire, Raven. But I'm beginning to understand my mother and my father a lot better. And there's more I don't know. Stuff my mother wouldn't tell me. She said...she said it's my father's story to tell. But she also said Indians were kind to them once." She let out a sigh. "My kind father, the preacher... Well, it turns out I really don't know him at all."

"You can never really know another person, Ella," Bear said from behind her. "Only the Great Spirit truly knows what's in a person's heart and a person's soul."

"Or a mate, brother." Raven smiled at Ella, his beautiful full lips lowering to hers. When he was just a hair's breadth away, he whispered, "You, my mate, my wife, my love, see everything within me. And I see everything within you." He crushed his mouth to hers and kissed her.

Her skin tingled as she parted her lips eagerly, drinking in his spicy taste, his essence. Her bodice still open, she pressed her body to his, her nipples tightening against his sculpted chest. Raven, her mind whirled. *Raven, how I love you.*

From somewhere, a throat cleared.

"Brother," came Bear's voice.

Raven's lips tensed slightly but he did not stop the kiss.

"Brother," Bear said again.

Raven's mouth slid away and he pressed moist kisses to Ella's cheek. She shuddered.

"We must go. Her father has no doubt missed her by now, and he will track us."

"You have not left him anything to track, have you?"

"No. But he is an excellent tracker, clearly. We must be on guard. It would be prudent to make haste back to camp."

"Agreed," Raven said. He moved away from Ella, but leaned down and nipped her earlobe. "When we reach camp," he whispered, "I have plans for you, my wife."

CHAPTER ELEVEN

Ella's nerves scuttled as she rode into the Lakota encampment that was Raven's home. Her bottom sore, she clenched her fingers tightly in the fabric of her ripped bodice, covered herself as best she could, and leaned backward into Raven's solid torso, hoping his closeness would ease her discomfort. Conical tent structures spotted the vast area. Horses grazed, and little brown children ran about, not seeming to notice Ella. Men and women, though, told a different story. Black eyes pierced her from every angle. She tensed and grabbed Raven's strong forearm.

"Do not be afraid, *tehila*," Raven said into her ear.

"But they're all staring."

He chuckled and pressed his lips to her neck. "That is because you are so beautiful."

"It's because I'm so pale," she hissed.

"Bear is as pale as you are." He motioned to his brother who rode beside them.

"No. He is tanned. From the sun. I am not. My mother always insists on my sunbonnet." She was babbling. She knew it. It didn't ease her nervousness. "Where are we going?"

"To my tipi."

"You really live in tipis? I didn't believe it, but now I've seen it with my own eyes."

"Some tribes call them lodges. But yes, we do live in tipis."

"Are they...comfortable?"

"I do not know that word, *tehila*. But the tipis serve us well. Now, in the heat of the summer, we cover them with a thin buffalo hide that helps them stay cool inside. In the winter, we drape heavier cloths around the inside to stay warm."

"But why not build a cabin? Surely that would serve your purpose just as well."

"Because the tipis can be taken down and transported easily."

"Why would that matter?"

"We follow the buffalo, *tehila*. When they leave an area, so do we. The buffalo provide us with meat, fur, hide. We go where they go. And then there are other times when..." His deep voice trailed off with words unsaid.

"What, Raven?"

"Sometimes we leave to avoid conflict with the white men."

Ella's stomach clenched, and she gripped Raven's forearm harder. Those black eyes that speared into her no doubt knew what the white people had done—were still doing—to them. And she was one of *them*.

"Why, Raven? Why do you leave? Why don't you fight the white men?"

"Some tribes do. Our chief, Black Wolf, is my grandfather. He chooses to exist in peace. He would rather leave than lose his people to a fight they cannot win."

Ella's stomach lurched again. Raven's people would despise her. "Can't we go away together, Raven? To a place where we'll both be accepted for who we are?"

"If I knew of such a place, *tehila*, I would take you there. I would hunt for you and our children, and I would need nothing more than your love to sustain me." He sighed, and his warm breath tickled the back of her neck. "But such a place does not exist for us. Fear not. My people will accept you."

Again the piercing stares stabbed Ella's prickled skin. "I'm not so sure about that."

"Trust me." He pressed a moist kiss to the side of her neck. "I have already told my father that I found you. Love is a mystery. A beautiful mystery that only the Great Spirit understands. My people will accept you, because I have accepted you as the mate of my spirit."

Wandering Bear edged his horse nearer. "I see your wife is attracting attention."

Raven replied to Bear in words Ella didn't understand, and then said, "I will take you to my tipi."

"Shouldn't we meet your father first? Or your mother? I really should pay my respect to them. Or...oh goodness, I'm afraid I don't know the correct etiquette for this situation. My mother would be mortified. She prided herself on teaching me how to behave in any circumstance, but I fear she neglected this one."

Raven's husky chuckle hummed in Ella's ears. "My mother and father can wait. Bear will tell them we are here. For now, I will take you to my tipi."

"But why?"

"You know why, *tehila*. I can wait not one minute longer to hold you, make love to you."

Ella trembled, and her skin rippled with awareness as she recalled the passion of their first joining.

She couldn't wait a minute longer either.

★ ★ ★ ★

Colored triangles and a painting of a raven covered the door flap to Raven's tipi.

"This is the place I've been assigned in the tribal circle, *tehila*." He pointed to a lodge with a bear painted on the door cover. "That is Bear's. Farther down is my parents' lodge. My sister, Singing Dove, lives with them.

"I'm anxious to meet all of them," Ella said. She shivered inside. She was anxious—afraid and anxious. She hoped her pulse would settle down when the time came.

As nervous as she was, her pulse raced now for a different reason. Raven helped her off his horse—Golden Feather was his name—and tied him to a post in back of the tipi. He led Ella through the colorful opening.

Inside, to the left of the doorway, lay a stack of firewood. In the middle of the dwelling, round gray stones surrounded a fireplace. Directly across from the opening was a bed covered in buffalo furs.

There, she and Raven would make love. Her heart sped, and she smiled. "I love it here. It's so cozy."

He grinned, and his raw male beauty tugged at her belly. So handsome, her Indian husband, with his bronze skin, full dusky lips, and hard muscled body.

"I am glad you like it," he said, taking her arm and leading her to the left, around in a circle. "When we have children, we will have a bigger lodge, but for now, this will do well for us."

"It's so interesting, to live in a circle. I've always lived in a cabin, which is square."

"The circle represents the earth beneath the heavens," Raven said. "The walls of the tipi represent the sky, and the poles that hold the tipi up are pathways that link us with the Great Spirit."

Ella's cheeks warmed. "I never thought of my home in quite such a reverent way, Raven. That's beautiful."

"We give thanks to the Great Spirit with all that we do, including the tipis we live in," Raven said. "It is our way."

"It's a very good way. A home *should* be sacred. All about our lives should be sacred. Our lives are a gift from God. Too many people forget that." Ella gazed into Raven's dark, mesmerizing eyes. They burned. For her. "I think I will like living with your people. I like your philosophy."

"Fil-ah-so-fee?"

"Your way of explaining things. It makes me feel warm inside. It makes...sense." She smiled. "I wish I could say it in a prettier way. I'm afraid words aren't my strong suit. I was never very good at composition in school. I was better with numbers."

"I think you use words very well, my *tehila*." He pulled her close, his gaze burning into hers. "Right now, there are only three words I want to hear from you, and I will say them first. *Techi' hhila*. I love you, Ella."

Her skin heated and prickled, as though a blazing inferno burned in the fireplace in the center of the dwelling. But the fireplace was bare. Only Raven's nearness scalded her. He moved closer and touched his forehead to hers. Energy—so palpable Ella could almost see it—crackled between them. Raw, feral, and steaming. Raven lowered his head and took her lips in a scorching kiss. She sighed into his questing mouth—he tasted dark and dangerous, but also like home. Sweet, soothing home.

His calloused fingers stroked her cheeks, cupped them,

and he devoured her with his lips, his teeth, his tongue. His moan hummed into her, and she responded with her own sighs of desire.

Her body blazed, and her clothes were suddenly an encumbrance. She wanted to fling them off, touch her naked body to his, lose herself in his raw male power until her soul became part of him.

She whimpered when his mouth trailed from hers and pressed moist kisses to her cheek, then below her ear.

"The words, *tehila*," he whispered, his breath hot against her flesh. His fingers crept down her cheeks, her neck, to cup and squeeze her full breasts. "Say the words."

Ella's insides spiraled and her mind whirled. Raven's hard muscled forearms felt glorious under her fingertips. Her hands traveled upward, over his broad shoulders and down the solid plane of his chest. His nipples hardened under her touch, and the rapid beat of his heart thundered against her palm.

The words. He wanted words. She stroked his chest, raised her hands to his beautiful masculine face, and caressed his chiseled jawline. She met his dark gaze with what she hoped was a look filled with joy and love. Love for her husband, her soulmate, the man who completed her. The man who stood before her, desiring her, needing her, loving her with all he was.

She swallowed, hoping with everything inside her that he understood how much he meant to her. How much she wished to give him. "I love you, Silver Raven. I love you, my wonderful, handsome, honorable husband. As long as I breathe, I'll never love another."

"Ella." He whispered her name as if in prayer, slowly undressed her and then himself. The afternoon sun shone through the thin buffalo hide. Her nakedness was not veiled by the dark of night this time, but Ella felt no shame. The contrast of her rosy skin with Raven's bronze beauty stole her breath and held her spellbound. His arousal stretched toward her, and her arm twitched with the urge to reach for it.

Raven let out a long breath. "You are beautiful, my wife."

He touched her breast, and one finger traced a lazy circle around her pebbled nipple.

Ella sucked in a gulp of air. Such a tiny touch, but sensation blazed through her. Raven led her to the bed, pulled the buffalo skin aside, and gently laid her down.

Beside her, he caressed every inch of her skin and covered her with teasing kisses. Ella writhed as the place between her legs grew moist and pulsed with need. When he touched her there, fingering her wetness, she whispered, "please."

One thick finger entered her, and she sighed at the pleasure.

"Raven?"

"Hmm?" He brushed his lips lightly over hers.

"I... That is, I want to touch you."

"You may touch any part of me, *tehila*."

"Even your...?"

"Especially that part." His raspy laugh tickled her neck.

With awkward timidity, Ella extended her arm and brushed her fingers against his arousal. He moaned.

She jerked away. "I'm sorry."

"No, *tehila*. It feels nice."

"But you..."

He chuckled. "That means it feels good. I want you to touch me."

He took her hand in his and led it back to his shaft. With his hand still covering hers, he showed her how to hold him and stroke him. The solid hardness, so warm to her touch, enraptured her. She wanted to kiss it, pleasure him with her mouth as he had her that first night under the stars.

But that would come later, because he rolled his body on top of hers with a breathy gasp. "I need you, Ella. I need to join with you."

"Yes, please, Raven." Her body pulsed with awareness. "I need you, too."

He entered her with a swift thrust, and a sigh escaped Ella's throat. Ah, so wonderful, so complete. Her whole body quaked as he pushed into her, and she cried out as the world exploded around her.

"Raven! I love you, Raven."

"I love you, Ella, my *tehila*." With one last thrust, he groaned and crushed his mouth to hers, enfolding her in a protective shield of love.

"I love you," she whispered again. "Forever, Raven. Forever."

As she closed her eyes and snuggled up to her husband's loving warmth, a wayward thought niggled at her and a chill crept along her neck.

Her father would come for her. It was only a matter of when.

CHAPTER TWELVE

"*Tehila*, I present my father, Standing Elk."

Ella's knees buckled, but she forced herself to remain steady. The Indian, a handsome older version of Raven, nodded to her.

"My son speaks highly of you. It is an honor to welcome you to our village. May I present my father, Black Wolf, the chief of our band."

Black Wolf's white hair hung in two long braids. His black eyes were sunken and wrinkled, but kind. "Welcome, wife of Silver Raven," he said.

"Th-Thank you, sir." Ella's voice wavered as she held out her hand.

"Damn it!" A voice came from outside the tent.

A familiar voice. A voice Ella had never before heard use a profane word. "You heathen redskins let me see my daughter or I swear I'll send your souls straight to hell."

The flap of buffalo hide swished open.

"Papa!" Ella gasped.

Raven gripped her shoulders and moved in front of her, shielding her body with his.

But it was Standing Elk who spoke. "Robert Morgan. After all these years, we meet again."

Her father's amber eyes widened and he dropped the rifle he held to his side. "You've got to be kiddin' me."

"You do not remember our first meeting?" Standing Elk walked toward him stealthily, shielding Raven and Ella, and extended his hand.

Did Indians shake hands? Ella wasn't sure. Her father didn't take Standing Elk's hand, though, and as Ella watched their interlude, she realized Raven's father wasn't asking for a handshake. It was a signal of friendship. Of peace.

Would her father accept? Questions jumbled in Ella's mind. How did Standing Elk know her father? Her mother had said Indians had been kind to them once. She shivered against Raven's hard body, gulped, and hoped with all her heart that Standing Elk and his band had been those Indians. If not...

"Yes"—her father lowered his head, but only slightly—"I remember."

Standing Elk's hand dropped to his side. "You are well?"

"As well as I can be. My wife and I want our daughter."

Her father's gaze burned into her. She held tighter to Raven.

Standing Elk nodded. "I understand."

Raven stepped forward, but Standing Elk gestured for him to remain still.

"It is not easy when a child leaves your home. But I assure you, my son loves your daughter and will take care of her. He will protect her and provide for her. He is a strong and able warrior."

"He's not her kind."

Standing Elk nodded again. "What is *kind*, Robert Morgan? His skin is darker. His clothing is different. But the two young people love each other. My grandmother was a white woman and she loved her Indian husband."

"You don't understand."

"I understand more than you know."

"He took her. You people just take what you want. It's not our way."

"That's not true!" Ella stormed from behind Raven to face her father's defeated gaze. "He didn't take me. I went with him willingly."

"Quiet, Ella!" Her father's voice thundered through the thick tension in the tipi.

Protective instinct rose within Ella. The hair on her skin bristled, chilling her. Like a she-bear defending her mate. "No, Papa. I'll not be quiet. This is my life you're deciding. Shouldn't I have some say in it? I love Raven. I want to be with him. I know it won't be easy. Every marriage has hardships. If we love each other, we can get through them."

"You're too young."

"I'm eighteen! Mama told me she was only nineteen when she married you. And she told me other things, Papa. How you kidnapped her while you were running from the law. Raven did not kidnap me. I came of my own accord. This is where I want to be."

"Your mother should not have told you how we met. It's... Well, it wasn't a normal courtship, I'll grant you that. But that's in the past. This is the present. Your mother needs you, Ella."

"No." Ella stood her ground, though her heart pounded against her breasts. "She'll let me go. She told me so. You can't hold onto me forever to ease your loss of David. It's been fifteen years. You need to let your son go."

"He wasn't just my son. He was your brother."

"I'm sorry, Papa." Ella sniffed back a tear. Not for David, but for her parents. "I don't remember him. I was too young. I ache for your loss. Truly I do. But I can't take his place for the rest of my life. My life is here now, with the man I love."

Her father sighed and lifted his gaze to Raven. "You are called?"

"Silver Raven."

"Silver Raven." His gaze shifted to Standing Elk. "This is the child I remember?"

"Yes."

"Raven?" Ella tugged at his arm. "I don't understand what they're talking about."

"I don't either, *tehila*." He turned to his father. "Father?"

"You are too young to remember," Standing Elk said. "You had seen three or four winters. Robert Morgan brought his woman to us. She had been shot. Summer Breeze healed her."

"Papa?"

"It's true, Ella. Your mother would have died otherwise. I owe these people more than I can ever repay." He sighed, and his rifle dropped to the soft dirt floor of the tipi. "I never thought payment would be my only child."

Ella warmed, and she couldn't help smiling. These *had* been the kind Indians. But so many questions haunted her. Her father had his own reasons for hating Indians, her mother had said. Reasons other than her brother's kidnapping?

"I told you then," Standing Elk said, "and I tell you now. We do not accept payment for what we have a duty to give."

"I'm not payment for anything, Papa." Ella's hands whipped to her hips as determination burned within her. "I'll not be treated as such. I've said before, I'm here of my own volition. This is where I want to be."

Her father's lips twitched. Was that a smile? At least the beginning of one? "You're the spittin' image of your mother at your age, darlin'. So beautiful and feisty."

"Thank you. That's a wonderful compliment, Papa."

"What will I tell your mama?"

"You'll tell her what she already knows. That I've found the man I love and I intend to marry him, live here with him, take care of him, and bear his children. This is the life I was meant to lead, Papa. Where is Mama, anyway?"

"She's outside the village with the wagon and team. I didn't want her to come here with me. I wasn't sure it'd be safe."

"You are safe here, Robert Morgan," Standing Elk said.

"Yes," Ella said. "Please go find Mama. I want to see her. I want her to meet my husband."

"Your husband? You have already married?"

"Not in our way, Papa, but in his. But I would like to marry in our way, also. Would you...marry us?"

Her father's amber eyes glistened. Tears? She'd never in her life seen her father cry. He didn't now, though she could see the tears threatened. He let out a sigh. "If it's what you wish, Ella."

"Oh, Papa!" Ella rushed toward her father and flung herself into his arms. "I promise you I'll come visit as often as you'd like. Right, Raven?"

"Of course. She is not a prisoner here. She is the wife of the grandson of our chief. She holds a position of honor."

"And you can come visit me whenever you want. I'll always be thrilled to see you."

Her father's arms tightened, and Ella's breath caught. This was so difficult for him, for reasons she still didn't completely understand. After a moment, his hold relaxed, and he spoke softly. "Ready yourself for a weddin', Ella. I'll be back with your mama."

Ella kissed her father's stubbled cheek. "Thank you, Papa.

Thank you so very much."

★ ★ ★ ★

"A white man's wedding?" Wandering Bear's golden gaze rested on Raven's face. His voice was deep as he spoke the Lakota words.

"Yes," Raven said, "and you must stand with me. Ella says we each need an attendant, and that it is customary for the man's attendant to be the brother or the best friend. You, Bear, are both to me."

"I am honored, Raven. What of Ella? You have told me she has no brothers and sisters."

"She had a brother, but he is gone. She has no sister and no close friends since she left Minnesota, so she has asked our sister, Singing Dove, to stand with her."

"That is kind of her."

"Singing Dove is very excited. She is helping Ella dress for our white man's wedding."

"Will she wear white man's clothing?"

"I do not know. According to Ella, I am not allowed to see her before the wedding. It is bad luck."

"That is ridiculous."

Raven laughed. "I agree. We have already mated. But she has agreed to live here with me and respect our ways. So I will respect hers."

Rays of sun shot into the tipi when Standing Elk entered.

"Reverend Morgan and his wife are here. And Ella and Singing Dove are ready to proceed. Are you ready, my son?"

Raven nodded. "I have never been more ready, Father. I wish to be mated to the woman I love in her way as well as ours."

Raven and Bear followed Standing Elk out of the tipi across the village to the camp circle, where the band held their ceremonies.

"Ella said we must hold this 'wedding' in a sacred place," Standing Elk said. "I told her we would go to her village, to her house of worship, but she was concerned for our safety." Standing Elk let out a chuckle. "I told her we were capable of taking care of ourselves, but she insisted you be married here. There is no more sacred place than our circle."

Raven looked toward the circle as they approached. Ella's father stood, looking sullen. Next to him was a lovely woman, an older version of Ella herself. Ella's mother. But for a few strands of silver highlighting her sable hair, she would be Ella's twin, right down to the violet eyes.

He and Bear walked slowly, solemnly, respectfully, toward Ella's parents. Robert Morgan's amber gaze rested on him. His demeanor was more of resignation than of happiness. As they came closer, the amber eyes widened and darkened.

Surprise?

Surprise and anger?

He pierced the gaze with his own, and it was then he realized Robert Morgan wasn't staring at him.

He was staring at Bear.

"Those eyes."

Robert Morgan's voice was soft and deep. The tone chilled Raven's skin.

"Of what do you speak, white man?" Bear turned away from his gaze. His discomfort trickled through Raven.

"Those eyes. They're the color of liquid gold. I only know of two others who had eyes like those."

"Who?" Raven asked, wondering why it mattered.

"My father"—the older man's eyes softened and he stared at Bear's face with a look of longing—"*and my son.*"

CHAPTER THIRTEEN

Raven steadied his breathing, forced his mouth closed when it wanted to drop open. He looked to Bear, who spoke no words as Ella's father continued to gaze at him. "Naomi."

"Bobby"—the older woman touched her fingers to her lips—"it can't be."

"This man is our son." Ella's father turned to Raven and Standing Elk. His handsome face burned red with anger. His amber eyes darkened and glowed.

Raven blinked. For a moment, time turned backward, and he recalled finding Bear, soon after his first vision quest, standing in the face of an Indian boy who dared to say he wasn't a true Lakota. The flesh on his face had burned scarlet and his eyes had darkened to an amber not unlike Robert Morgan's.

The man was tall and muscular like Bear. His hair was the same light brown of chestnuts.

No. No, it cannot be.

Robert Morgan's hands curled into fists and he walked toward Standing Elk. His teeth clenched, his voice even lower, even icier, he said, "You stole my son, you heathen redskin."

Bear moved in front of Raven and Standing Elk. "You will not speak to my father in that manner. I assure you I am not your son, white man."

Raven fingered for his dagger at his side and then remembered Ella had asked him not to wear a weapon to their wedding. He inhaled, again forced to steady himself in the face of his pounding heart. What would he do, anyway? Threaten Ella's father? Kill him? What would that do to his wife?

Standing Elk, though wearing a dagger, did not reach for it. He faced Ella's father, his black stare never wavering. "I stole nothing from you or any other white man."

"My brother wandered into our camp when he was a young boy," Raven said. "My father took him in, adopted him as his son, and I as my brother."

"Raven." Standing Elk's voice was firm.

Though he said no more, Raven ceased his explanation. He would let his father speak.

The woman, Ella's mother, walked toward Bear, tears glistening in her amethyst eyes. They were lighter than Ella's, Raven noticed, lighter, like the hue of the violet right before it wilted and died.

Her gaze traveled over Bear, from the top of his head to his moccasin-clad feet, and then returned to rest on his face. "Those eyes, they are David's, and the nose, it's mine. Mine and Ella's. You are tall, like your father and mine. Dear God..." Her body trembled, and she fell backward into her husband's arms. "David," she said, and her eyes closed.

"Where is Summer Breeze?" Standing Elk said in Lakota.

"She is with Ella and Singing Dove," Raven said.

"Fetch her," Standing Elk said to a young warrior standing nearby. He turned to Morgan. "Your wife has fainted. Summer Breeze will see to her needs. Then you will come to my tipi, and I will tell you about my son, Wandering Bear."

"I'll stay with my wife," Morgan said. "I can't leave her."

Standing Bear gripped Morgan's shoulder. Morgan tensed. Just a bit, but Raven noticed.

"You forget, friend. I know how you love your wife. I was there the first time she was injured. When she lingered near death. Summer Breeze helped her then, and she will help her now. Trust me."

"Trust you? Are you serious? You stole my child! And now you're taking the only one I have left. Do you have any idea what this has done to Naomi? To me? Losing David nearly killed us."

Standing Bear nodded. "I understand more than you know."

"Raven!"

Raven turned at Ella's voice. Ella, Singing Dove, and Summer Breeze came running.

"What's going on?" Ella gasped when her gaze landed on her mother. "Mama? Papa, what happened to Mama?"

"Your mother only fainted, Ella," Standing Elk said. Then, to Summer Breeze in Lakota, "We will take her to the healing tent, and you can see to her there."

Summer Breeze nodded.

"Follow me, Robert Morgan."

Morgan lifted his wife into his arms as if she weighed no more than a feather.

"Raven," Standing Elk continued, "take Ella to my tipi. You go too, Bear. When I return with Morgan, we will speak."

Raven nodded and looked at his beautiful wife. She wore a buckskin dress and her lovely hair hung in two braids. She had dressed for him, for his people, even though the wedding was her tradition.

At that moment, he had never loved her more.

His heart raced. Who was Bear, really? Was he Ella's brother? And if he was, what would that do to his marriage to

Ella? He could share Bear with Ella. Indeed, he'd share all that he had, all that he was, with Ella. But what of Ella's parents? Of Ella herself? What blame might she cast upon him for keeping her from her brother all these years? He shook his head. He'd make her understand, somehow. He had to.

He smiled into her beautiful face—her eyes the color of violets at first bloom, her hair the hue of the soft dirt under his feet after a rain storm, her lips pretty and sweet as red currants.

He would not give her up.

★ ★ ★ ★

"He wandered into our camp one day, starved and beaten. We called him Wandering Bear."

Ella sat, mesmerized by the melodic, throaty sound of her father-in-law's voice.

"Though I knew he was old enough to speak, he did not. Not for several weeks. Summer Breeze and her mother, Laughing Sun, may she rest in peace, nursed him back to health."

Ella rested her gaze on Bear, the man who could be her brother by blood, and now by marriage. She had mistaken him for her father the night she'd nearly been raped. At the time, she'd blamed it on her muddled mind, but now, looking him over, the resemblance was uncanny. His height, his build, his hair and eye color. His facial characteristics—mostly her father, but her mother's straight nose.

Ella's fingers wandered to her face and she traced the straight line of her own nose. So like her mother's.

So like Bear's.

"In time, he spoke to Raven," Standing Bear said. "Raven

had seen ten winters at the time, and I had begun to teach him the white man's tongue. When he and Bear began to communicate, they spoke to each other in their own languages, and each learned the other. Summer Breeze and I were amazed at how quickly they learned. Bear told Raven he had seen five winters. That he had run away from his family one night in Indian territory looking for arrowheads. Some bad white men caught him."

"Dear God."

The pain in her father's voice lanced through Ella. What must it be like to lose a child? To wonder where he was? Who he was with? She trembled and hoped she never knew the answer to those questions.

"Dear God," her father said again. "I hadn't let him look for arrowheads. We had chores, and then we went to bed early that night because we needed to get an early start in the morning. Naomi was busy with Ella, and I"—he gulped—"was too busy to take my son to look for arrowheads." He shook his head, his gaze resting on Bear, who had said nothing so far. "It can't be."

"Do you believe Bear is your son, Robert Morgan?"

Her father nodded. "I do."

Ella shuddered. Her father's eyes, amber and sunken, held years of sorrow, years of regret.

"Bear never told us his white man's name." Standing Elk cleared his throat. "Summer Breeze felt"—he hedged—"he had willed himself not to remember his former life. He had been badly mistreated by those who captured him."

"Thank God Naomi isn't here to hear this," her father said.

Standing Elk turned to Bear. "Does this bring anything back to you? Do you remember your white man's name?"

Ella fidgeted, nervous, waiting for Bear's deep voice, but

he didn't speak.

Ella could remain silent no longer. She wasn't one to sit idly by. She stood and went to the man who was her brother now, perhaps in more ways than one. She sat next to him.

"I'm truly sorry, Bear, that we didn't get to grow up together. But you are my brother. I feel it in my bones. She fingered a strand of his chestnut hair. "You look just like Papa. Tell me"—she took his hand—"tell me you feel it, too."

Bear grasped her hand. "I should have been there," he said. "I should have been there to take care of you, little sister."

Ella flung her arms around his neck and hugged him. He stiffened, but within a few seconds, he softened and hugged her back.

"I'm fine. Mama and Papa took care of me. And you were here, taking care of Singing Dove. You did your duties. You did them well, Bear." She swallowed. "*David.*"

"David," he said. "David Robert Charles Morgan. That is my name."

Ella released her brother and looked to her father.

His eyes softened. "David, for a man who was kind to me once when I was on my own as a youngun'. Robert for me, Charles for your mother's father." He turned to Standing Elk. "It seems I am in your debt once again."

"You owe me nothing, Robert Morgan. I love Bear as if he were my own. He filled a void for Summer Breeze and me." Standing Elk's voice cracked. "You see, I understand what it is to lose a child. Raven had twin brothers, born when he had seen five winters. When they had seen no more than four winters, they wandered away from camp, content in each other's company, as twins are. We searched and searched, but we never saw them again."

Ella's eyes stung with tears. So much loss. What could have happened to Raven's brothers? She chilled to think about it.

"A year later, when Bear wandered into our camp, he wandered into my heart as well. A few years later, the Great Spirit blessed us with Singing Dove, and our family was complete."

For several moments, no one spoke. Ella felt the ominous silence in the depths of her soul. So much pain. For her parents, for her in-laws. For Bear. For Raven's little brothers, may they rest in peace.

Finally her father spoke, his gaze resting on Bear. "Can you ever forgive me?"

"For what?"

"For not taking you to look for arrowheads that day. For making you go to bed." He swiped at his forehead and raked his fingers through his chestnut hair sprinkled with silver. "I'm sorry."

"Forgive yourself," Bear said. "You had my forgiveness a long time ago."

"You were happy here?"

"Very happy. I will not leave here."

Her father nodded. "I won't ask you to." He turned to Standing Elk. "You told me once that there were good and bad Indians, just as there are good and bad white men. Indians raped my mother and then slaughtered her and my father. I was ten years old, and I saw the whole thing through a window."

Ella gasped. Her belly lurched. Vivid half-formed images scattered through her mind. She swallowed back the nausea in her throat. She knew so little about her father. He sat, his amber eyes sunken and wet. Her strong, handsome father, brought to his knees by these Indians—her new family.

"But then you saved Naomi. I tried to change my thinkin' about Indians, but when David was taken, and Indians had been in the area that night, I just assumed..."

"You assumed Indians had taken him. And some Indians might have. Just like some white men might have. There are evil among all types of people, Robert Morgan."

"Yes, I know. I forgave the Indians. Truly I did. That's why I became a preacher. But when I saw your son with Ella, and I thought I would lose another child to Indians... Well, it all came back to me. The slaughter of my parents, the loss of David."

"I understand."

"Yes, I think you do." Again her father turned to Bear. "I hope you will let your mother and me be part of your life. You can come visit us anytime. And we will come to visit you and Ella here, if we are welcome."

"You are welcome," Standing Elk said.

Bear simply nodded.

Tears stung Ella's eyes, but she had heard enough about pain and loss for one day. She took her place at Raven's side.

"Papa. In light of these developments, I think maybe we should postpone the wedding for a few days."

Bobby nodded. "When your mama can travel, we'll go back to the claim. This will be a lot for her to digest. We'll come back day after tomorrow."

"That would be wonderful."

Raven nodded. "Yes, two days. And then Ella will be mine in our way and yours."

His arms wrapped around her and he gave her a searing kiss right in front of everyone.

★ ★ ★ ★

"Dearly Beloved, we are gathered here today to join this man and this woman in the bonds of holy matrimony."

Her father's deep voice resonated throughout the camp, and after Raven spoke his vows to Ella, she gazed into his black eyes, love coursing through her.

"I, Ella Ruth Morgan, take thee, Silver Raven, as my lawful husband."

Her insides warmed as she spoke the words of love and devotion to her beautiful groom. Clad in buckskins, his bronze chest bare, his raven hair accented with white feathers, he was as noble and handsome as any man alive.

"I now pronounce you man and wife."

Raven clasped her to him, and her breath caught at the hardness of his sculpted chest. She would never tire of looking at him.

"We will celebrate the marriage of Raven and Ella with a feast," Standing Elk announced.

"And your mother and I have a wedding gift for you," her father said. "I sent a young brave to retrieve it. It's not much, but it's all we have to give right now."

"A gift isn't necessary, Papa. You've given us so much already."

"Nonsense. We need to give you something. Ah, here it comes."

Ella looked over her shoulder and her tummy tumbled. She rolled her eyes.

"Oh, Raven," she whispered to her husband. "It's that dratted cow, Sukie."

THE END

MESSAGE FROM HELEN HARDT

Dear Reader,

Thank you for reading *The Daughters of the Prairie Series*. If you want to find out about my current backlist and future releases, please like my Facebook page: facebook.com/HelenHardt and join my mailing list: helenhardt.com/signup/. I often do giveaways. If you're a fan and would like to join my street team to help spread the word about my books, you can do so here: facebook.com/groups/hardtandsoul/. I regularly do awesome giveaways for my street team members.

If you enjoyed the story, please take the time to leave a review on a site like Amazon or Goodreads. I welcome all feedback.

I wish you all the best!
Helen

ALSO BY HELEN HARDT

The Misadventures Series
Misadventures of a Good Wife

The Sex and the Season Series
Lily and the Duke
Rose in Bloom
Lady Alexandra's Lover
Sophie's Voice
The Perils of Patricia (Coming Soon)

The Temptation Saga:
Tempting Dusty
Teasing Annie
Taking Catie
Taming Angelina
Treasuring Amber
Trusting Sydney
Tantalizing Maria

The Steel Brothers Saga
Craving
Obsession
Possession
Melt
Burn
Surrender
Shattered (Coming August 29th, 2017)
Twisted (December 26th, 2017)

More Titles
Destination Desire
The Daughter of the Prairie Series
Her Two Lovers

ABOUT THE AUTHOR

#1 *New York Times* and *USA Today* Bestselling author Helen Hardt's passion for the written word began with the books her mother read to her at bedtime. She wrote her first story at age six and hasn't stopped since. In addition to being an award winning author of contemporary and historical romance and erotica, she's a mother, a black belt in Taekwondo, a grammar geek, an appreciator of fine red wine, and a lover of Ben and Jerry's ice cream. She writes from her home in Colorado, where she lives with her family. Helen loves to hear from readers.

Visit her here:
www.facebook.com/HelenHardt

ALSO AVAILABLE FROM
HELEN HARDT

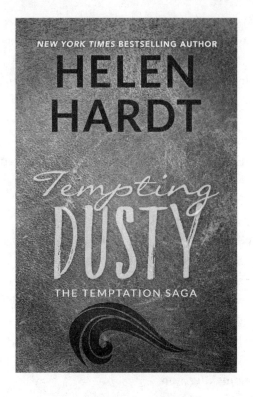

Keep reading for an excerpt!

CHAPTER ONE

Seventeen years later

"He doesn't look so tough," Dusty said to Sam as she eyed El Diablo, the stud bull penned up outside the Western Stock Show grounds in Denver. She winced at the pungent aroma of dust and animals.

"No man's been able to stay on him more than two seconds, Dust," her brother said.

"He just needs a woman's touch." Dusty looked into the bull's menacing eyes. Oh, he was mad all right, but she had no doubt she could calm him. The ranchers in Montana didn't call her the Bull Whisperer for nothing.

"I don't know. I'm not sure you should try it. Papa wouldn't like it."

"Papa's dead, Sam, and you can't tell me what to do." She pierced her brother's dark gaze with her own. "Besides, the purse for riding him would save our ranch, and you know it."

"Hell, Dusty." Sam shoved his hands in his denim pockets. "I plan to win a few purses bronc busting. You don't need to worry about making money."

"I want to make the money, Sam."

"That's silly."

"No, it's not."

"Look, you don't need to feel any obligation. What happened couldn't be helped. It wasn't your fault. You know that."

"Whatever." She shrugged her shoulders and turned back to the bull. "Besides, if I ride old Diablo here, I can make five hundred thousand dollars in eight seconds. That's"—she did some rapid calculations in her head—"two hundred and twenty-five million dollars an hour. Can you beat that?" She grinned, raising her eyebrows.

"Your math wizardry is annoying, Dust. Always has been. And yeah, I might be able to come away from this rodeo with half a mill, though I won't do it in eight seconds. Besides, Diablo's owner will never let a woman ride him."

"Who's his owner? I haven't had a chance to look through the program yet."

"Zach McCray."

"No fooling?" Dusty smiled as she remembered the lanky teenager with the odd-colored eyes. Yes, he had tormented her, but he had been kind that last day when the O'Donovans left for Montana. At thirteen, Zach had no doubt understood the magnitude of Mollie's illness much better than Dusty. "I figured the McCrays would be here. Think they'll remember us?"

"Sure. Chad and I are blood brothers." Sam held up his palm. "Seriously, though, they may not. Ranch hands come and go all the time around a place as big as McCray Landing."

"It's Sam O'Donovan!"

Dusty turned toward the deep, resonating voice. A tall broad man with a tousled shock of brown hair ambled toward them.

"Chad? I'll be damned. It *is* you." Sam held out his hand. "We were just talking about you, wondering if you'd remember us."

"A man doesn't forget his first and only blood brother."

Chad slapped Sam on the back. "And is this the little twerp?"

"Yeah, it's me, Chad." Dusty held out her hand.

Chad grabbed it and pulled her toward him in a big bear hug. "You sure turned out to be a pretty thing. " He turned back to Sam. "I bet you got your work cut out for you, keeping the flies out of the honey."

"Yeah, so don't get any ideas," Sam said.

Chad held up his hands in mock surrender. "Wouldn't dream of it, bro. So how are you all? I'd heard you might be back in town. I was sorry to hear about your pa."

"I didn't know the news made it down here," Sam said.

"Yeah, there was a write up in the Bakersville Gazette. The old lady who runs it always kept a list of the hands hired at the nearby ranches. Once she discovered the Internet five years ago, there was no stopping her." Chad grinned. "She found every one of them. Needs a new hobby, I guess. So what are you all up to?"

"Here for the rodeo. Dusty and I are competing."

"No kidding?"

"Yep. I'm bronc busting, and Dusty's a barrel racer. And..." Sam chuckled softly.

"And what?"

"She thinks she's gonna take Diablo here for a ride."

Chad's eyes widened as he stared at Dusty. Warmth crept up her neck. Clearly her five-feet-five-inch frame didn't inspire his confidence.

"You ride bulls?"

Her facial muscles tightened. "You bet I do."

Chad let out a breathy chortle. "Good joke."

"No joke, Chad," Sam said. "She's pretty good, actually. But she's never ridden a bull as big as Diablo. She's tamed some pretty nasty studs in Montana, though never during competition."

"I hate to tell you this, Gold Dust, but this rodeo doesn't allow female bull riding."

"I'll just have to get them to change their minds then," Dusty said.

"Good luck with that," Chad said. "In fact, can I go with you? I think the whole affair might be funny."

"Fine, come along then. Who do I speak to?"

"Honey, why don't you stick to female riding? I'm sure the WPRA will be happy to hear your pleas. But this here's a *man's* rodeo."

Dusty's nostrils flared as anger seethed in her chest. "I'm as good a bull rider as any man. Tell him, Sam."

"I already told him you're good."

"But tell him what they call me back home."

"Dust—"

"Tell him, or I will!"

"They call her the Bull Whisperer. She's good, I tell you."

"Bull Whisperer?" Chad scoffed. "So you're the Cesar Millan of cattle, huh? Ain't no whisper gonna calm Diablo. Even Zach hasn't been able to ride him, and he's the best."

"Yeah, well, he hasn't seen me yet." Dusty stood with her hands on her hips, wishing her presence were more imposing. Both her brother and Chad were nearly a foot taller than she was. "I'm going to ride that bull and win that purse!"

"Seriously, Dusty," Chad said, "I was teasing you. But you can't try to ride Diablo. He'll kill you. Trust me, I know. He damn near killed me. I was out all last season recovering from injuries I got from him."

"I have a way with animals," Dusty said.

"So do I, honey."

Sam rolled his eyes, laughing. "Whatever you say, McCray."

"Hey, dogs love me," Chad said.

"I'm not surprised," Dusty said, smiling sardonically. "I'm sure you make a nice tall fire hydrant. Now tell me, who do I need to talk to about riding the bull?"

"You need to talk to me, darlin'."

Dusty shuddered at the sexy western drawl, the hot whisper of breath against the back of her neck.

"And there ain't a woman alive who can ride that bull."

Continue Reading in Tempting Dusty

Visit www.helenhardt.com for more info!

Kate and Price Lewis had the perfect marriage—love, fulfilling careers, and a great apartment in the city. But when Price's work takes him overseas and his plane goes down, their happily-ever-after goes down with it.

A year later, Kate is still trying to cope. She's tied to her grief as tightly as she was bound to Price. When her sister-in-law coaxes her into an extended girls' trip—three weeks on a remote Caribbean island—Kate agrees. At a villa as secluded as the island, they're the only people in sight, until Kate sees a ghost walking toward them on the beach. Price is alive.

Their reunion is anything but picture perfect. Kate has been loyal to the husband she thought was dead, but she needs answers. What she gets instead is a cryptic proposal—go back home in three weeks, or disappear with Price...forever.

Emotions run high, passions burn bright, and Kate faces an impossible choice. Can Price win back his wife? Or will his secrets tear them apart?

Visit Misadventures.com for more information!

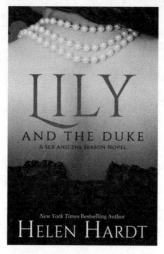